Jim Henson's FRAGGLE ROCK™

JOURNEY TO THE EVERSPRING

Published by
ARCHAIA™

**JIM HENSON'S FRAGGLE ROCK: JOURNEY TO THE EVERSPRING,
OCTOBER 2018.** Published by Archaia, a division of Boom Entertainment, Inc. © 2018
The Jim Henson Company. JIM HENSON's mark & logo, FRAGGLE ROCK, mark & logo, and
all related characters and elements are trademarks of The Jim Henson Company. Originally
published in single magazine form as JIM HENSON'S FRAGGLE ROCK: JOURNEY TO THE
EVERSPRING No. 1-4. ™ & © 2014, 2015 The Jim Henson Company. All Rights Reserved.
Archaia™ and the Archaia logo are trademarks of Boom Entertainment, Inc., registered in
various countries and categories. All characters, events, and institutions depicted herein
are fictional. Any similarity between any of the names, characters, persons, events, and/or
institutions in this publication to actual names, characters, and persons, whether living or
dead, events, and/or institutions is unintended and purely coincidental.

BOOM! Studios, 5670 Wilshire Boulevard, Suite 400, Los Angeles, CA 90036-5679.
Printed in China. First Printing.

ISBN: 978-1-68415-250-6, eISBN: 978-164144-112-4

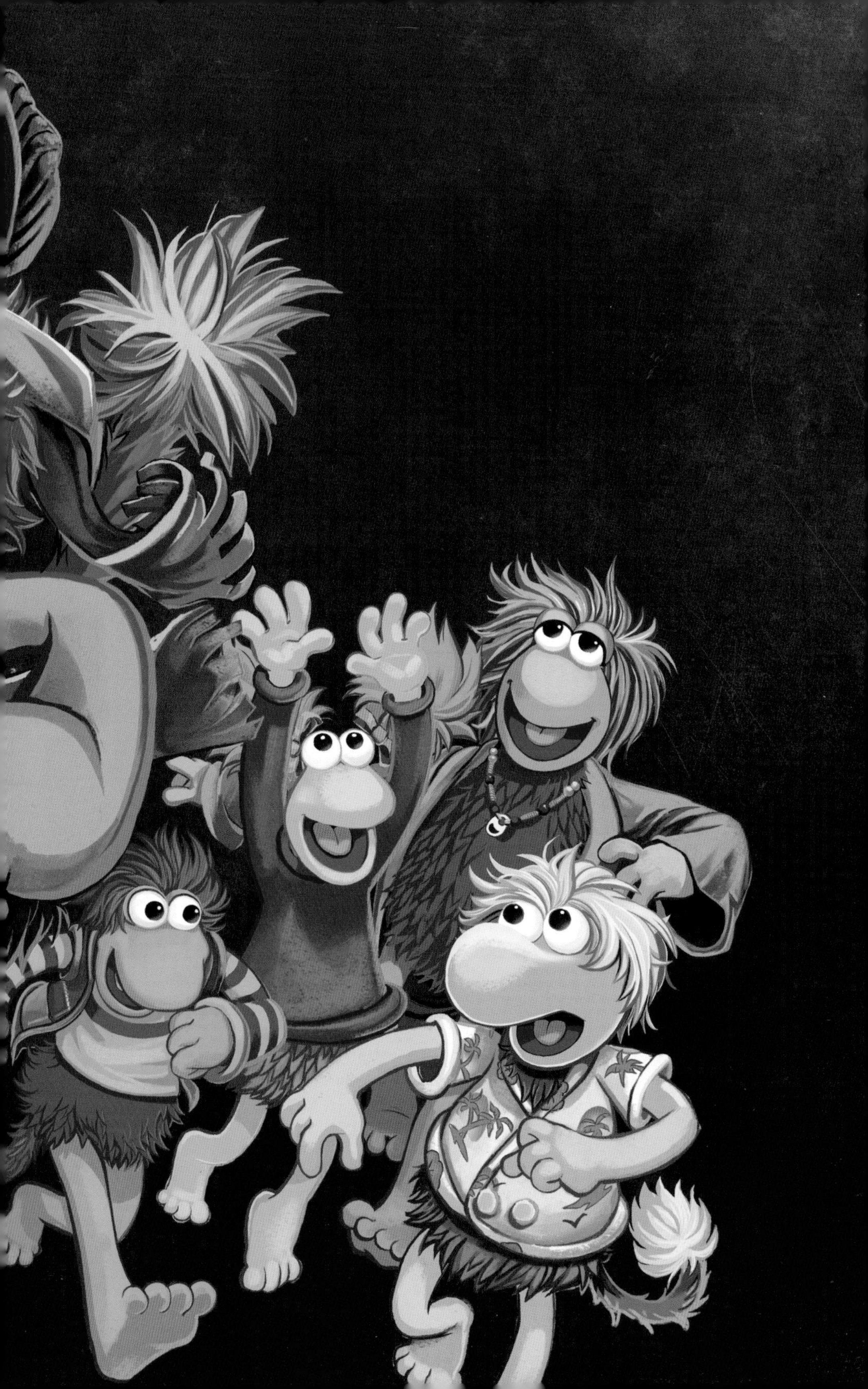

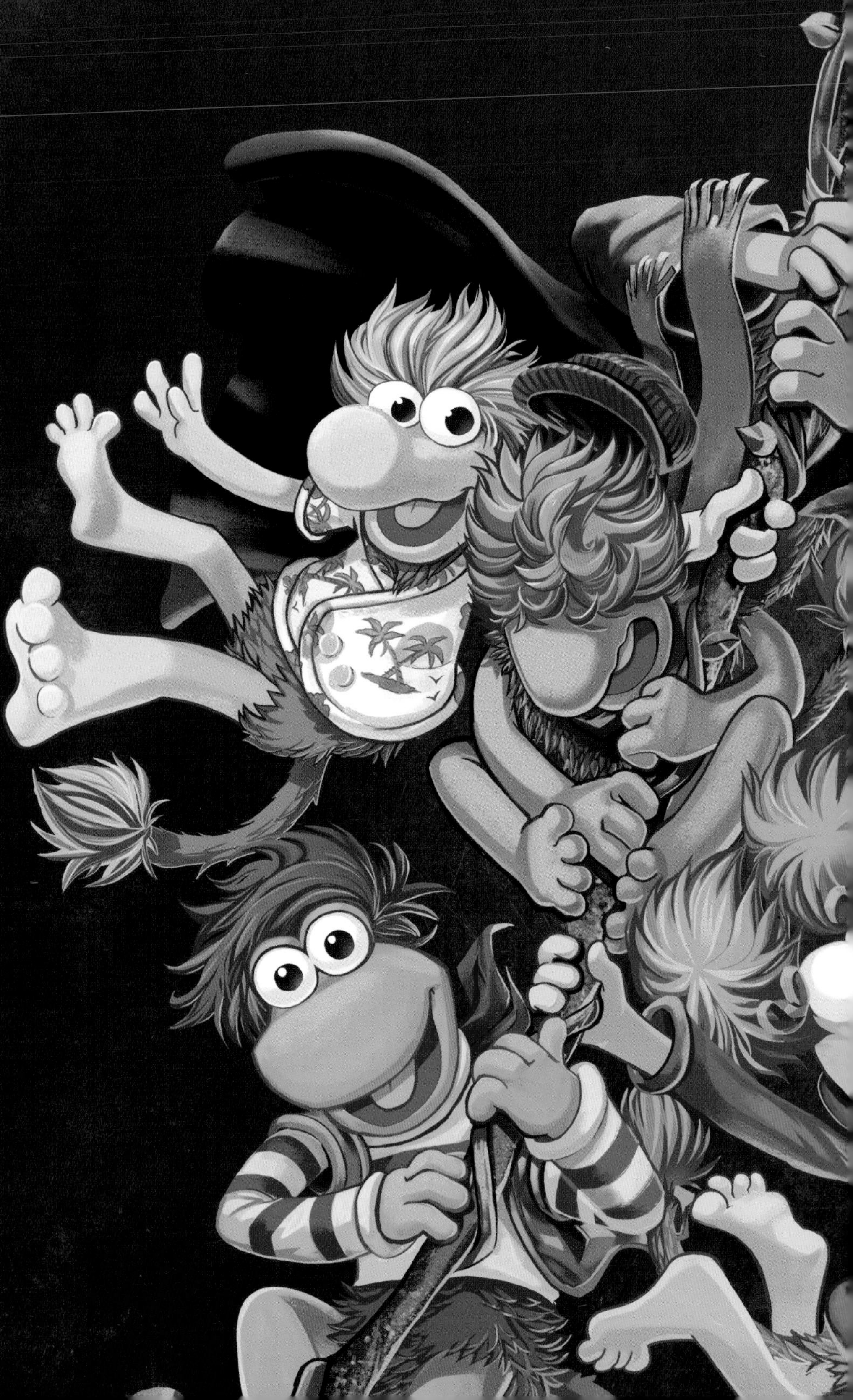

Jim Henson's
FRAGGLE ROCK™
JOURNEY TO THE EVERSPRING

WRITTEN BY **KATE LETH**
ILLUSTRATED BY **JAKE MYLER**
LETTERED BY **COREY BREEN**

COVER BY **JAKE MYLER**

DESIGNER **KARA LEOPARD**
ORIGINAL SERIES EDITOR **REBECCA TAYLOR**
COLLECTION ASSISTANT EDITOR **GAVIN GRONENTHAL**
COLLECTION EDITOR **CAMERON CHITTOCK**

SPECIAL THANKS TO BRIAN HENSON, LISA HENSON, JIM FORMANEK, NICOLE GOLDMAN, MARYANNE PITTMAN, CARLA DELLAVEDOVA, JUSTIN HILDEN, KAREN FALK, BLANCA LISTA, AND THE ENTIRE JIM HENSON COMPANY TEAM.

DANCE YOUR CARES AWAY

CHAPTER ONE

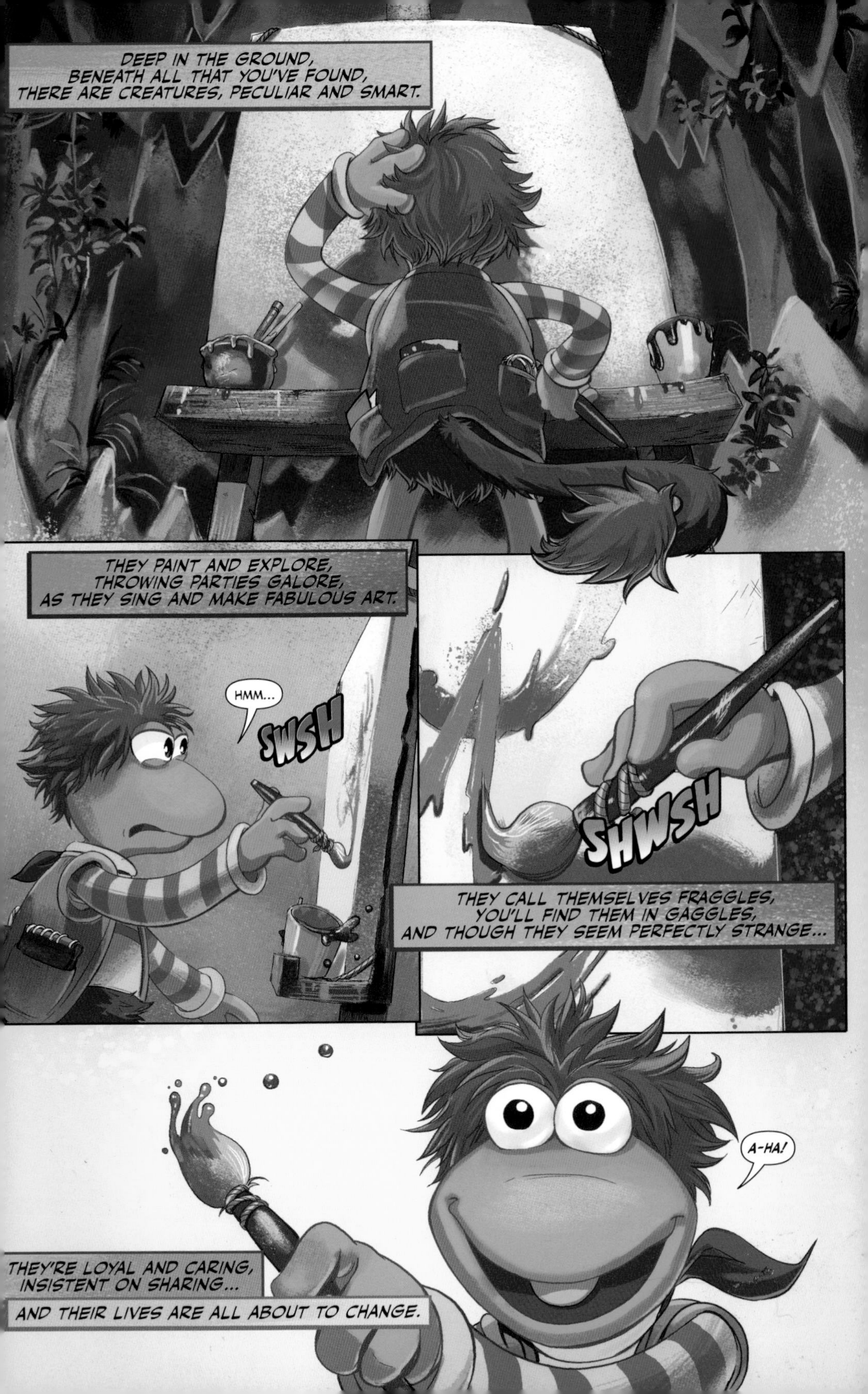

DEEP IN THE GROUND,
BENEATH ALL THAT YOU'VE FOUND,
THERE ARE CREATURES, PECULIAR AND SMART.
THEY PAINT AND EXPLORE,
THROWING PARTIES GALORE,
AS THEY SING AND MAKE FABULOUS ART.
HMM...
SWSH
SHWSH
THEY CALL THEMSELVES FRAGGLES,
YOU'LL FIND THEM IN GAGGLES,
AND THOUGH THEY SEEM PERFECTLY STRANGE...
A-HA!
THEY'RE LOYAL AND CARING,
INSISTENT ON SHARING...
AND THEIR LIVES ARE ALL ABOUT TO CHANGE.

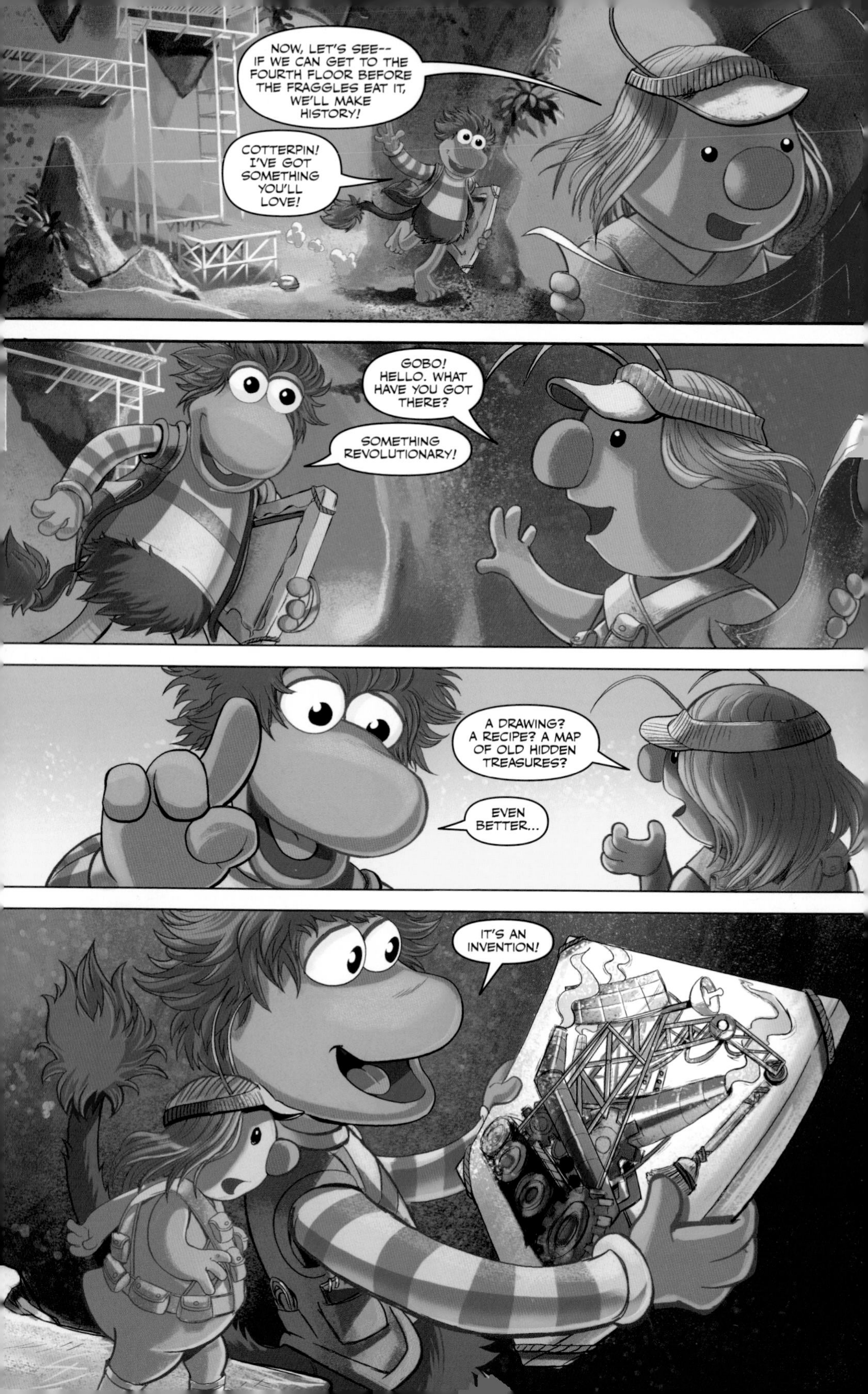
NOW, LET'S SEE-- IF WE CAN GET TO THE FOURTH FLOOR BEFORE THE FRAGGLES EAT IT, WE'LL MAKE HISTORY!
COTTERPIN! I'VE GOT SOMETHING YOU'LL LOVE!
GOBO! HELLO. WHAT HAVE YOU GOT THERE?
SOMETHING REVOLUTIONARY!
A DRAWING? A RECIPE? A MAP OF OLD HIDDEN TREASURES?
EVEN BETTER...
IT'S AN INVENTION!

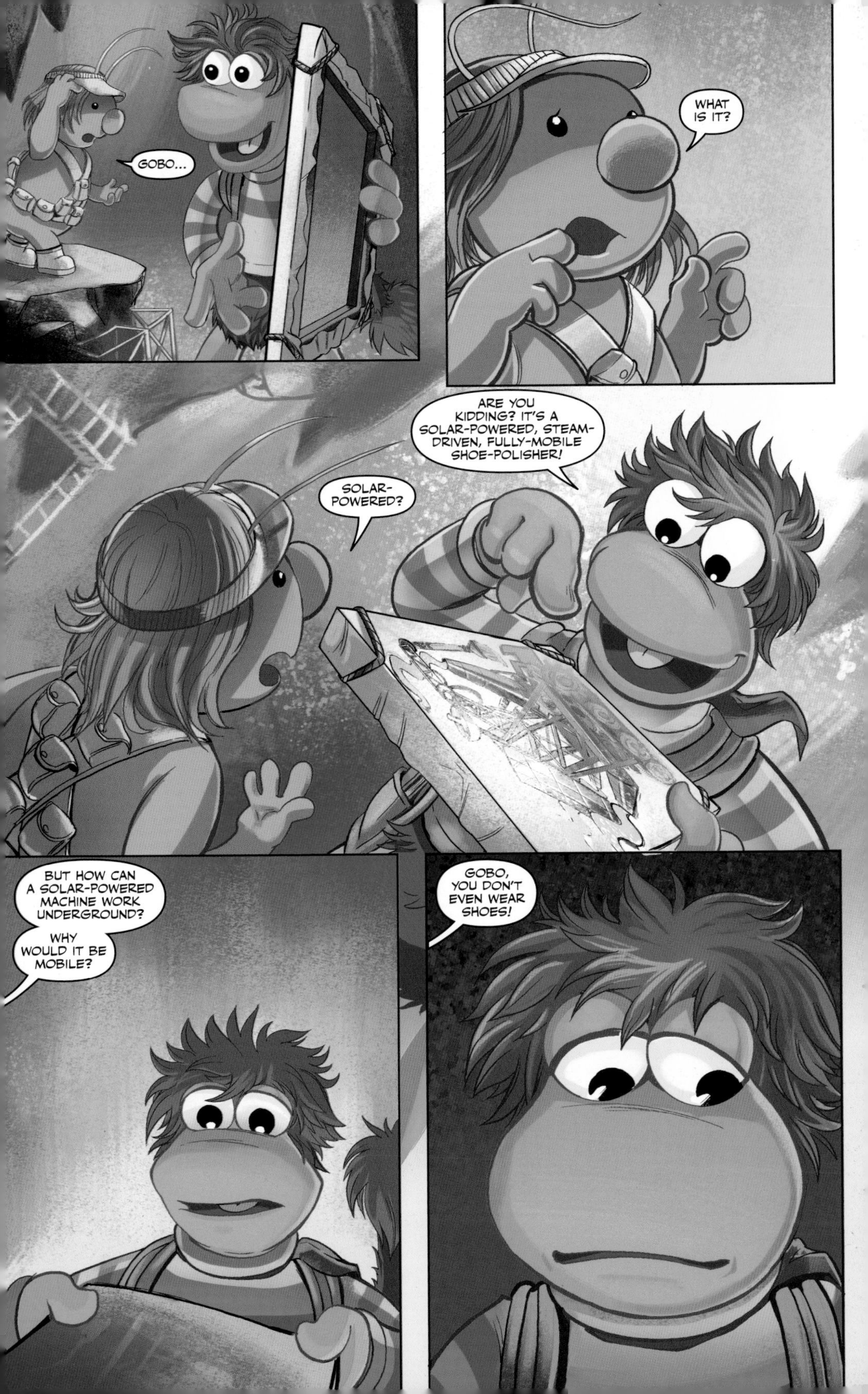
GOBO...
WHAT IS IT?
ARE YOU KIDDING? IT'S A SOLAR-POWERED, STEAM-DRIVEN, FULLY-MOBILE SHOE-POLISHER!
SOLAR-POWERED?
BUT HOW CAN A SOLAR-POWERED MACHINE WORK UNDERGROUND?
WHY WOULD IT BE MOBILE?
GOBO, YOU DON'T EVEN WEAR SHOES!

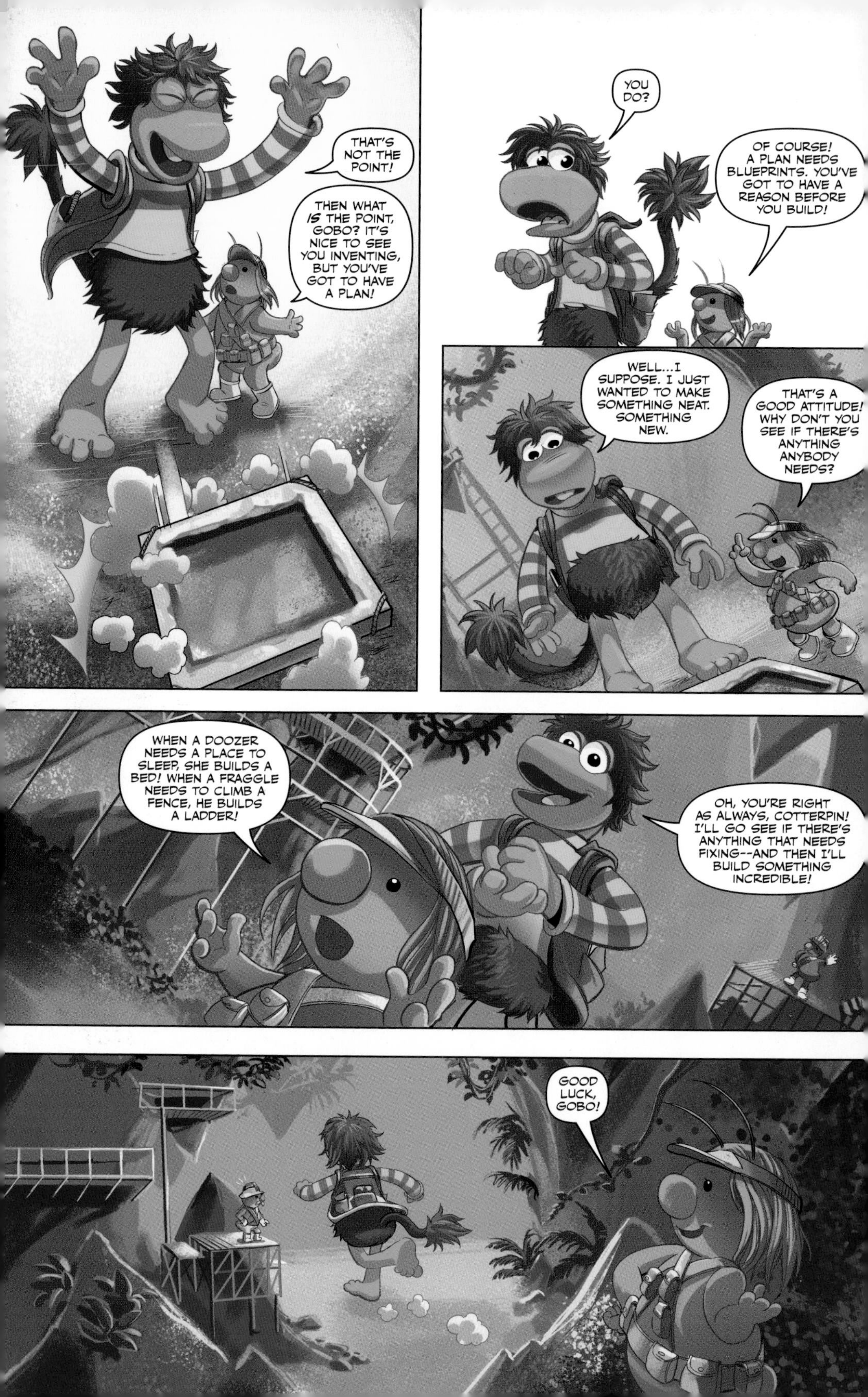
THAT'S NOT THE POINT!
THEN WHAT *IS* THE POINT, GOBO? IT'S NICE TO SEE YOU INVENTING, BUT YOU'VE GOT TO HAVE A PLAN!
YOU DO?
OF COURSE! A PLAN NEEDS BLUEPRINTS. YOU'VE GOT TO HAVE A REASON BEFORE YOU BUILD!
WELL...I SUPPOSE. I JUST WANTED TO MAKE SOMETHING NEAT. SOMETHING NEW.
THAT'S A GOOD ATTITUDE! WHY DON'T YOU SEE IF THERE'S ANYTHING ANYBODY NEEDS?
WHEN A DOOZER NEEDS A PLACE TO SLEEP, SHE BUILDS A BED! WHEN A FRAGGLE NEEDS TO CLIMB A FENCE, HE BUILDS A LADDER!
OH, YOU'RE RIGHT AS ALWAYS, COTTERPIN! I'LL GO SEE IF THERE'S ANYTHING THAT NEEDS FIXING--AND THEN I'LL BUILD SOMETHING INCREDIBLE!
GOOD LUCK, GOBO!

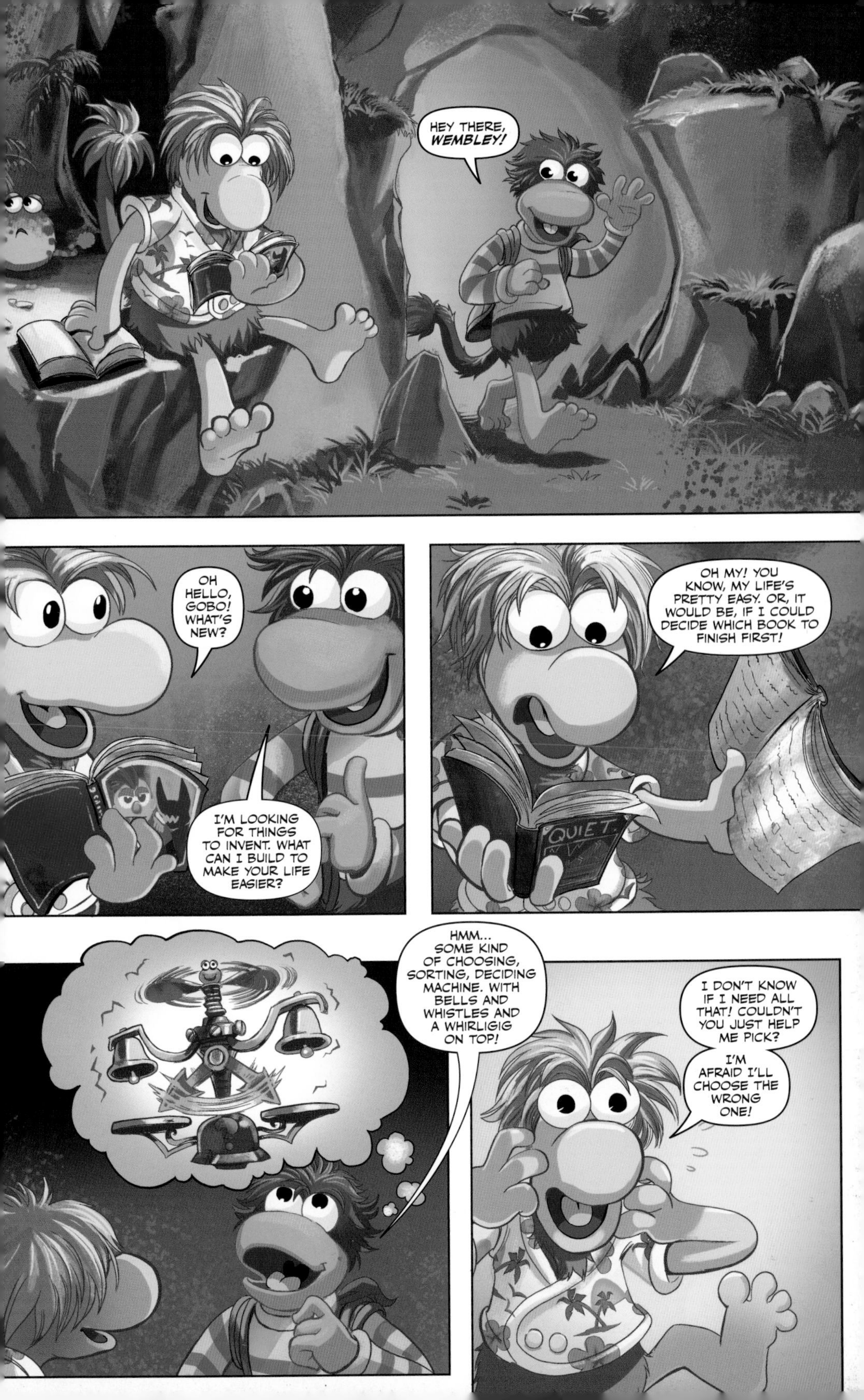
HEY THERE, WEMBLEY!
OH HELLO, GOBO! WHAT'S NEW?
I'M LOOKING FOR THINGS TO INVENT. WHAT CAN I BUILD TO MAKE YOUR LIFE EASIER?
OH MY! YOU KNOW, MY LIFE'S PRETTY EASY. OR, IT WOULD BE, IF I COULD DECIDE WHICH BOOK TO FINISH FIRST!
QUIET
HMM... SOME KIND OF CHOOSING, SORTING, DECIDING MACHINE. WITH BELLS AND WHISTLES AND A WHIRLIGIG ON TOP!
I DON'T KNOW IF I NEED ALL THAT! COULDN'T YOU JUST HELP ME PICK?
I'M AFRAID I'LL CHOOSE THE WRONG ONE!

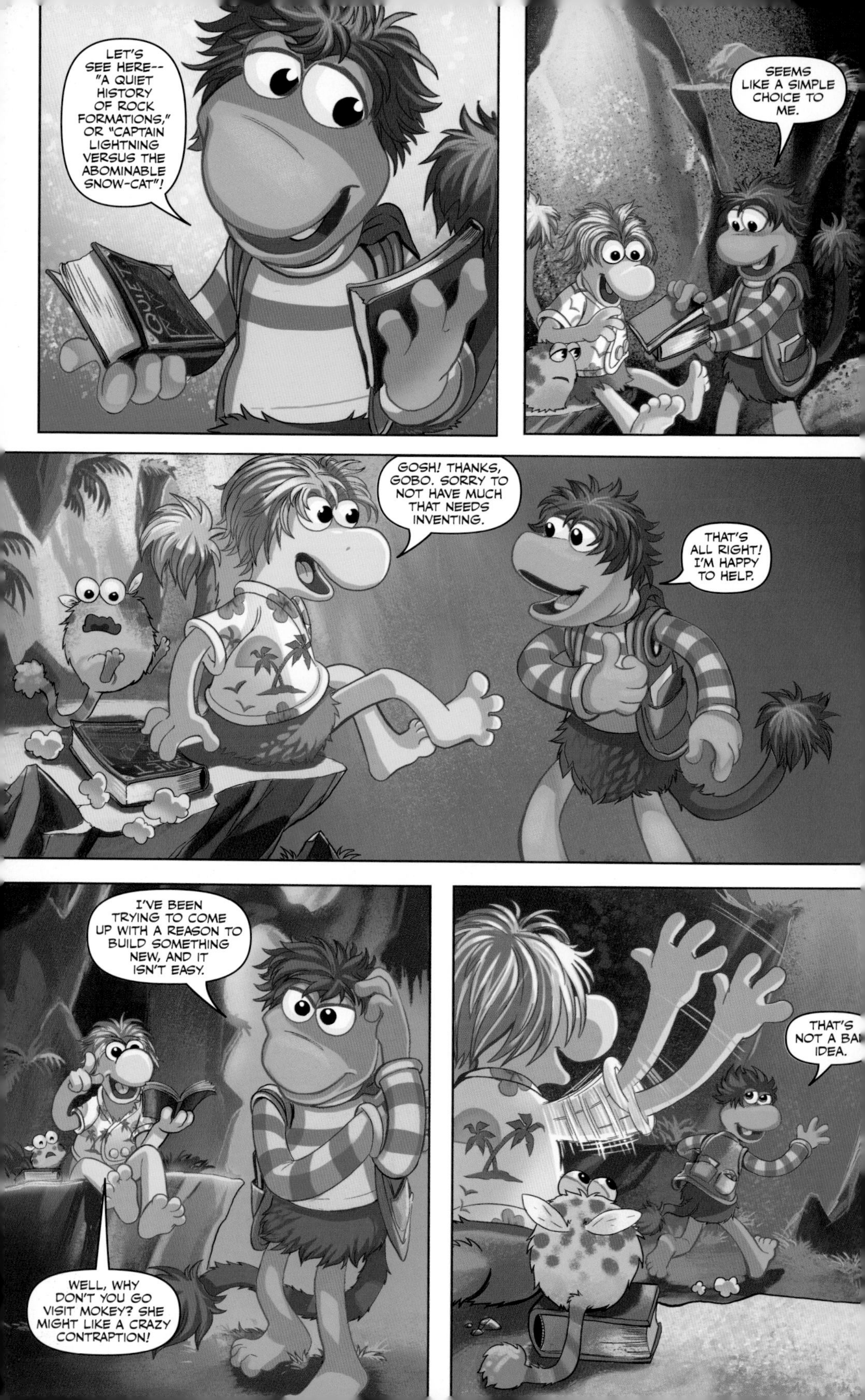

LET'S SEE HERE-- "A QUIET HISTORY OF ROCK FORMATIONS," OR "CAPTAIN LIGHTNING VERSUS THE ABOMINABLE SNOW-CAT"!
SEEMS LIKE A SIMPLE CHOICE TO ME.
GOSH! THANKS, GOBO. SORRY TO NOT HAVE MUCH THAT NEEDS INVENTING.
THAT'S ALL RIGHT! I'M HAPPY TO HELP.
I'VE BEEN TRYING TO COME UP WITH A REASON TO BUILD SOMETHING NEW, AND IT ISN'T EASY.
WELL, WHY DON'T YOU GO VISIT MOKEY? SHE MIGHT LIKE A CRAZY CONTRAPTION!
THAT'S NOT A BA IDEA.

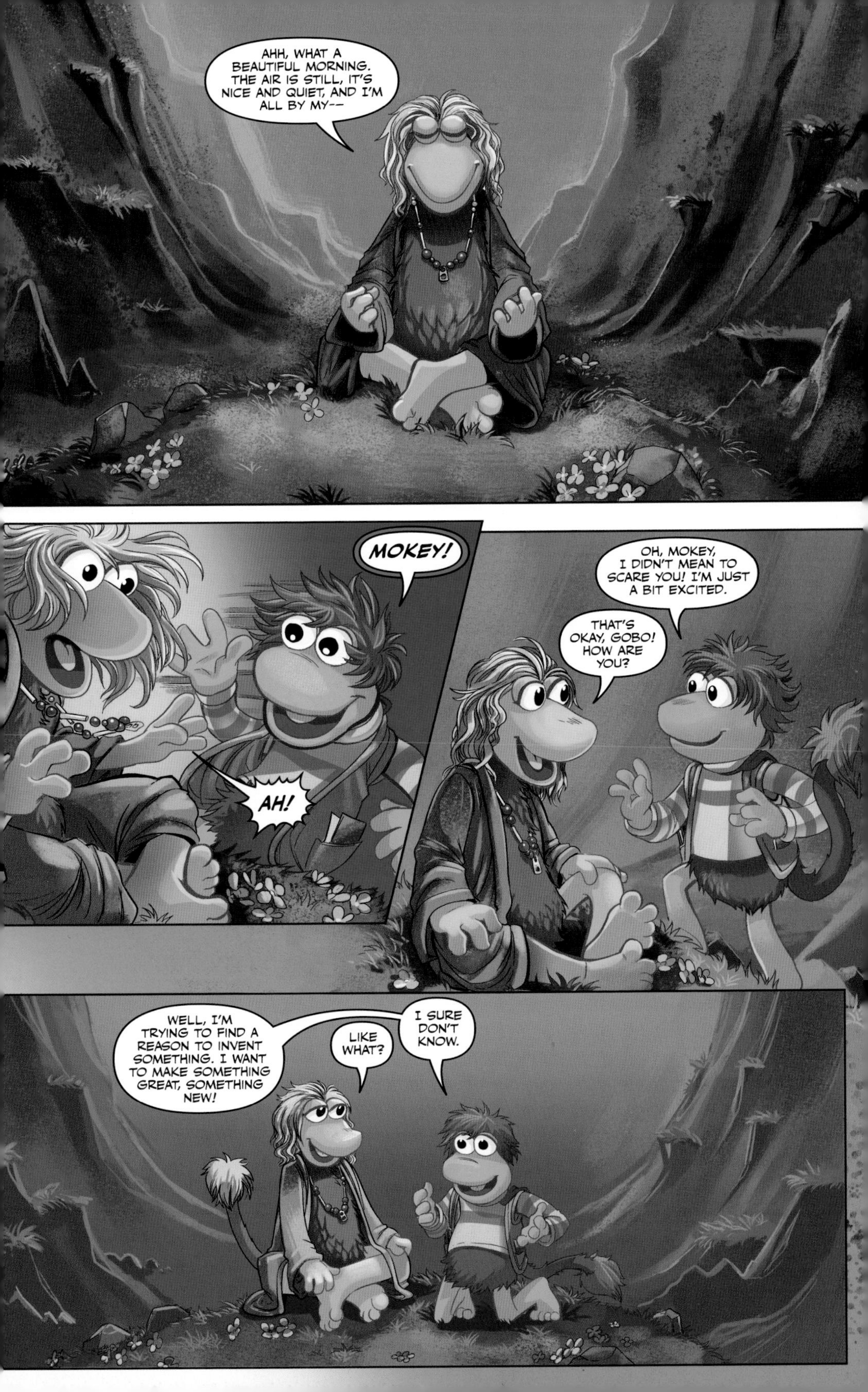
AHH, WHAT A BEAUTIFUL MORNING. THE AIR IS STILL, IT'S NICE AND QUIET, AND I'M ALL BY MY--
MOKEY!
AH!
OH, MOKEY, I DIDN'T MEAN TO SCARE YOU! I'M JUST A BIT EXCITED.
THAT'S OKAY, GOBO! HOW ARE YOU?
WELL, I'M TRYING TO FIND A REASON TO INVENT SOMETHING. I WANT TO MAKE SOMETHING GREAT, SOMETHING NEW!
LIKE WHAT?
I SURE DON'T KNOW.

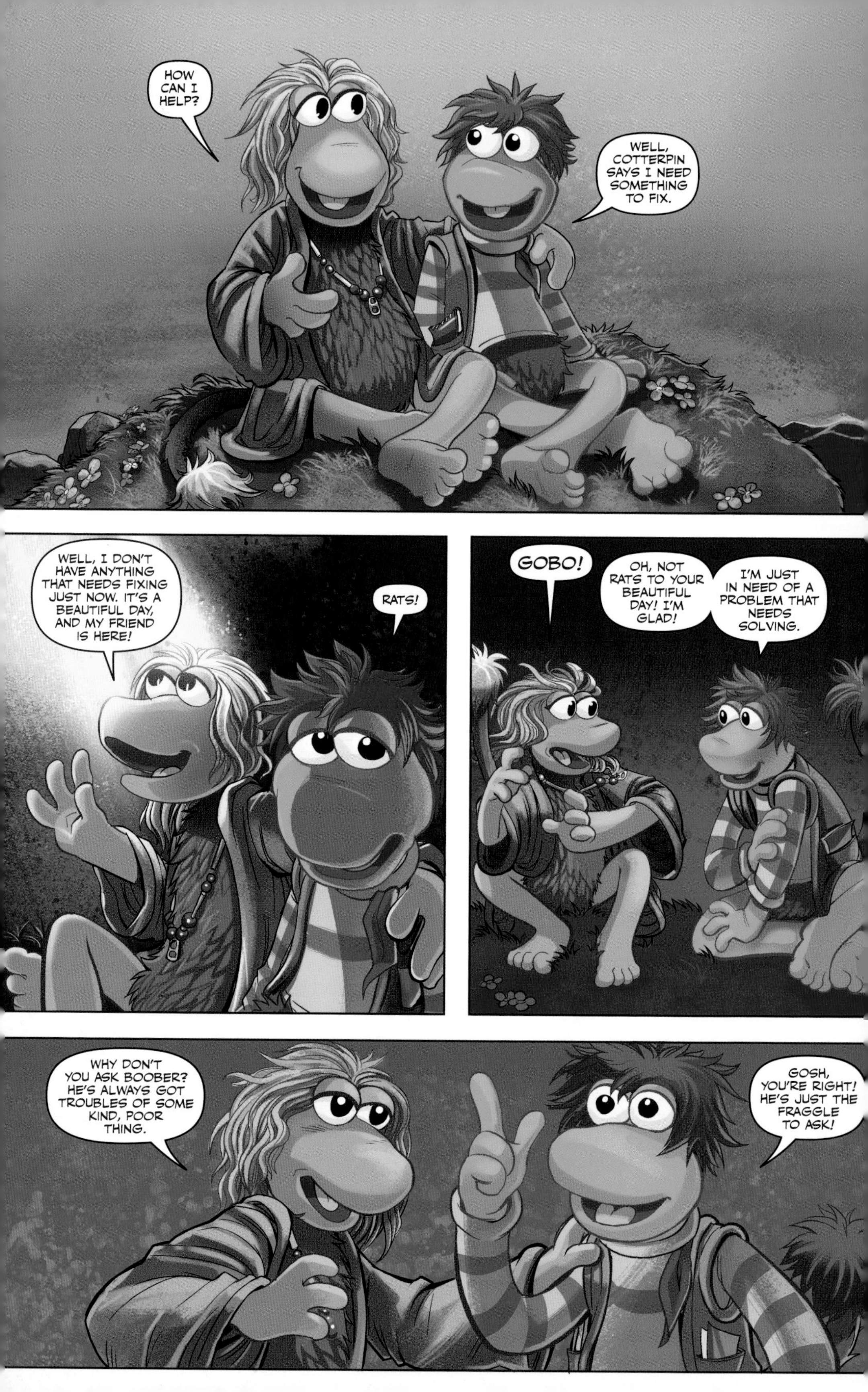
HOW CAN I HELP?
WELL, COTTERPIN SAYS I NEED SOMETHING TO FIX.
WELL, I DON'T HAVE ANYTHING THAT NEEDS FIXING JUST NOW. IT'S A BEAUTIFUL DAY, AND MY FRIEND IS HERE!
RATS!
GOBO!
OH, NOT RATS TO YOUR BEAUTIFUL DAY! I'M GLAD!
I'M JUST IN NEED OF A PROBLEM THAT NEEDS SOLVING.
WHY DON'T YOU ASK BOOBER? HE'S ALWAYS GOT TROUBLES OF SOME KIND, POOR THING.
GOSH, YOU'RE RIGHT! HE'S JUST THE FRAGGLE TO ASK!

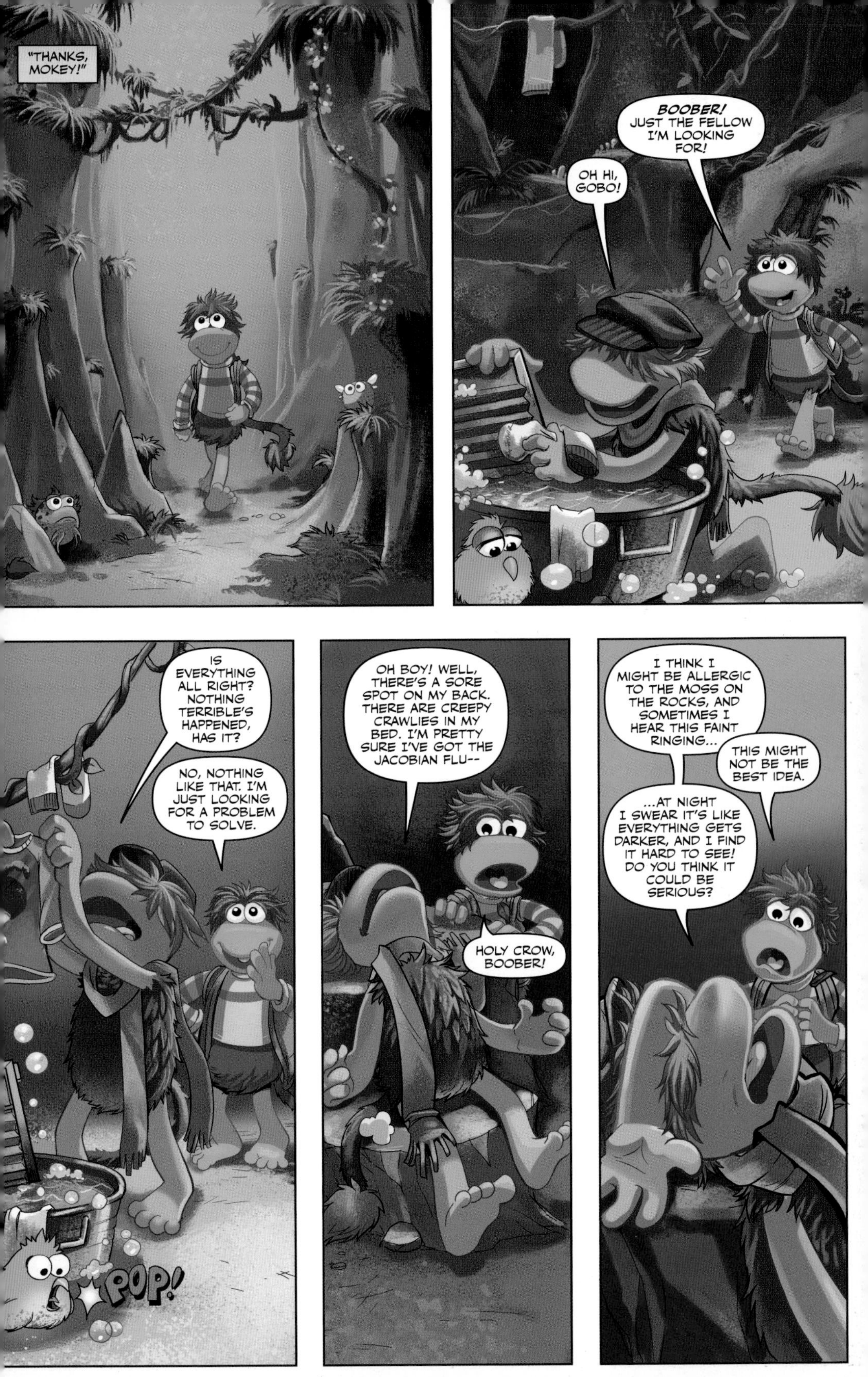
"THANKS, MOKEY!"
BOOBER! JUST THE FELLOW I'M LOOKING FOR!
OH HI, GOBO!
IS EVERYTHING ALL RIGHT? NOTHING TERRIBLE'S HAPPENED, HAS IT?
NO, NOTHING LIKE THAT. I'M JUST LOOKING FOR A PROBLEM TO SOLVE.
POP!
OH BOY! WELL, THERE'S A SORE SPOT ON MY BACK. THERE ARE CREEPY CRAWLIES IN MY BED. I'M PRETTY SURE I'VE GOT THE JACOBIAN FLU--
HOLY CROW, BOOBER!
I THINK I MIGHT BE ALLERGIC TO THE MOSS ON THE ROCKS, AND SOMETIMES I HEAR THIS FAINT RINGING...
THIS MIGHT NOT BE THE BEST IDEA.
...AT NIGHT I SWEAR IT'S LIKE EVERYTHING GETS DARKER, AND I FIND IT HARD TO SEE! DO YOU THINK IT COULD BE SERIOUS?

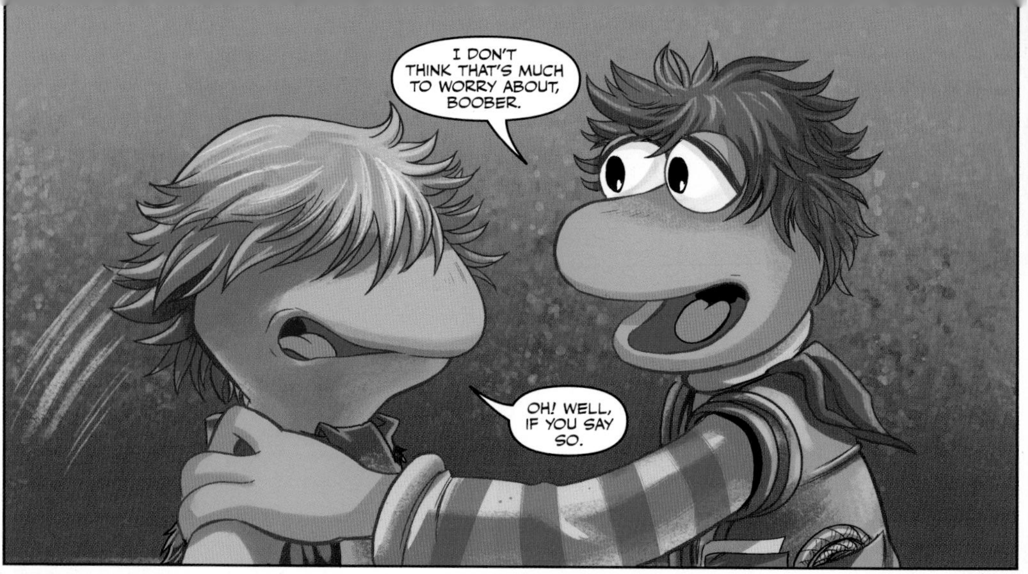
I DON'T THINK THAT'S MUCH TO WORRY ABOUT, BOOBER.
OH! WELL, IF YOU SAY SO.

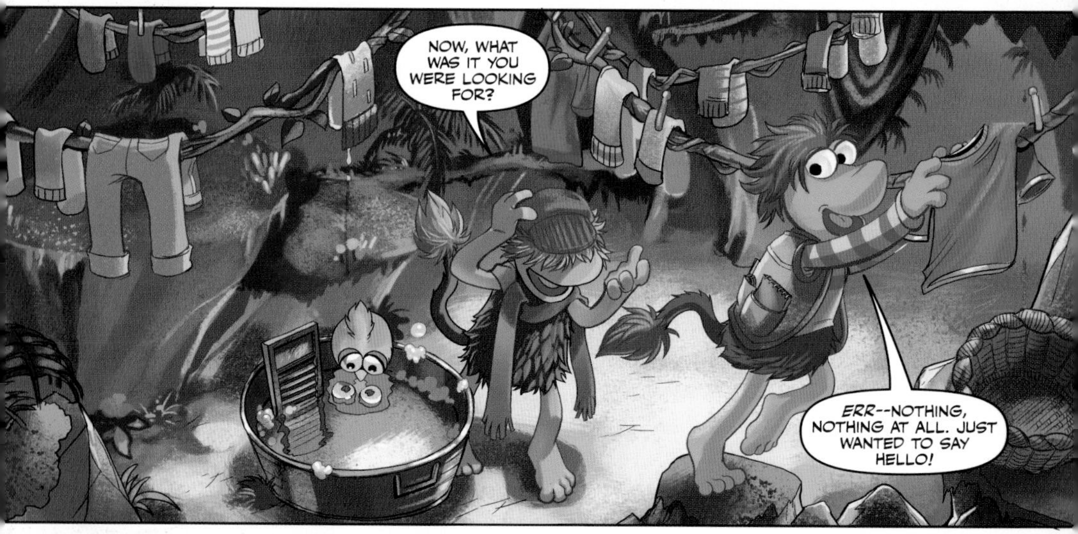
NOW, WHAT WAS IT YOU WERE LOOKING FOR?
ERR--NOTHING, NOTHING AT ALL. JUST WANTED TO SAY HELLO!

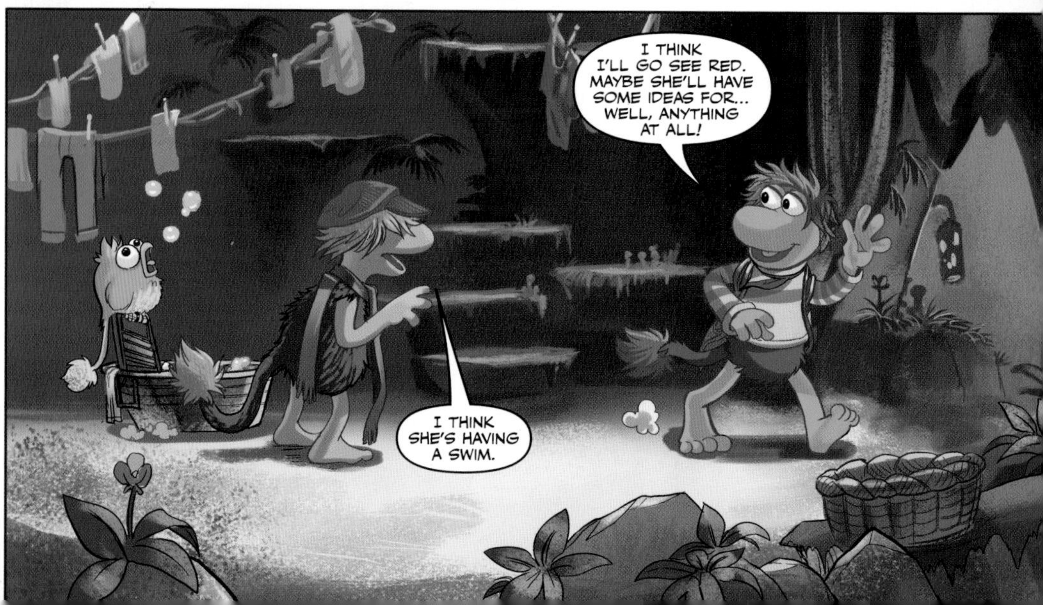
I THINK I'LL GO SEE RED. MAYBE SHE'LL HAVE SOME IDEAS FOR... WELL, ANYTHING AT ALL!
I THINK SHE'S HAVING A SWIM.

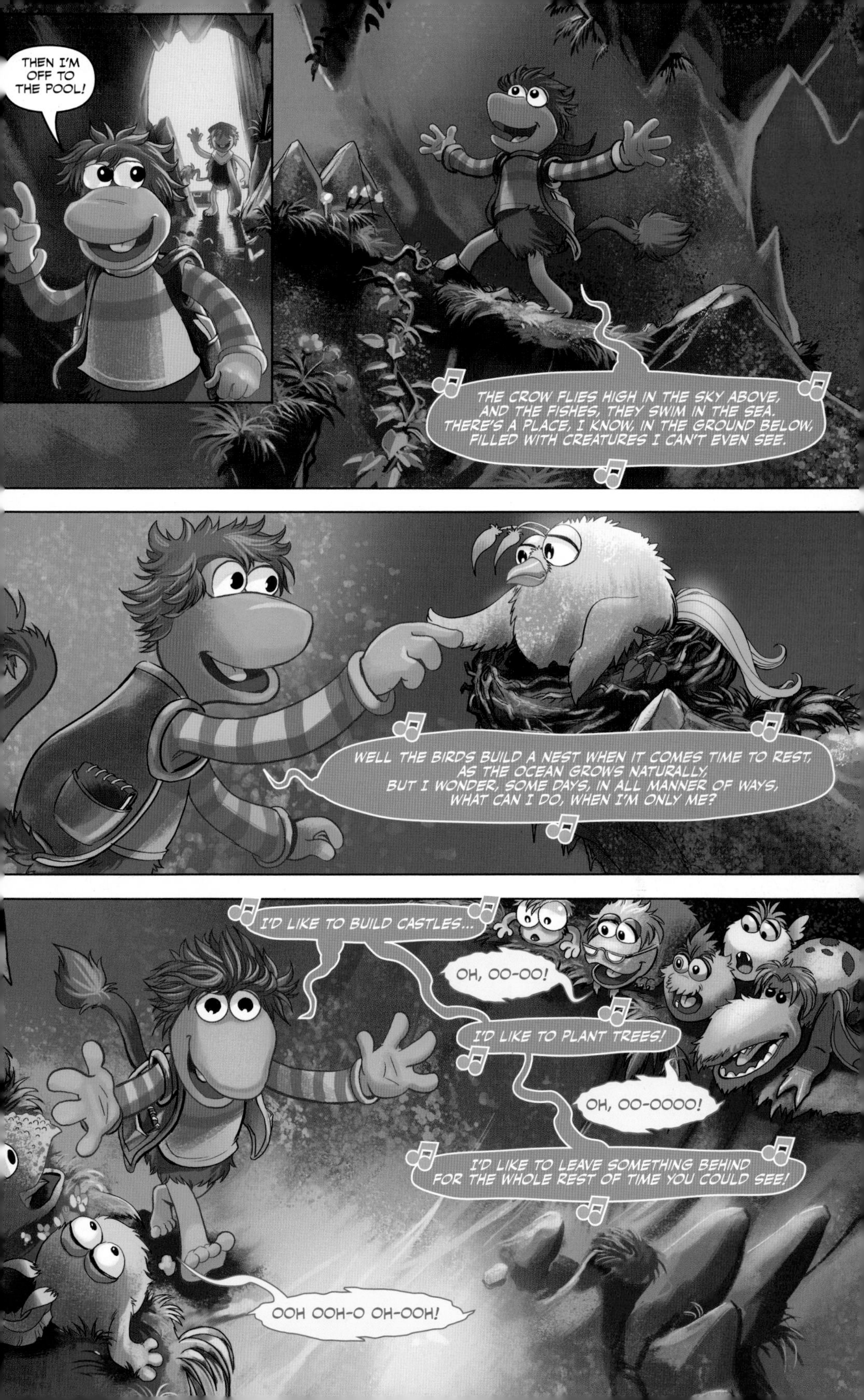
THEN I'M OFF TO THE POOL!
THE CROW FLIES HIGH IN THE SKY ABOVE,
AND THE FISHES, THEY SWIM IN THE SEA.
THERE'S A PLACE, I KNOW, IN THE GROUND BELOW,
FILLED WITH CREATURES I CAN'T EVEN SEE.
WELL THE BIRDS BUILD A NEST WHEN IT COMES TIME TO REST,
AS THE OCEAN GROWS NATURALLY.
BUT I WONDER, SOME DAYS, IN ALL MANNER OF WAYS,
WHAT CAN I DO, WHEN I'M ONLY ME?
I'D LIKE TO BUILD CASTLES...
OH, OO-OO!
I'D LIKE TO PLANT TREES!
OH, OO-OOOO!
I'D LIKE TO LEAVE SOMETHING BEHIND
FOR THE WHOLE REST OF TIME YOU COULD SEE!
OOH OOH-O OH-OOH!

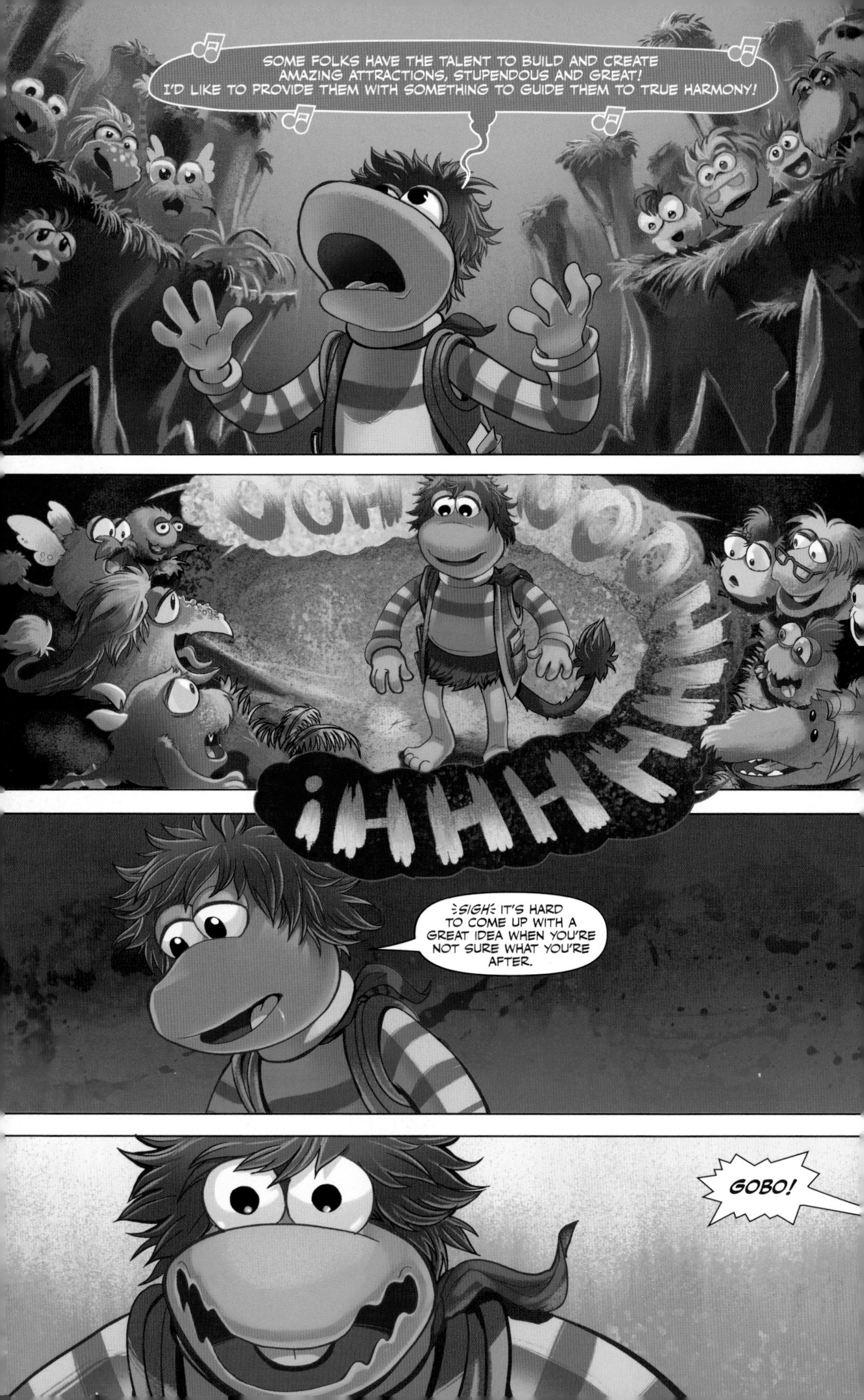
SOME FOLKS HAVE THE TALENT TO BUILD AND CREATE AMAZING ATTRACTIONS, STUPENDOUS AND GREAT! I'D LIKE TO PROVIDE THEM WITH SOMETHING TO GUIDE THEM TO TRUE HARMONY!
SIGH IT'S HARD TO COME UP WITH A GREAT IDEA WHEN YOU'RE NOT SURE WHAT YOU'RE AFTER.
GOBO!

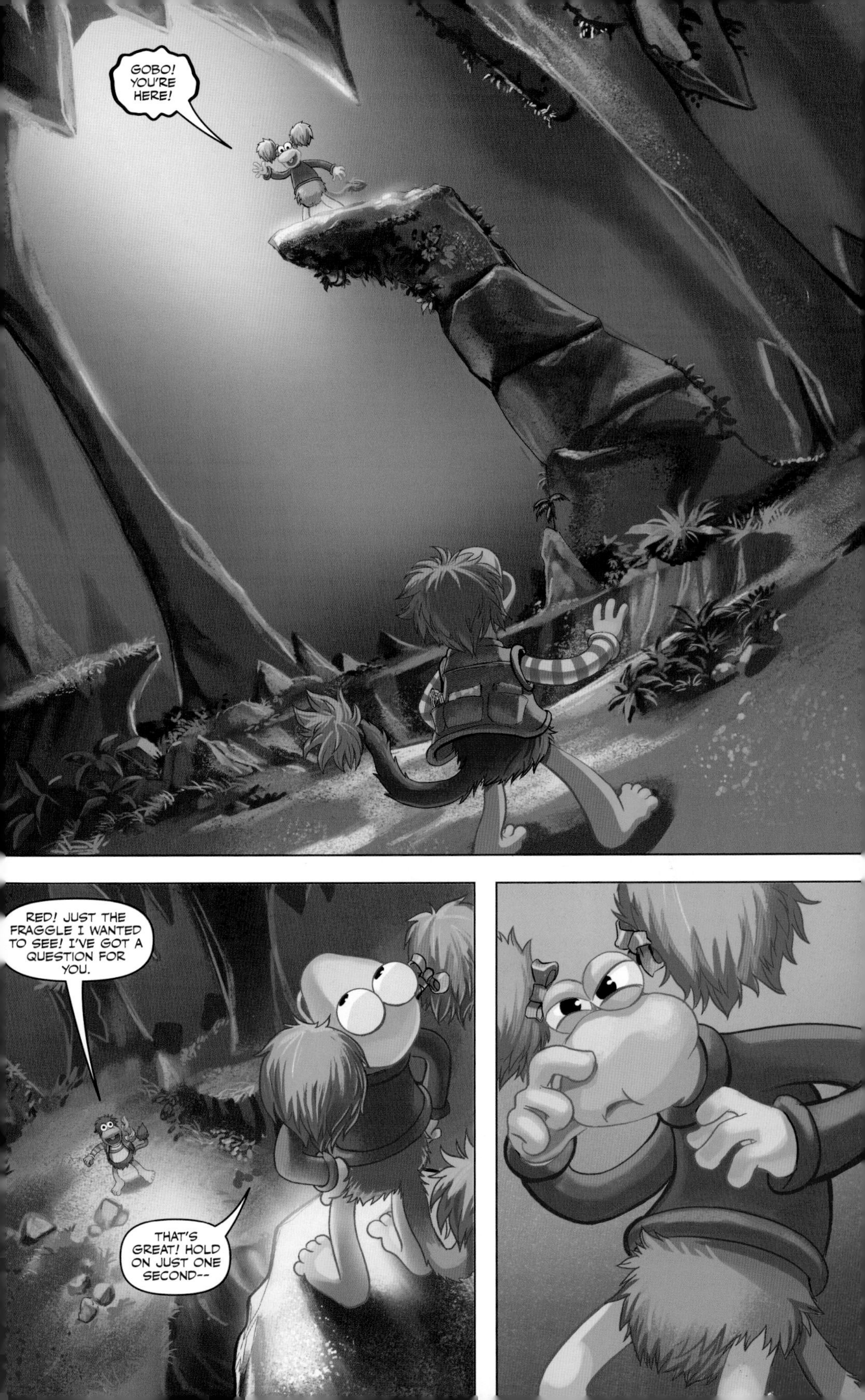
GOBO! YOU'RE HERE!
RED! JUST THE FRAGGLE I WANTED TO SEE! I'VE GOT A QUESTION FOR YOU.
THAT'S GREAT! HOLD ON JUST ONE SECOND--

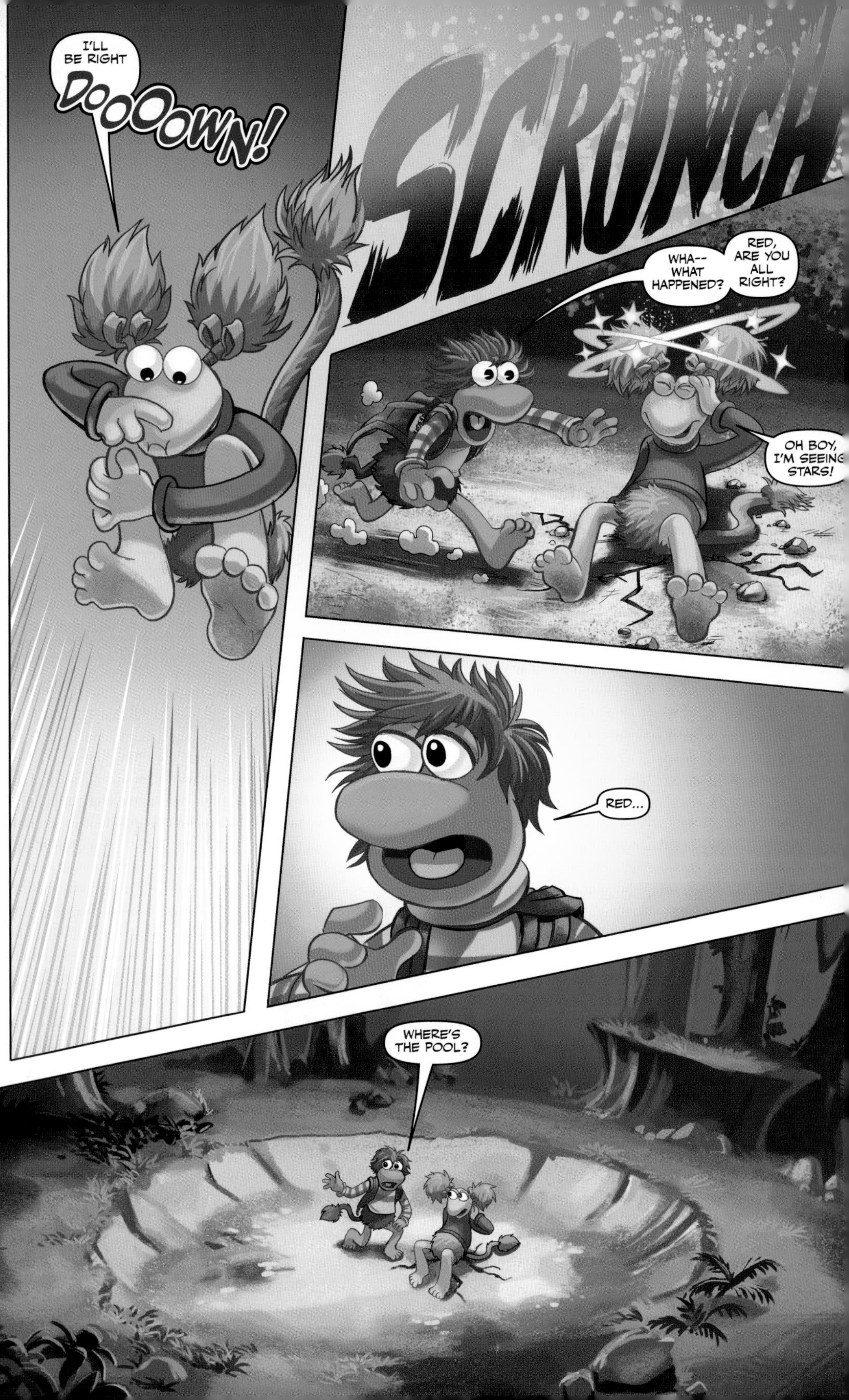
I'LL BE RIGHT DOOOOOWN!
SCRUNCH
RED, ARE YOU ALL RIGHT?
WHA-- WHAT HAPPENED?
OH BOY, I'M SEEING STARS!
RED...
WHERE'S THE POOL?

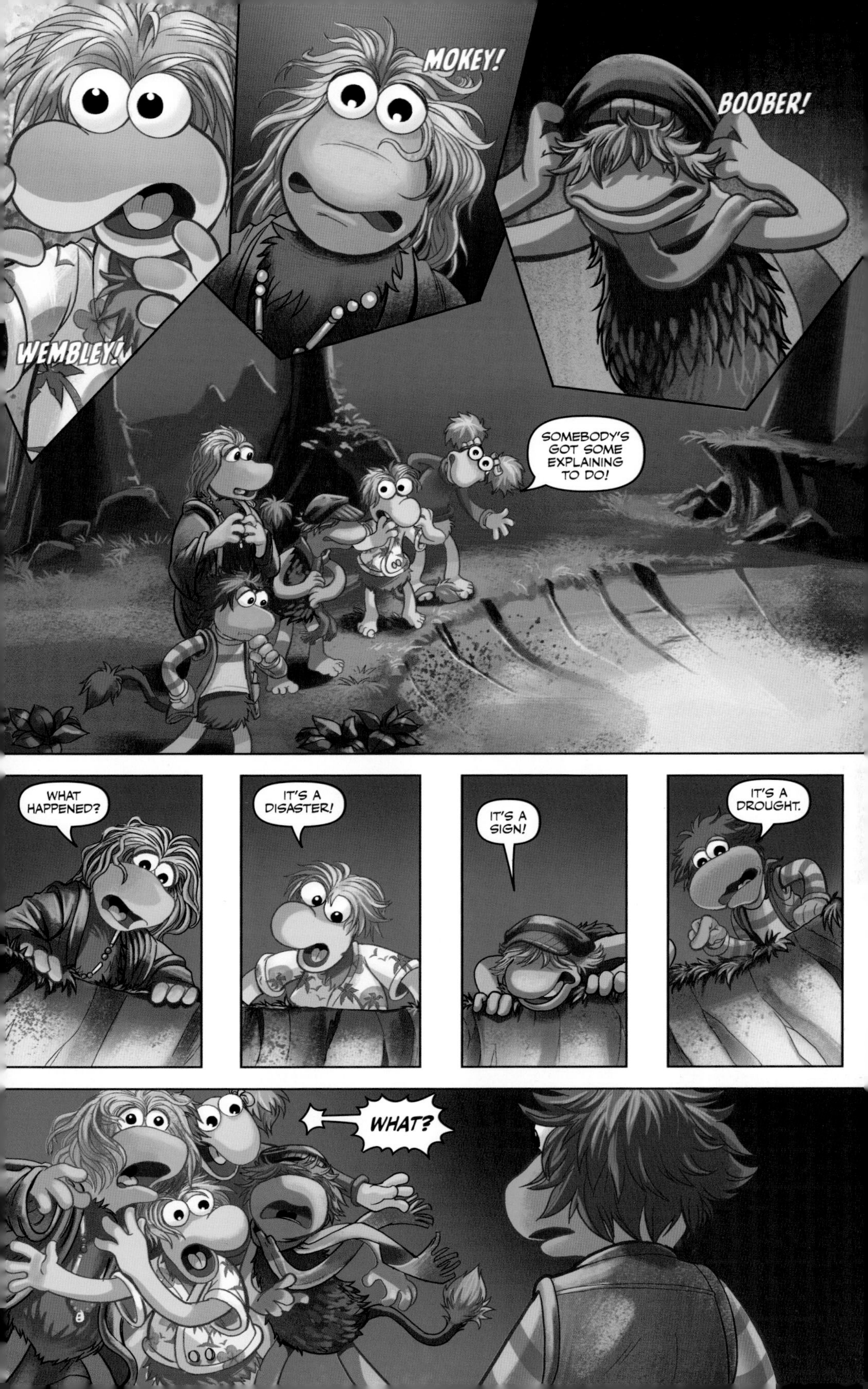
WEMBLEY!
MOKEY!
BOOBER!
SOMEBODY'S GOT SOME EXPLAINING TO DO!
WHAT HAPPENED?
IT'S A DISASTER!
IT'S A SIGN!
IT'S A DROUGHT.
WHAT?

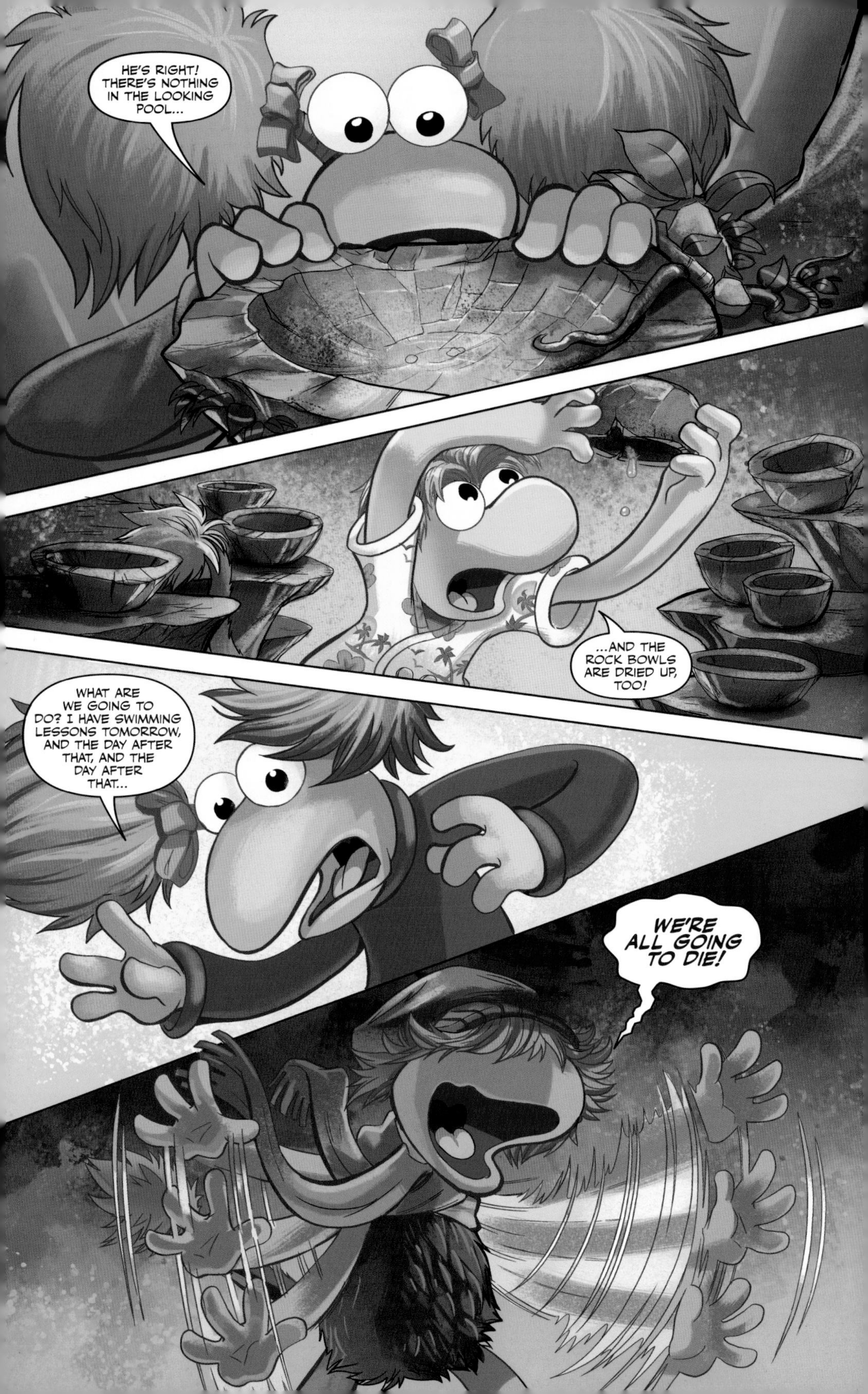
HE'S RIGHT! THERE'S NOTHING IN THE LOOKING POOL...
...AND THE ROCK BOWLS ARE DRIED UP, TOO!
WHAT ARE WE GOING TO DO? I HAVE SWIMMING LESSONS TOMORROW, AND THE DAY AFTER THAT, AND THE DAY AFTER THAT...
WE'RE ALL GOING TO DIE!

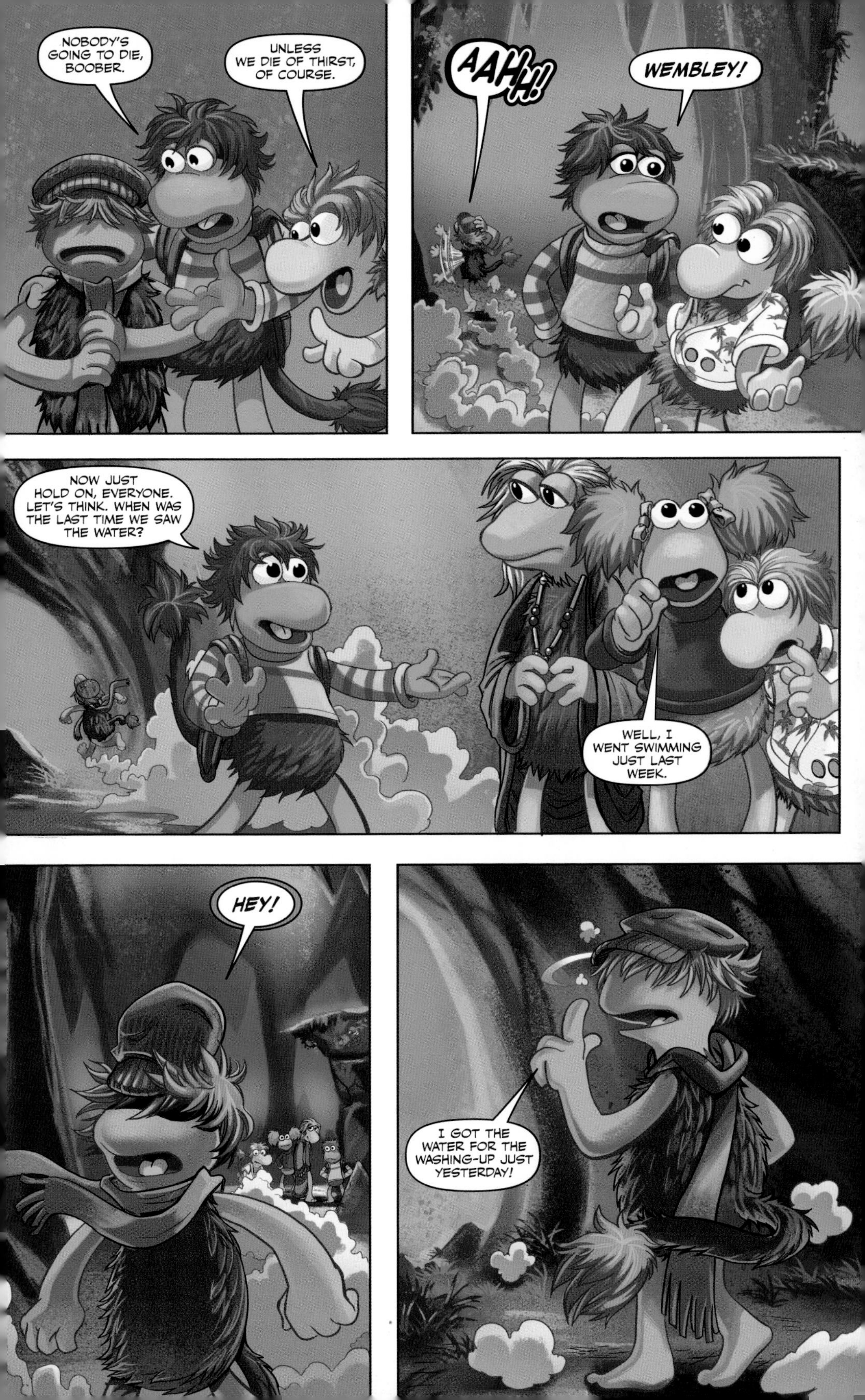
NOBODY'S GOING TO DIE, BOOBER.
UNLESS WE DIE OF THIRST, OF COURSE.
AAHH!
WEMBLEY!
NOW JUST HOLD ON, EVERYONE. LET'S THINK. WHEN WAS THE LAST TIME WE SAW THE WATER?
WELL, I WENT SWIMMING JUST LAST WEEK.
HEY!
I GOT THE WATER FOR THE WASHING-UP JUST YESTERDAY!

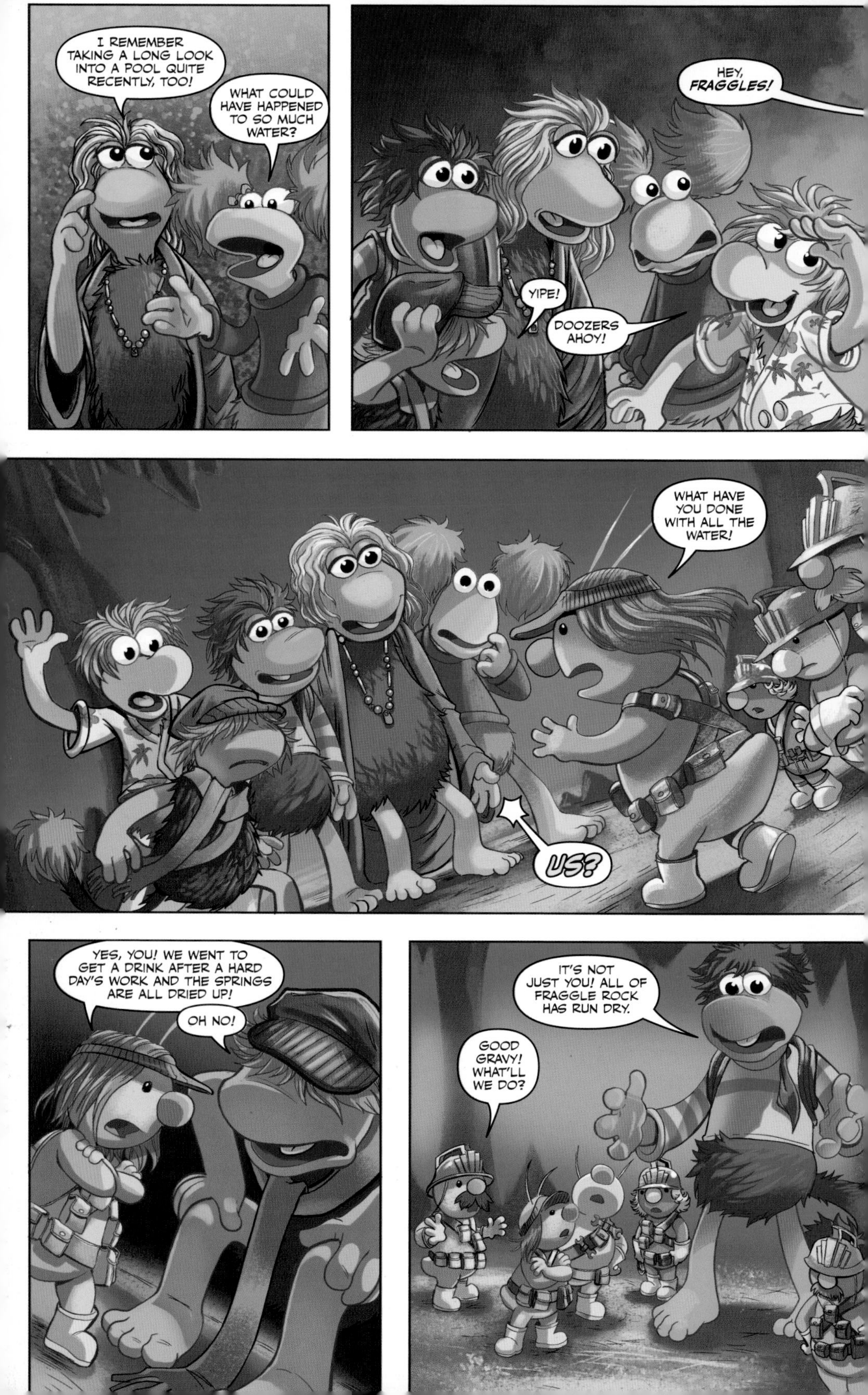
I REMEMBER TAKING A LONG LOOK INTO A POOL QUITE RECENTLY, TOO!
WHAT COULD HAVE HAPPENED TO SO MUCH WATER?
HEY, *FRAGGLES!*
YIPE!
DOOZERS AHOY!
WHAT HAVE YOU DONE WITH ALL THE WATER!
US?
YES, YOU! WE WENT TO GET A DRINK AFTER A HARD DAY'S WORK AND THE SPRINGS ARE ALL DRIED UP!
OH NO!
IT'S NOT JUST YOU! ALL OF FRAGGLE ROCK HAS RUN DRY.
GOOD GRAVY! WHAT'LL WE DO?

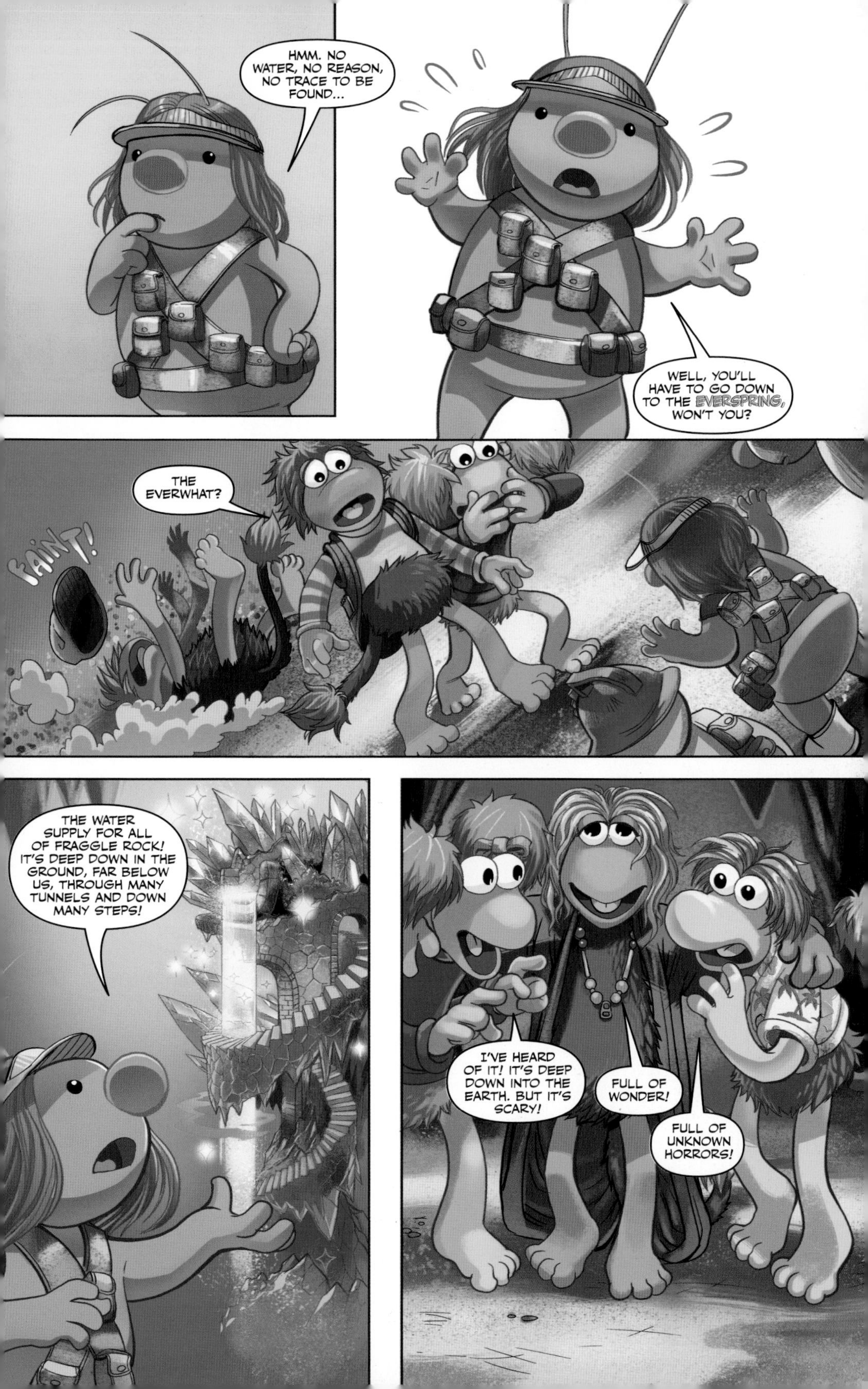
HMM. NO WATER, NO REASON, NO TRACE TO BE FOUND...
WELL, YOU'LL HAVE TO GO DOWN TO THE EVERSPRING, WON'T YOU?
THE EVERWHAT?
FAINT!
THE WATER SUPPLY FOR ALL OF FRAGGLE ROCK! IT'S DEEP DOWN IN THE GROUND, FAR BELOW US, THROUGH MANY TUNNELS AND DOWN MANY STEPS!
I'VE HEARD OF IT! IT'S DEEP DOWN INTO THE EARTH. BUT IT'S SCARY!
FULL OF WONDER!
FULL OF UNKNOWN HORRORS!

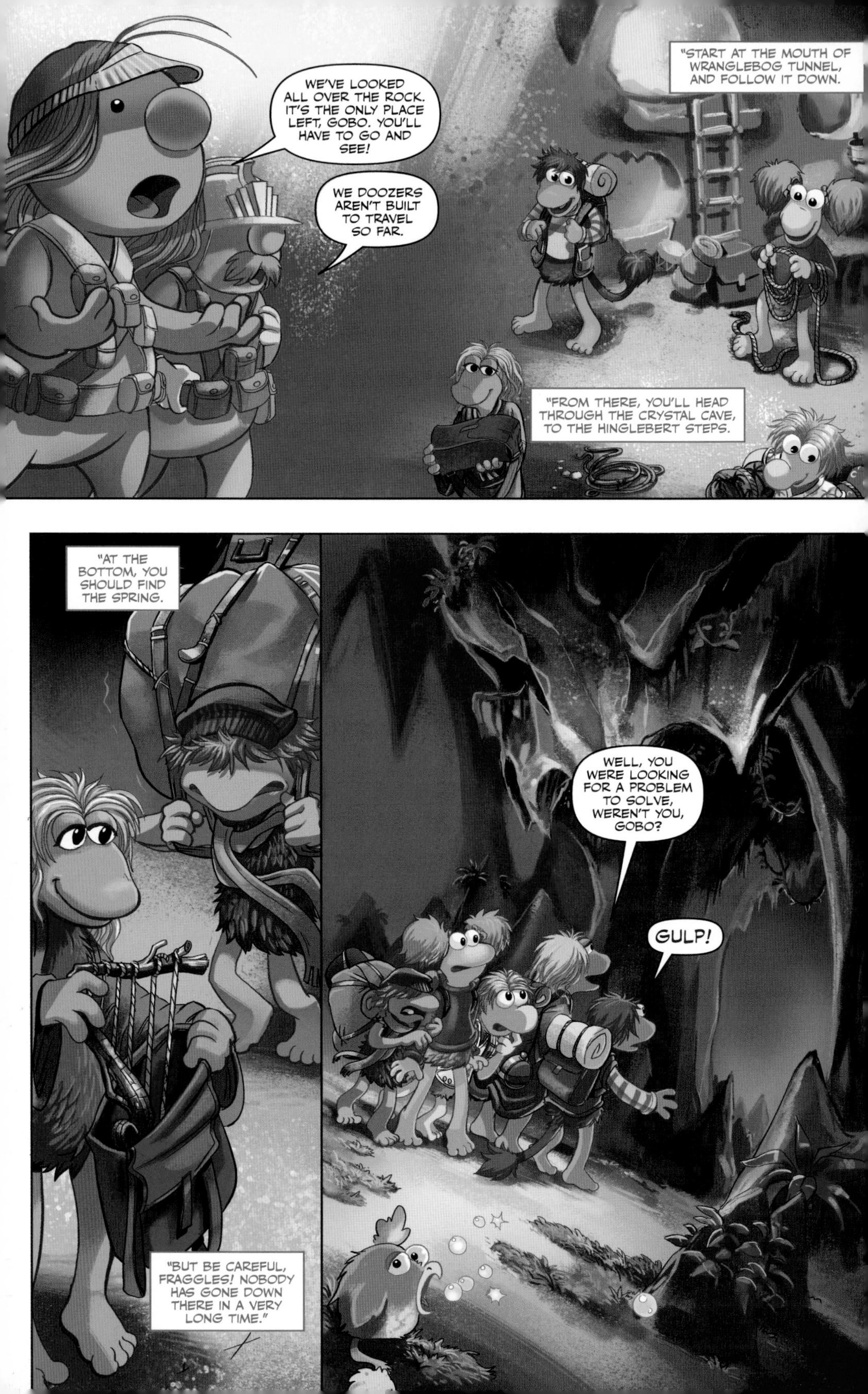
WE'VE LOOKED ALL OVER THE ROCK. IT'S THE ONLY PLACE LEFT, GOBO. YOU'LL HAVE TO GO AND SEE!
WE DOOZERS AREN'T BUILT TO TRAVEL SO FAR.
"START AT THE MOUTH OF WRANGLEBOG TUNNEL, AND FOLLOW IT DOWN.
"FROM THERE, YOU'LL HEAD THROUGH THE CRYSTAL CAVE, TO THE HINGLEBERT STEPS.
"AT THE BOTTOM, YOU SHOULD FIND THE SPRING.
"BUT BE CAREFUL, FRAGGLES! NOBODY HAS GONE DOWN THERE IN A VERY LONG TIME."
WELL, YOU WERE LOOKING FOR A PROBLEM TO SOLVE, WEREN'T YOU, GOBO?
GULP!

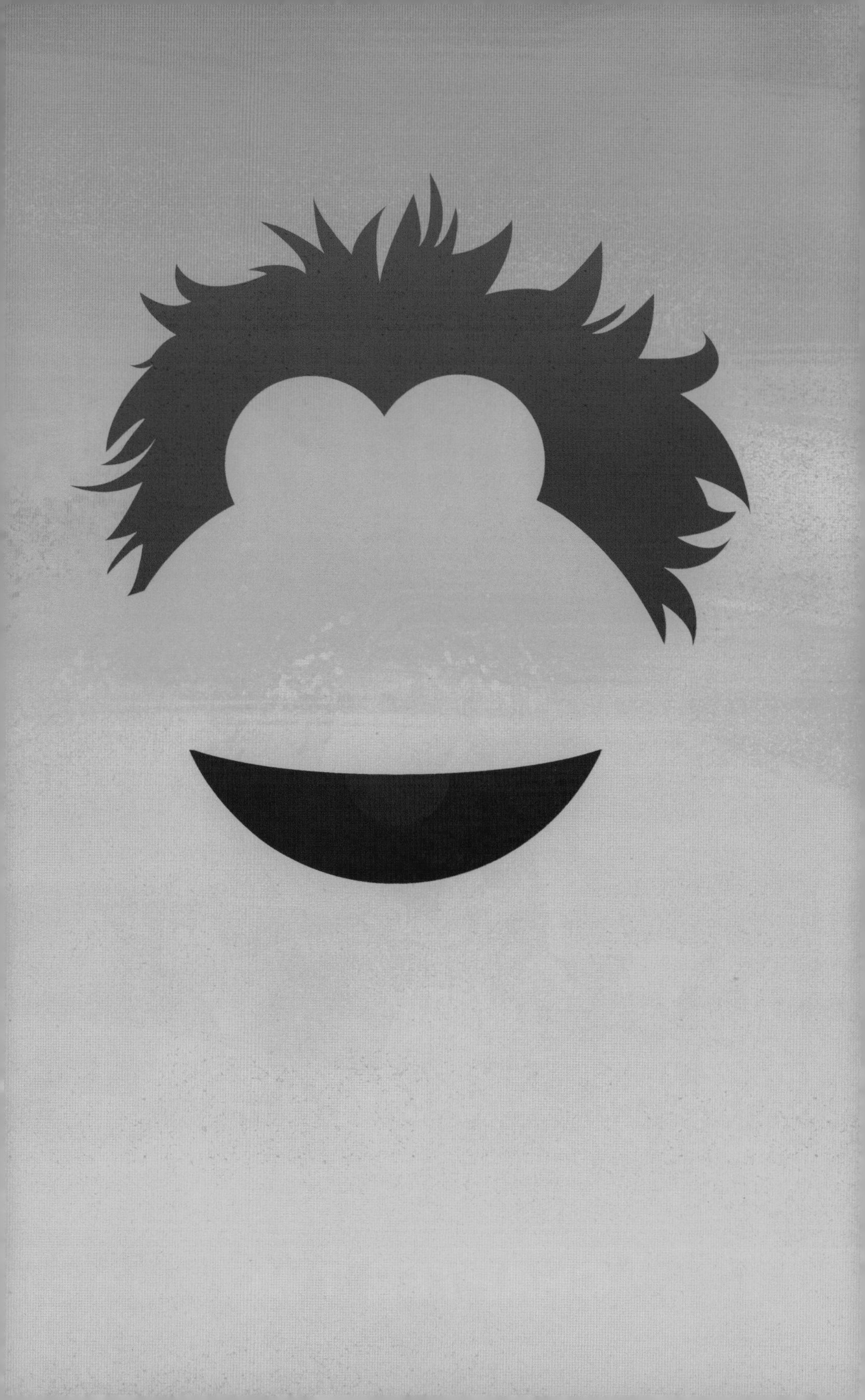

WORRY'S FOR ANOTHER DAY

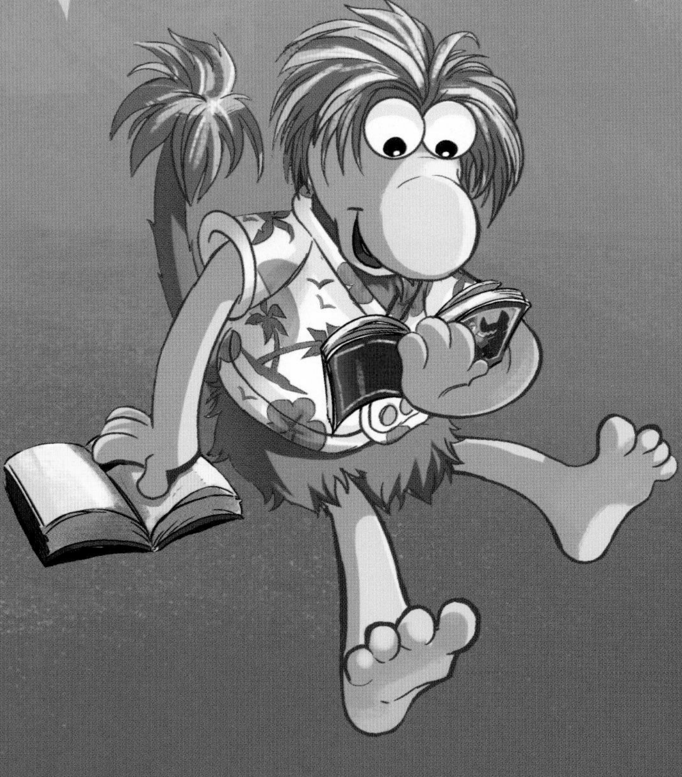

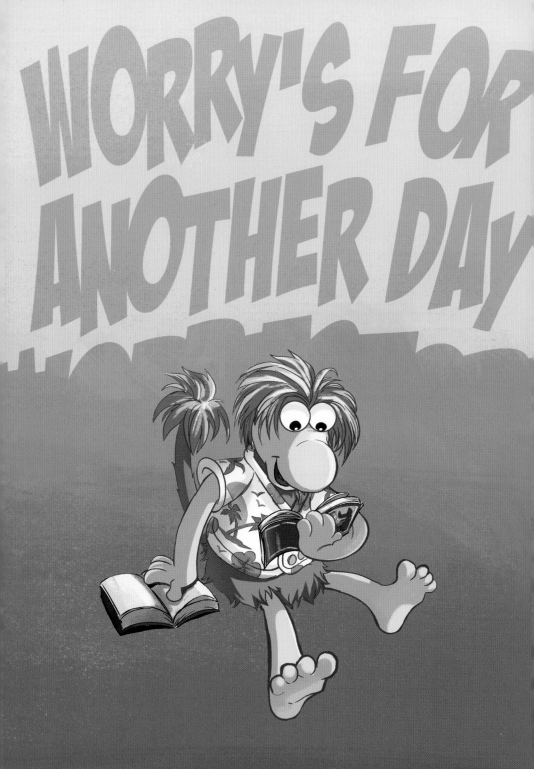

CHAPTER TWO

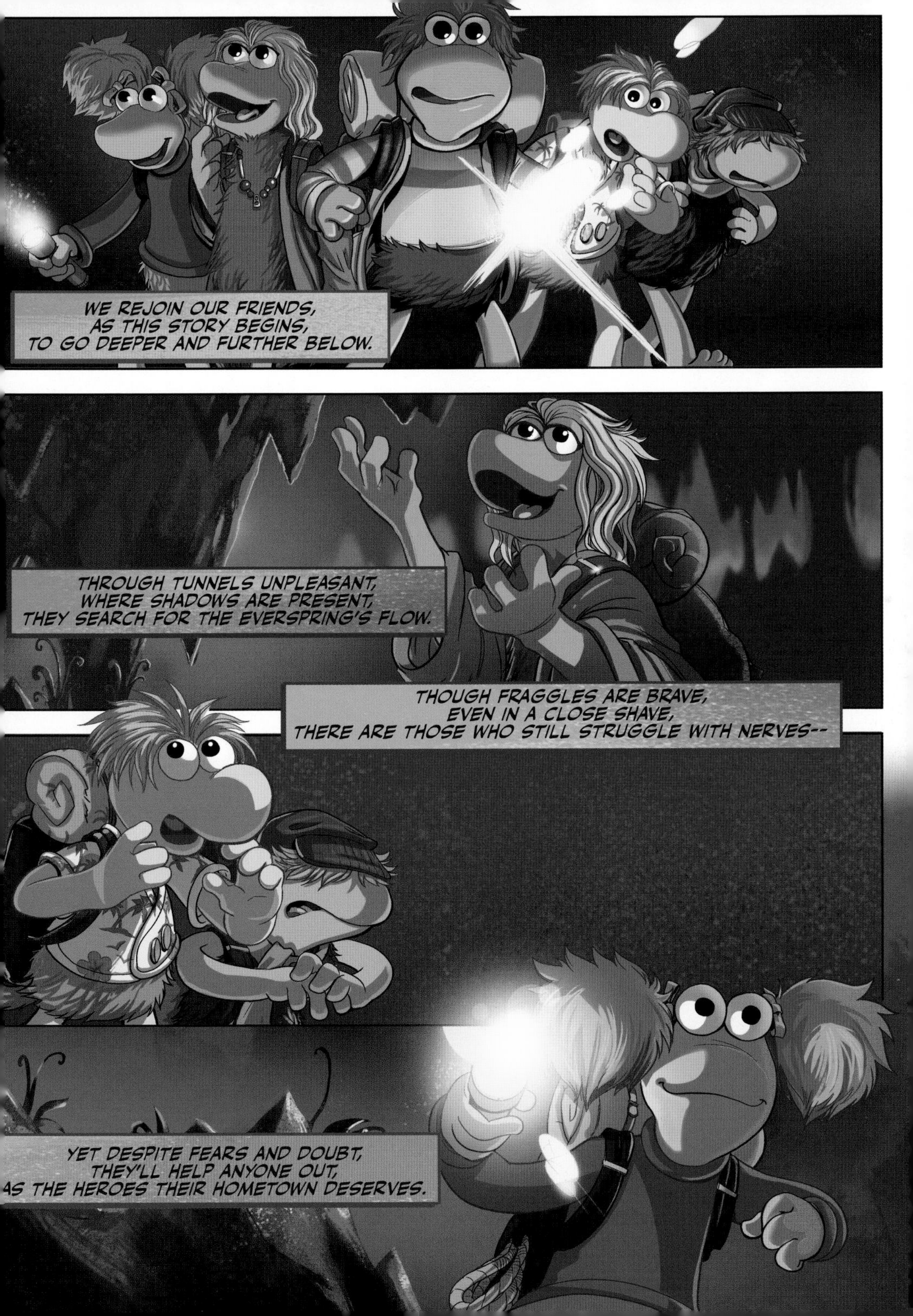
WE REJOIN OUR FRIENDS, AS THIS STORY BEGINS, TO GO DEEPER AND FURTHER BELOW.
THROUGH TUNNELS UNPLEASANT, WHERE SHADOWS ARE PRESENT, THEY SEARCH FOR THE EVERSPRING'S FLOW.
THOUGH FRAGGLES ARE BRAVE, EVEN IN A CLOSE SHAVE, THERE ARE THOSE WHO STILL STRUGGLE WITH NERVES--
YET DESPITE FEARS AND DOUBT, THEY'LL HELP ANYONE OUT, AS THE HEROES THEIR HOMETOWN DESERVES.

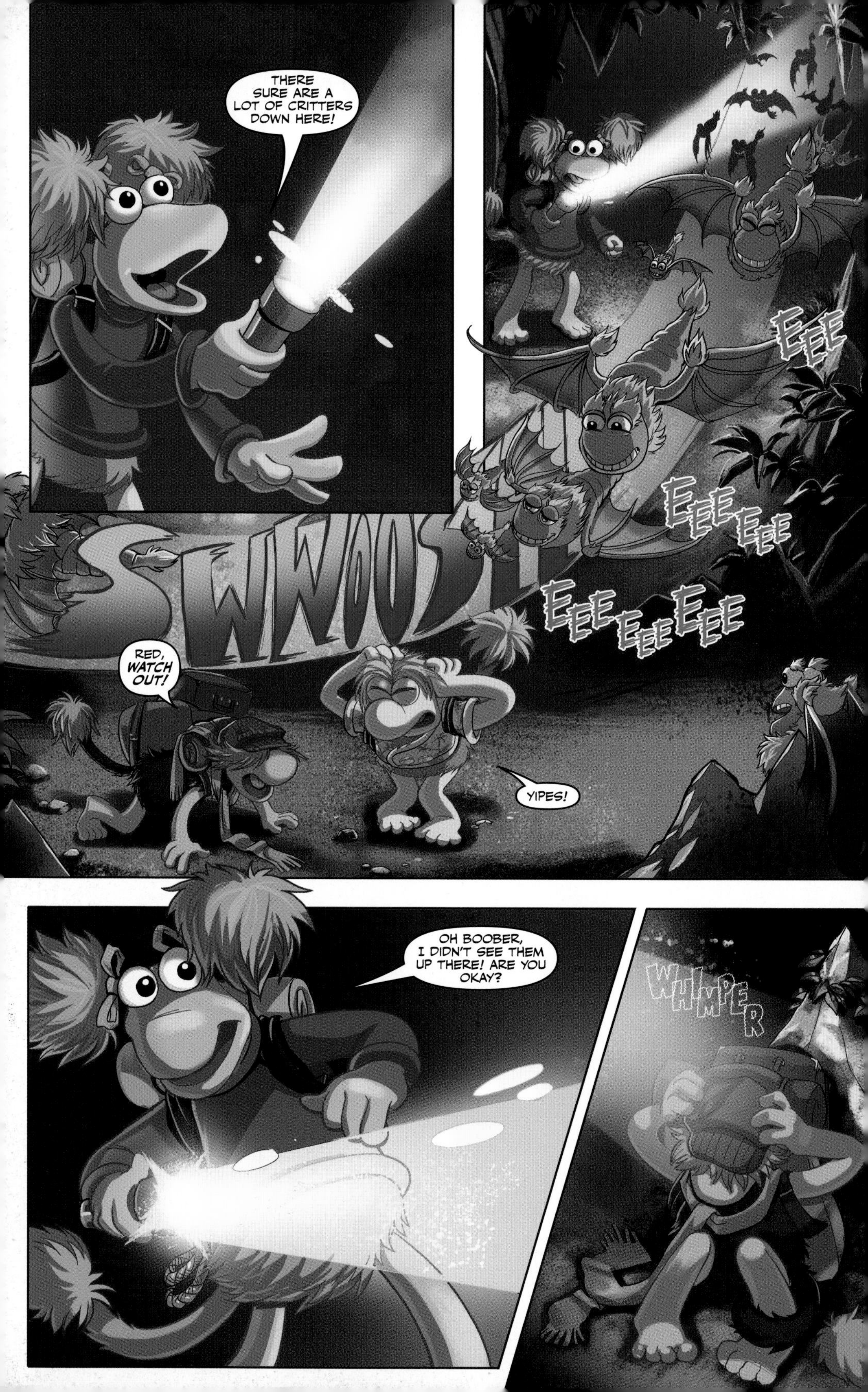
THERE SURE ARE A LOT OF CRITTERS DOWN HERE!
EEE
EEEEEE
SWWOOSH
EEEEEEEEE
RED, WATCH OUT!
YIPES!
OH BOOBER, I DIDN'T SEE THEM UP THERE! ARE YOU OKAY?
WHIMPER

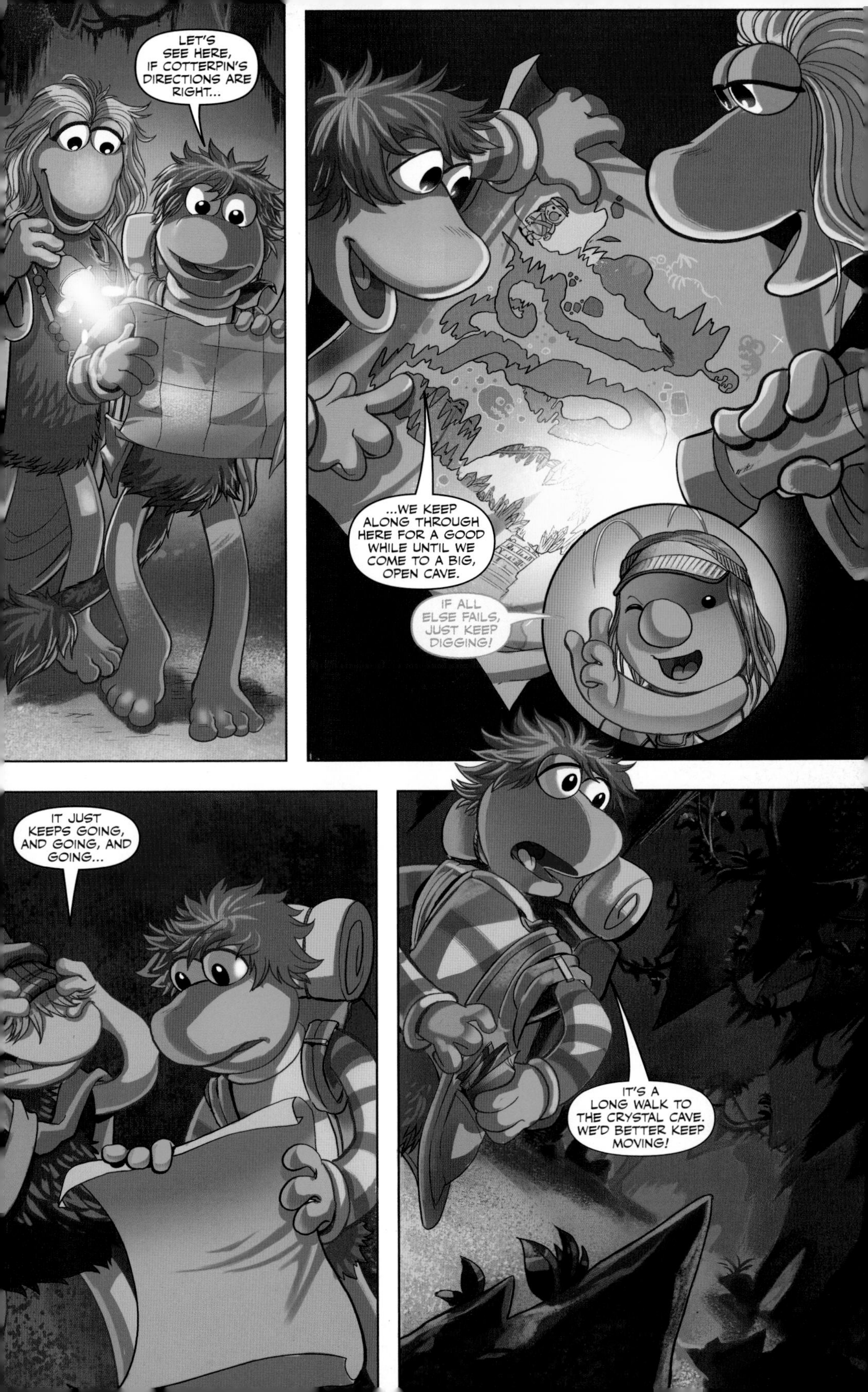
LET'S SEE HERE, IF COTTERPIN'S DIRECTIONS ARE RIGHT...
...WE KEEP ALONG THROUGH HERE FOR A GOOD WHILE UNTIL WE COME TO A BIG, OPEN CAVE.
IF ALL ELSE FAILS, JUST KEEP DIGGING!
IT JUST KEEPS GOING, AND GOING, AND GOING...
IT'S A LONG WALK TO THE CRYSTAL CAVE. WE'D BETTER KEEP MOVING!

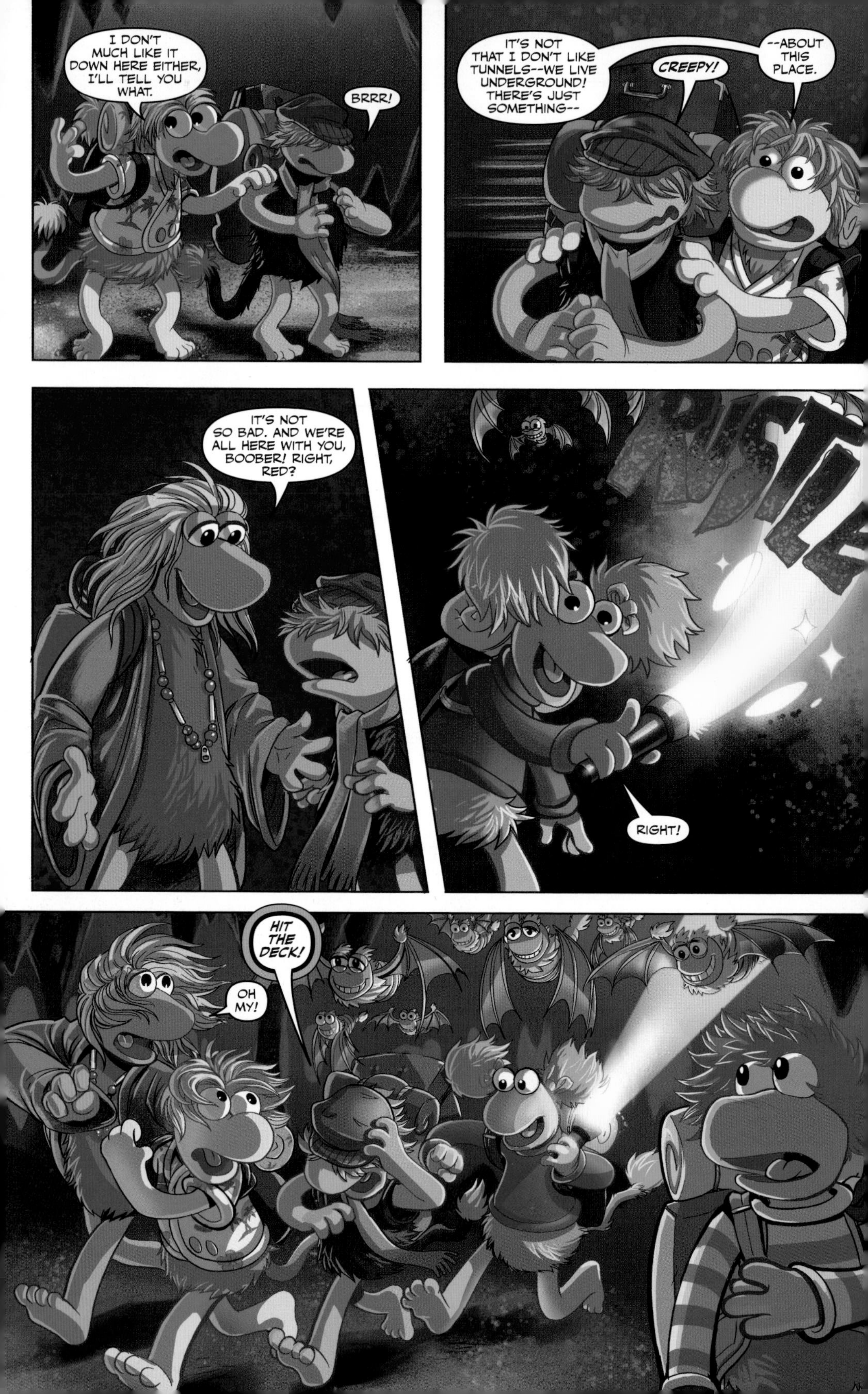
I DON'T MUCH LIKE IT DOWN HERE EITHER, I'LL TELL YOU WHAT.
BRRR!
IT'S NOT THAT I DON'T LIKE TUNNELS--WE LIVE UNDERGROUND! THERE'S JUST SOMETHING--
CREEPY!
--ABOUT THIS PLACE.
IT'S NOT SO BAD. AND WE'RE ALL HERE WITH YOU, BOOBER! RIGHT, RED?
RIGHT!
HIT THE DECK!
OH MY!

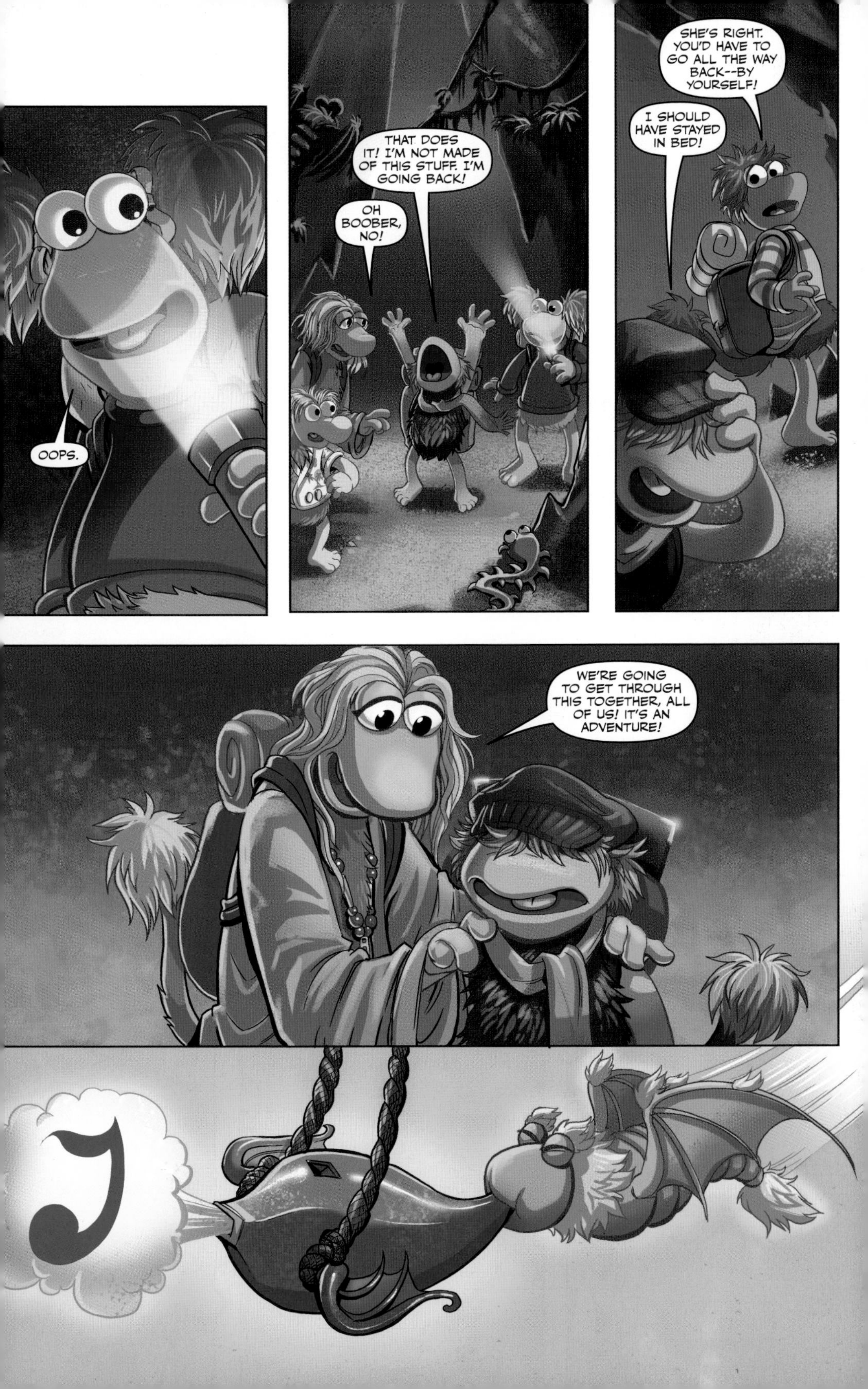
OOPS.
THAT DOES IT! I'M NOT MADE OF THIS STUFF. I'M GOING BACK!
OH BOOBER, NO!
SHE'S RIGHT. YOU'D HAVE TO GO ALL THE WAY BACK--BY YOURSELF!
I SHOULD HAVE STAYED IN BED!
WE'RE GOING TO GET THROUGH THIS TOGETHER, ALL OF US! IT'S AN ADVENTURE!

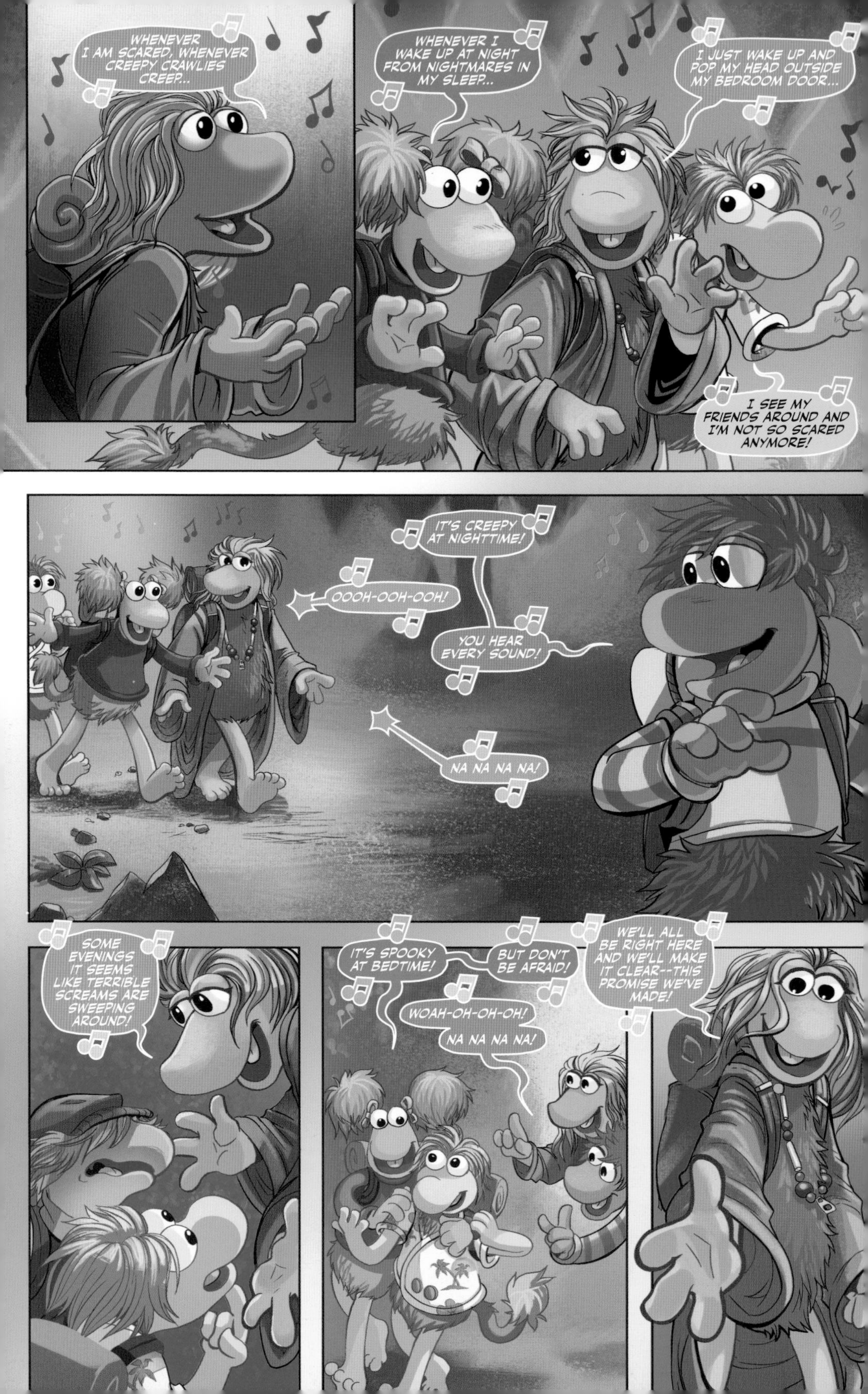

WHENEVER I AM SCARED, WHENEVER CREEPY CRAWLIES CREEP...
WHENEVER I WAKE UP AT NIGHT FROM NIGHTMARES IN MY SLEEP...
I JUST WAKE UP AND POP MY HEAD OUTSIDE MY BEDROOM DOOR...
I SEE MY FRIENDS AROUND AND I'M NOT SO SCARED ANYMORE!
IT'S CREEPY AT NIGHTTIME!
OOOH-OOH-OOH!
YOU HEAR EVERY SOUND!
NA NA NA NA!
SOME EVENINGS IT SEEMS LIKE TERRIBLE SCREAMS ARE SWEEPING AROUND!
IT'S SPOOKY AT BEDTIME!
BUT DON'T BE AFRAID!
WOAH-OH-OH-OH!
NA NA NA NA!
WE'LL ALL BE RIGHT HERE AND WE'LL MAKE IT CLEAR--THIS PROMISE WE'VE MADE!

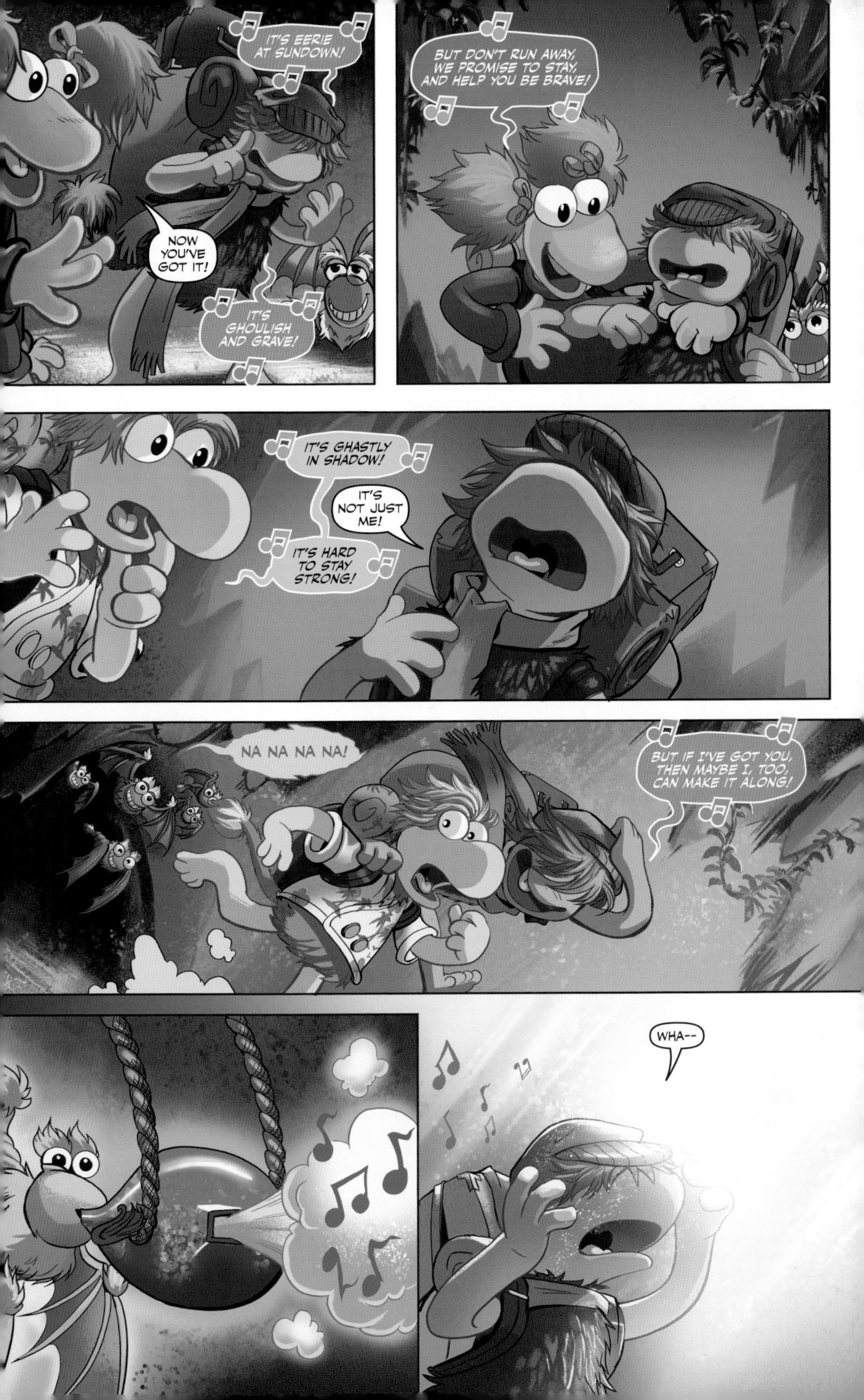
IT'S EERIE AT SUNDOWN!
NOW YOU'VE GOT IT!
IT'S GHOULISH AND GRAVE!
BUT DON'T RUN AWAY, WE PROMISE TO STAY, AND HELP YOU BE BRAVE!
IT'S GHASTLY IN SHADOW!
IT'S HARD TO STAY STRONG!
IT'S NOT JUST ME!
NA NA NA NA!
BUT IF I'VE GOT YOU, THEN MAYBE I, TOO, CAN MAKE IT ALONG!
WHA--

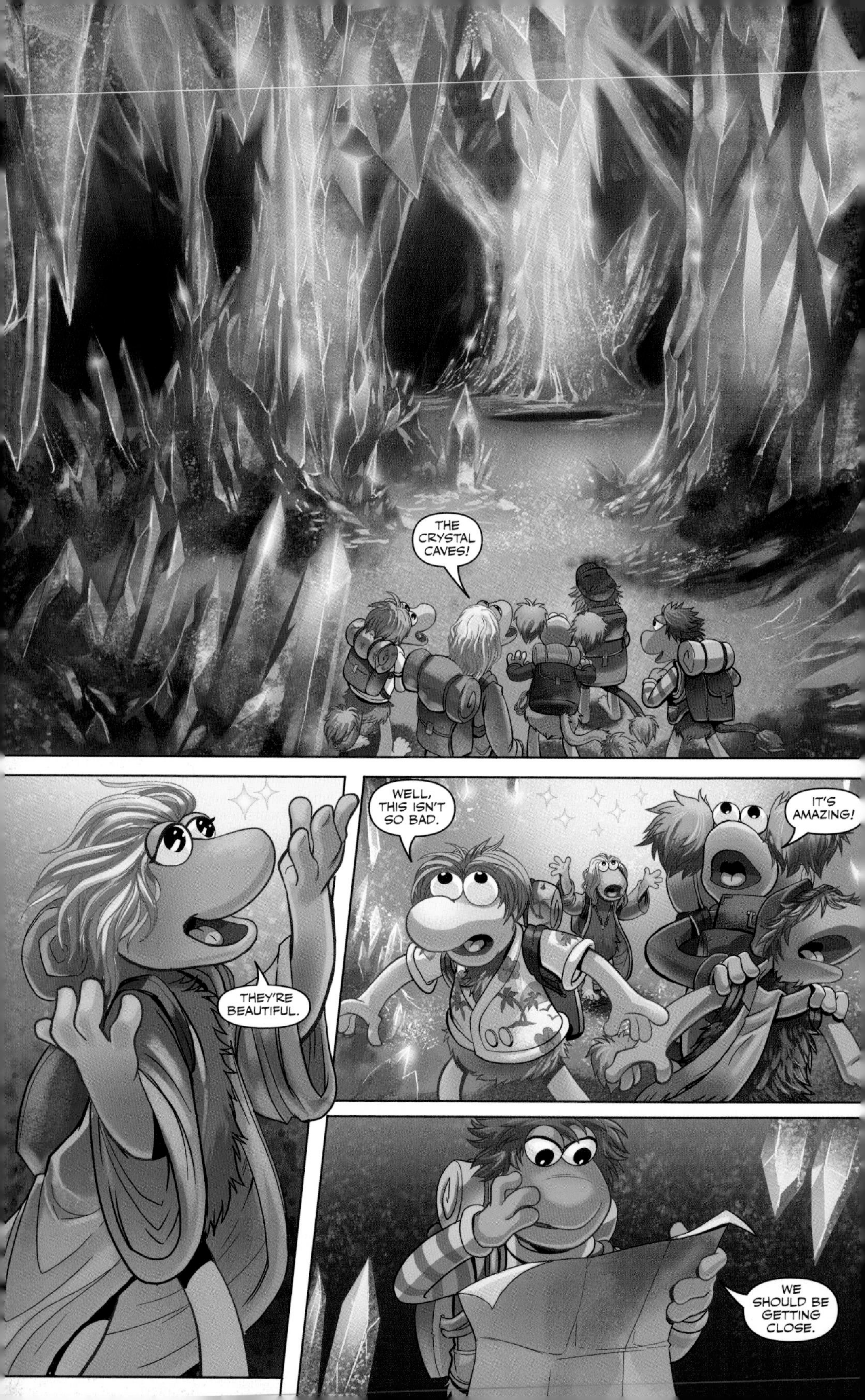
THE CRYSTAL CAVES!
THEY'RE BEAUTIFUL.
WELL, THIS ISN'T SO BAD.
IT'S AMAZING!
WE SHOULD BE GETTING CLOSE.

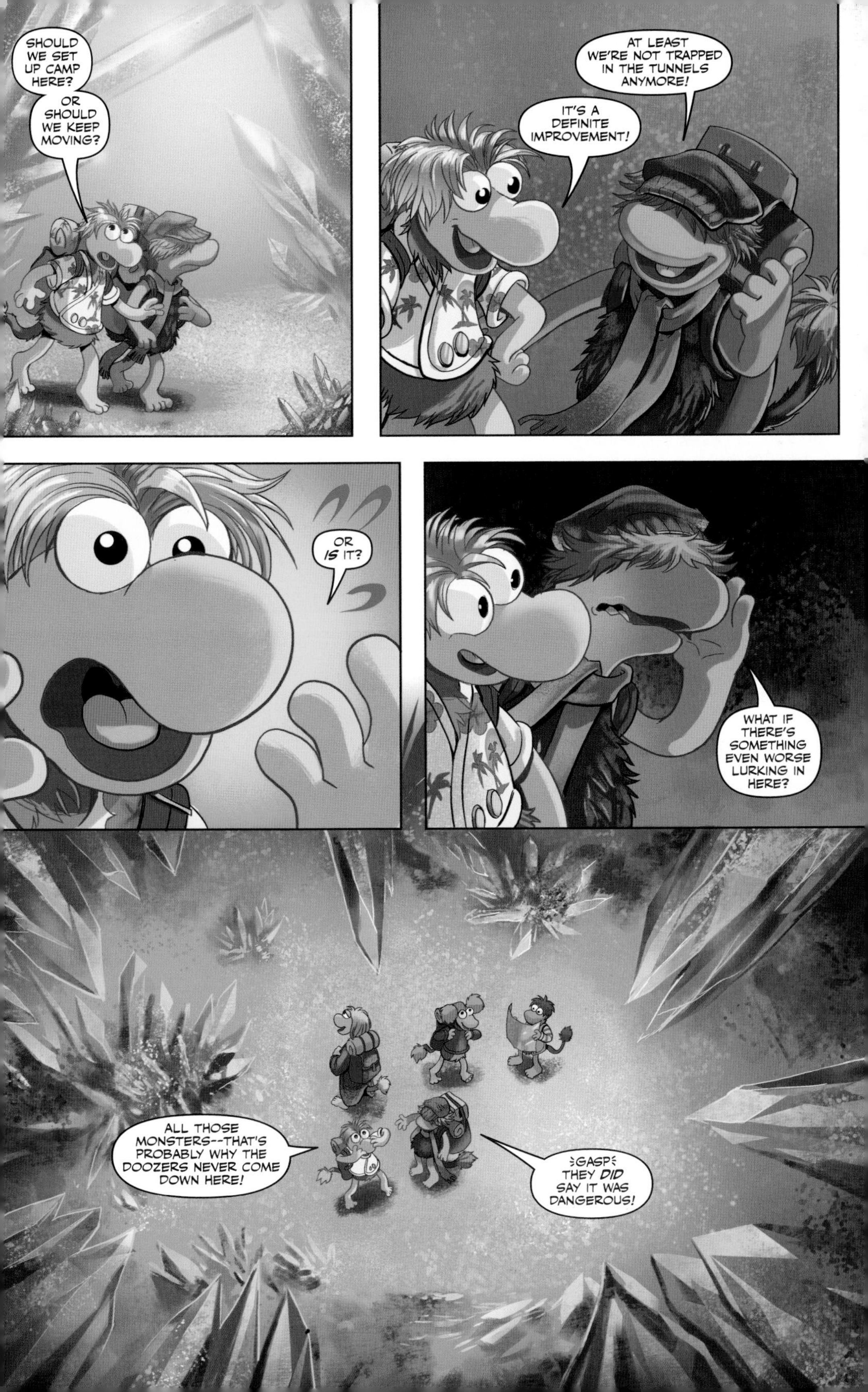
SHOULD WE SET UP CAMP HERE?
OR SHOULD WE KEEP MOVING?
AT LEAST WE'RE NOT TRAPPED IN THE TUNNELS ANYMORE!
IT'S A DEFINITE IMPROVEMENT!
OR *IS* IT?
WHAT IF THERE'S SOMETHING EVEN WORSE LURKING IN HERE?
ALL THOSE MONSTERS--THAT'S PROBABLY WHY THE DOOZERS NEVER COME DOWN HERE!
GASP THEY *DID* SAY IT WAS DANGEROUS!

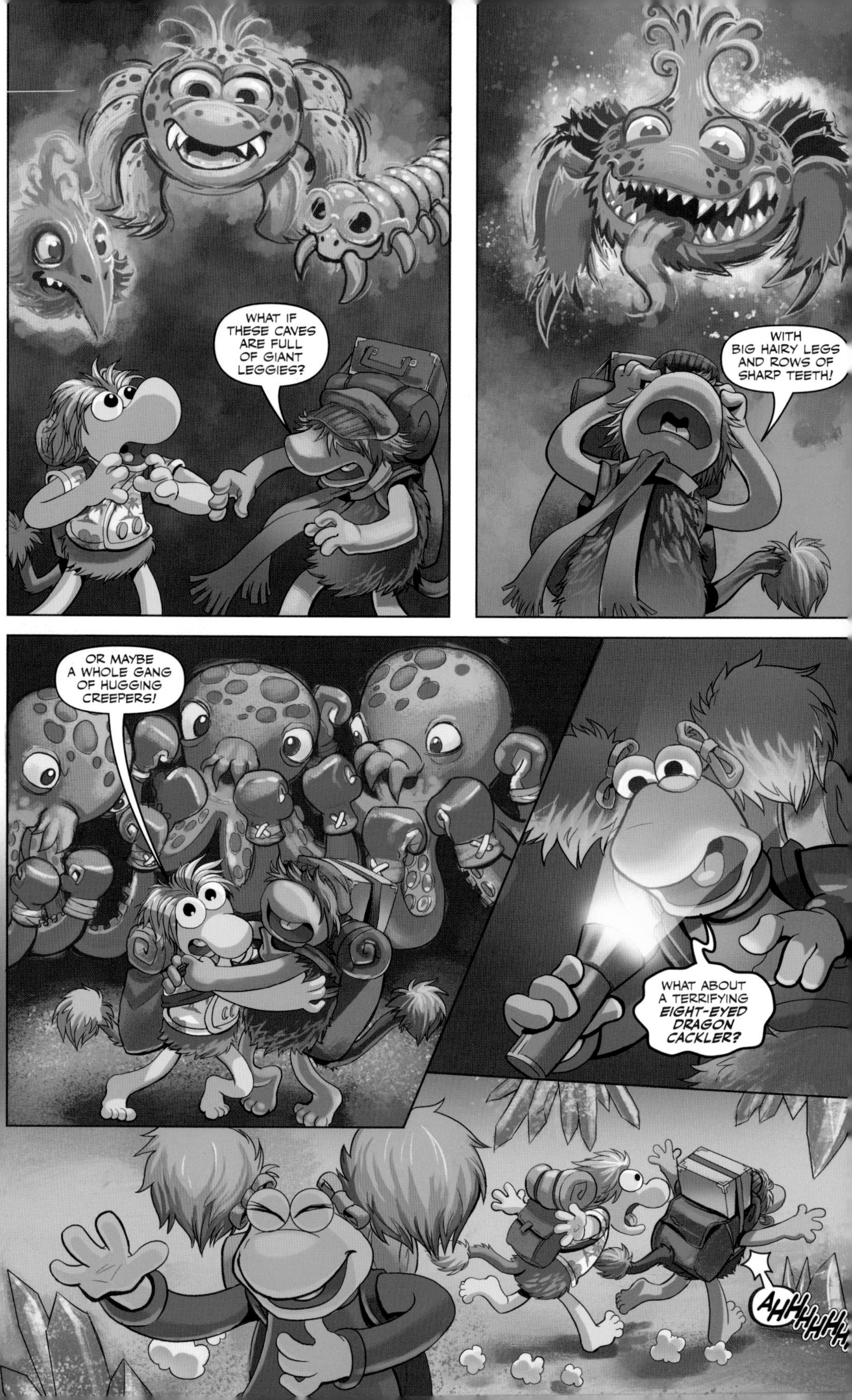
WHAT IF THESE CAVES ARE FULL OF GIANT LEGGIES?
WITH BIG HAIRY LEGS AND ROWS OF SHARP TEETH!
OR MAYBE A WHOLE GANG OF HUGGING CREEPERS!
WHAT ABOUT A TERRIFYING *EIGHT-EYED DRAGON CACKLER?*
AHHHHHH

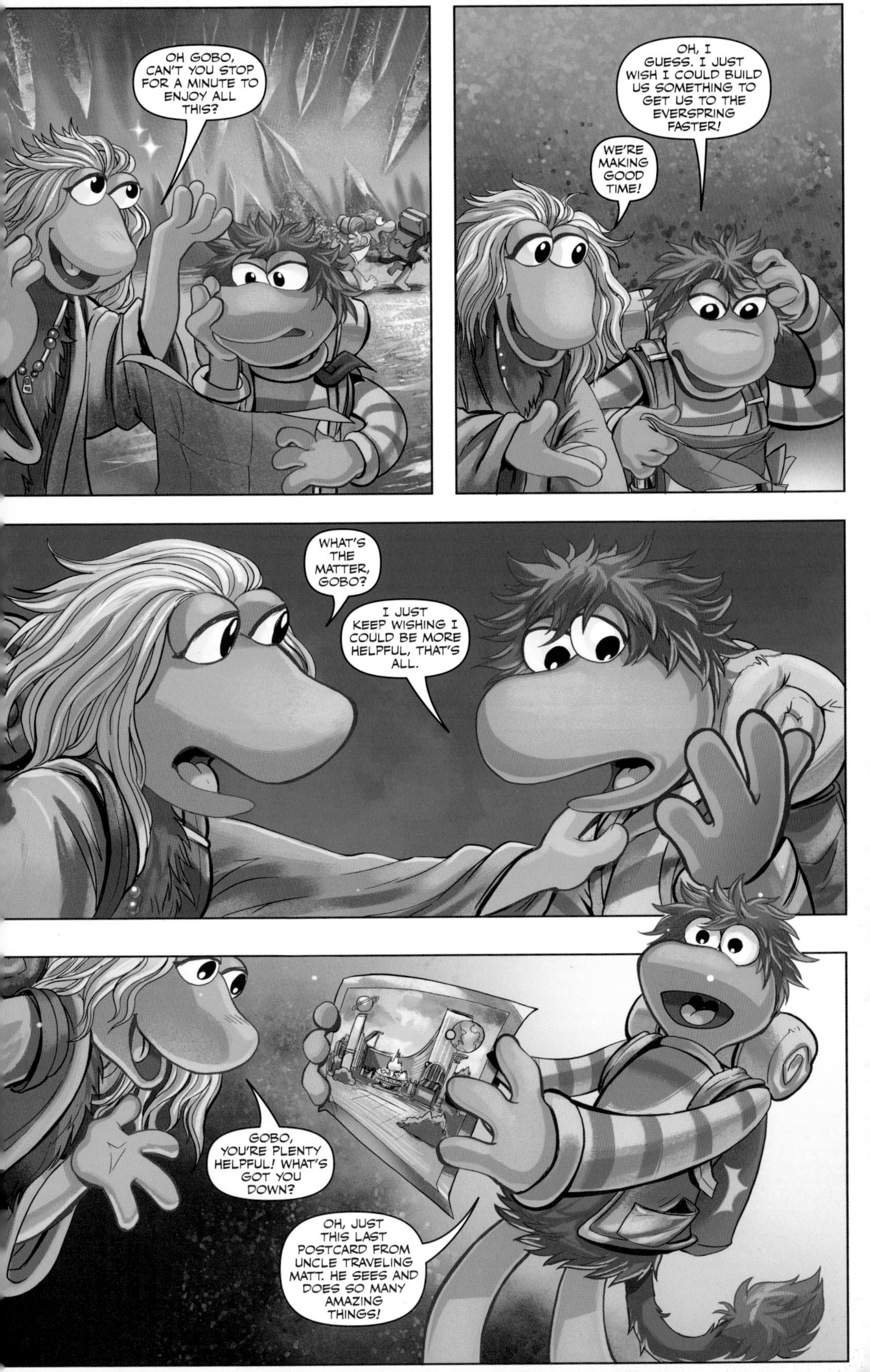
OH GOBO, CAN'T YOU STOP FOR A MINUTE TO ENJOY ALL THIS?
OH, I GUESS. I JUST WISH I COULD BUILD US SOMETHING TO GET US TO THE EVERSPRING FASTER!
WE'RE MAKING GOOD TIME!
WHAT'S THE MATTER, GOBO?
I JUST KEEP WISHING I COULD BE MORE HELPFUL, THAT'S ALL.
GOBO, YOU'RE PLENTY HELPFUL! WHAT'S GOT YOU DOWN?
OH, JUST THIS LAST POSTCARD FROM UNCLE TRAVELING MATT. HE SEES AND DOES SO MANY AMAZING THINGS!

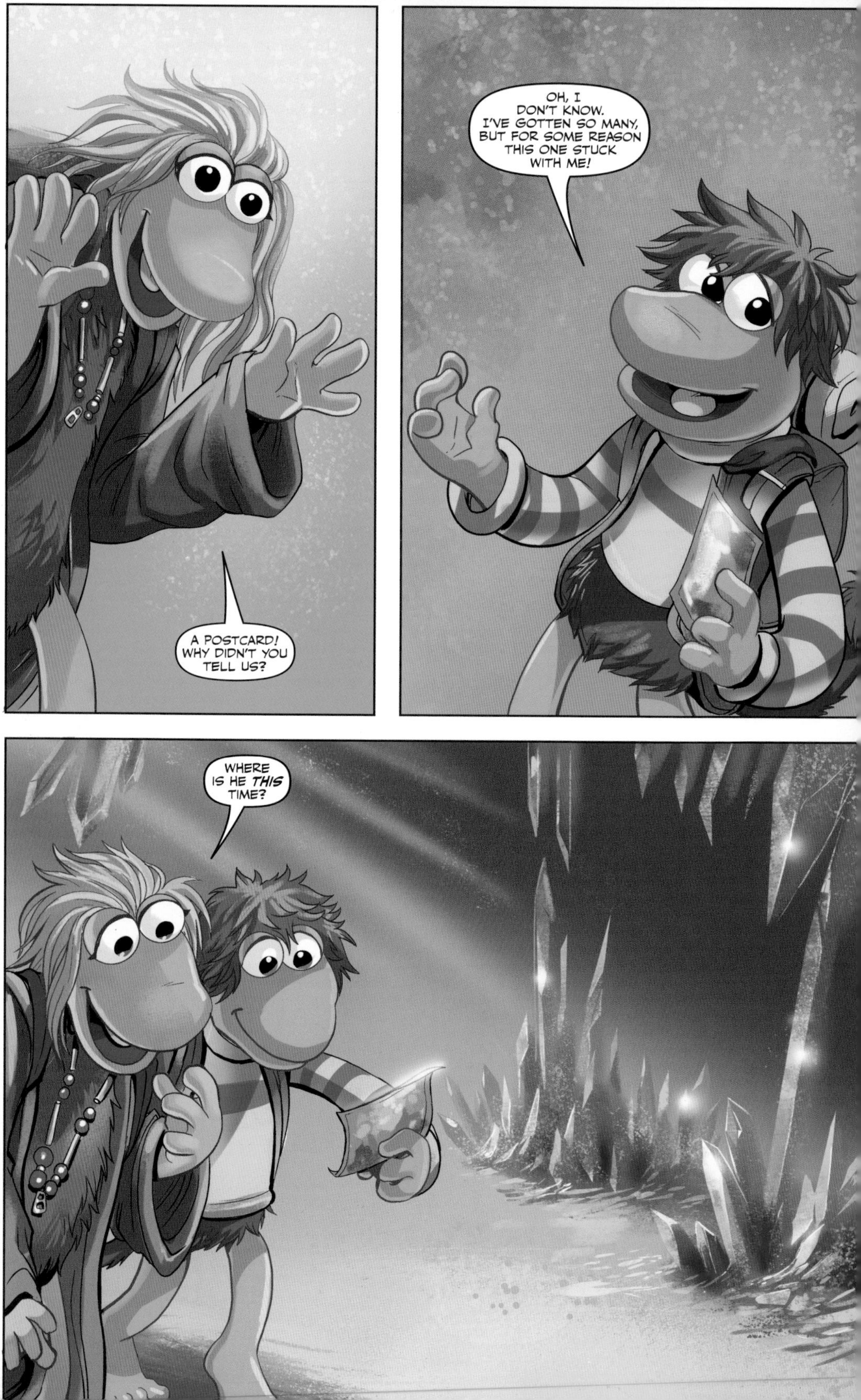
A POSTCARD! WHY DIDN'T YOU TELL US?
OH, I DON'T KNOW. I'VE GOTTEN SO MANY, BUT FOR SOME REASON THIS ONE STUCK WITH ME!
WHERE IS HE *THIS* TIME?

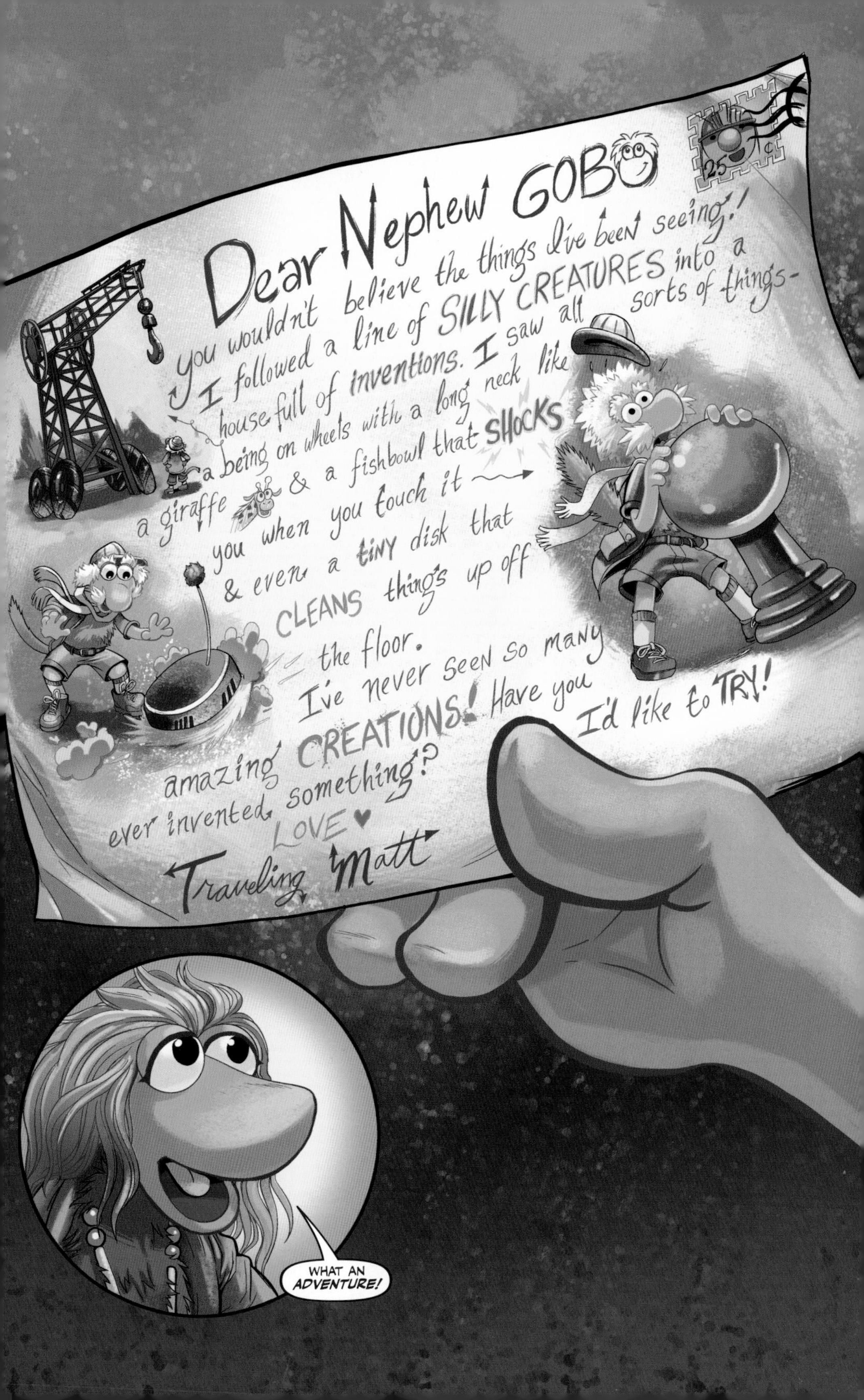
Dear Nephew GOBO
You wouldn't believe the things I've been seeing!
I followed a line of SILLY CREATURES into a house full of inventions. I saw all sorts of things-
a being on wheels with a long neck like a giraffe & a fishbowl that SHOCKS you when you touch it
& even a tiny disk that CLEANS things up off the floor.
I've never seen so many amazing CREATIONS! Have you ever invented something?
I'd like to TRY!
LOVE
Traveling Matt
25¢
WHAT AN ADVENTURE!

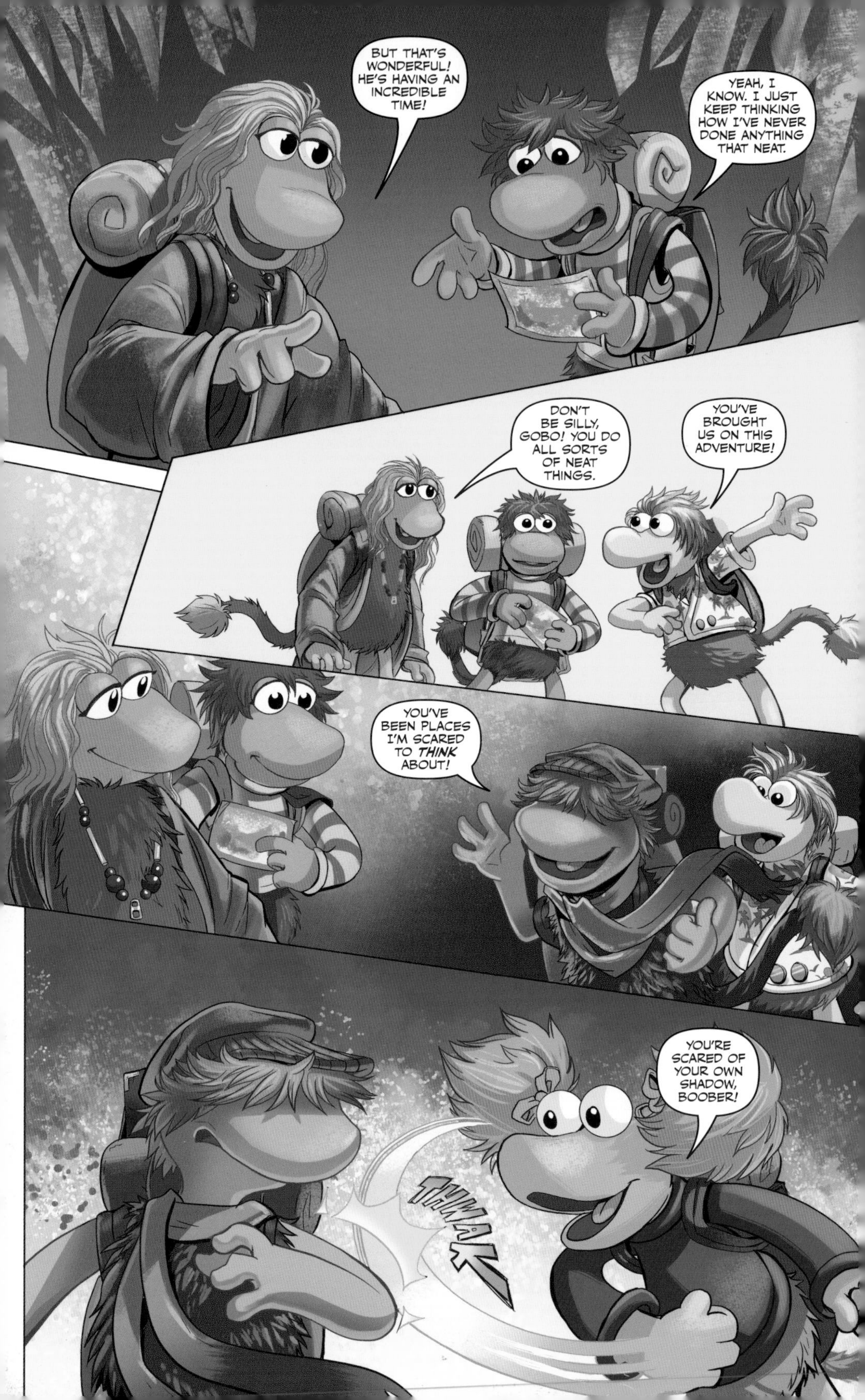
BUT THAT'S WONDERFUL! HE'S HAVING AN INCREDIBLE TIME!
YEAH, I KNOW. I JUST KEEP THINKING HOW I'VE NEVER DONE ANYTHING THAT NEAT.
DON'T BE SILLY, GOBO! YOU DO ALL SORTS OF NEAT THINGS.
YOU'VE BROUGHT US ON THIS ADVENTURE!
YOU'VE BEEN PLACES I'M SCARED TO *THINK* ABOUT!
YOU'RE SCARED OF YOUR OWN SHADOW, BOOBER!
THWAK

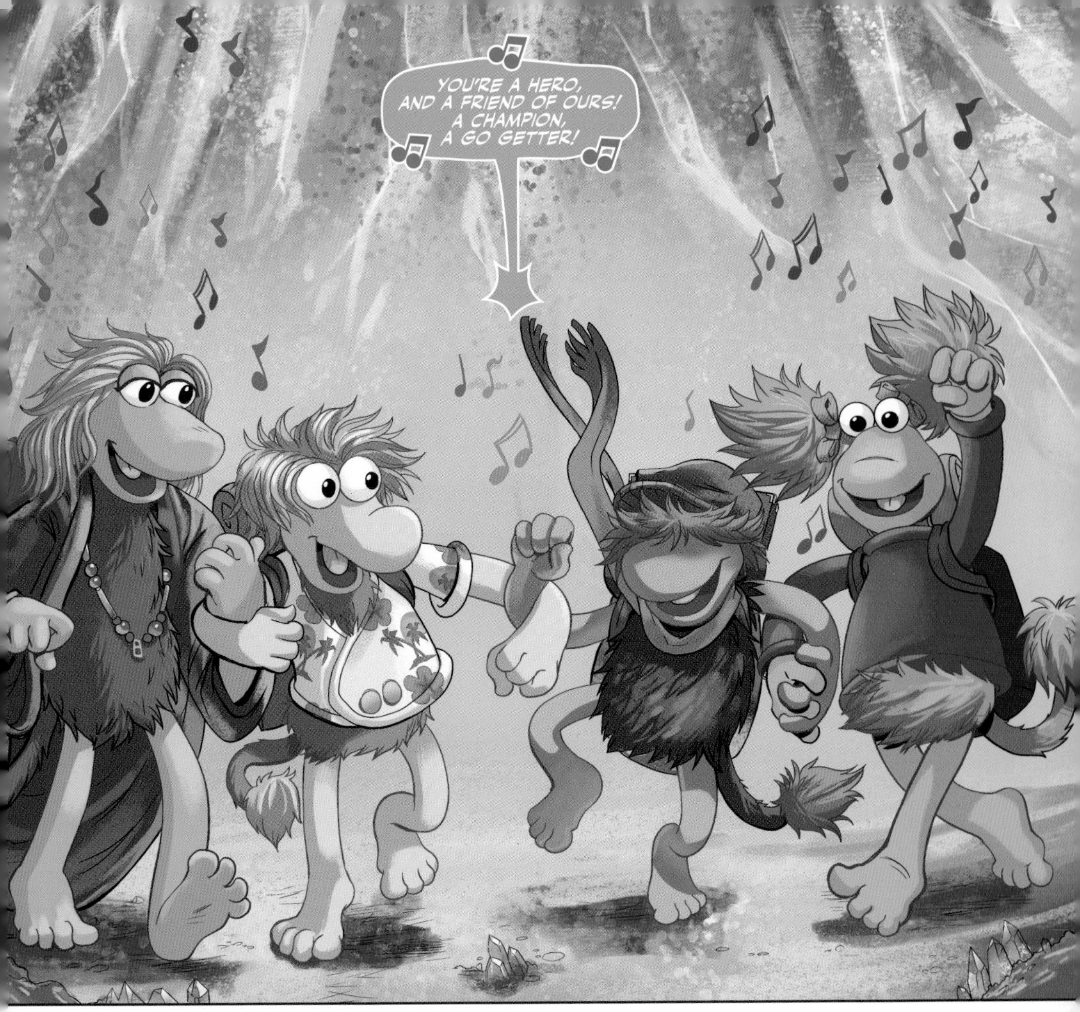
YOU'RE A HERO, AND A FRIEND OF OURS! A CHAMPION, A GO GETTER!

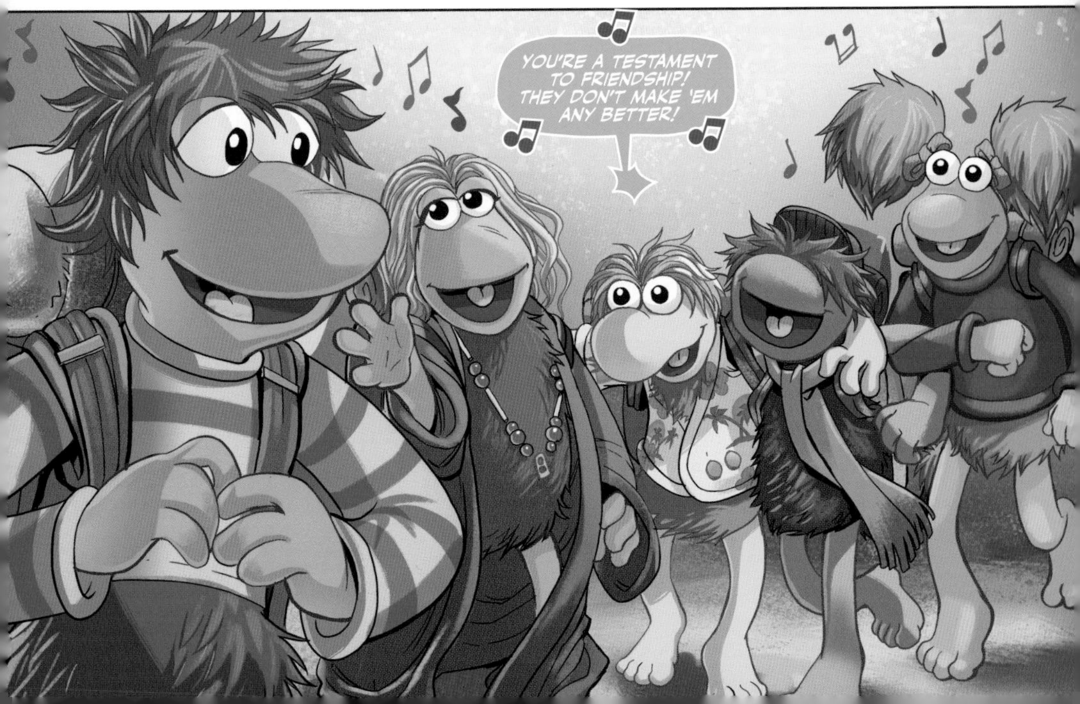
YOU'RE A TESTAMENT TO FRIENDSHIP! THEY DON'T MAKE 'EM ANY BETTER!

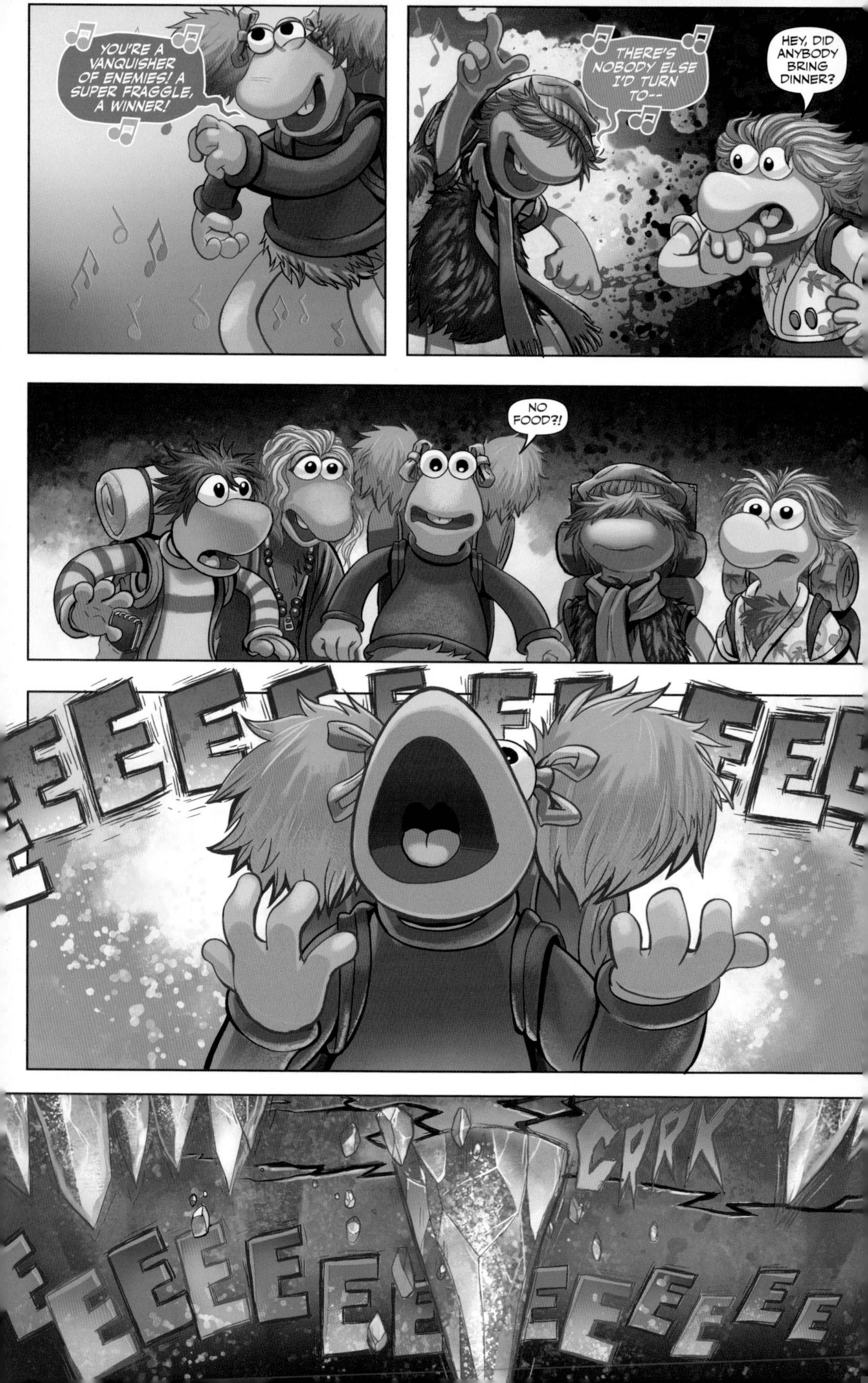
YOU'RE A VANQUISHER OF ENEMIES! A SUPER FRAGGLE, A WINNER!
THERE'S NOBODY ELSE I'D TURN TO--
HEY, DID ANYBODY BRING DINNER?
NO FOOD?!
EEEEEEEEE
CRRK
EEEEEEEEEEEEEE

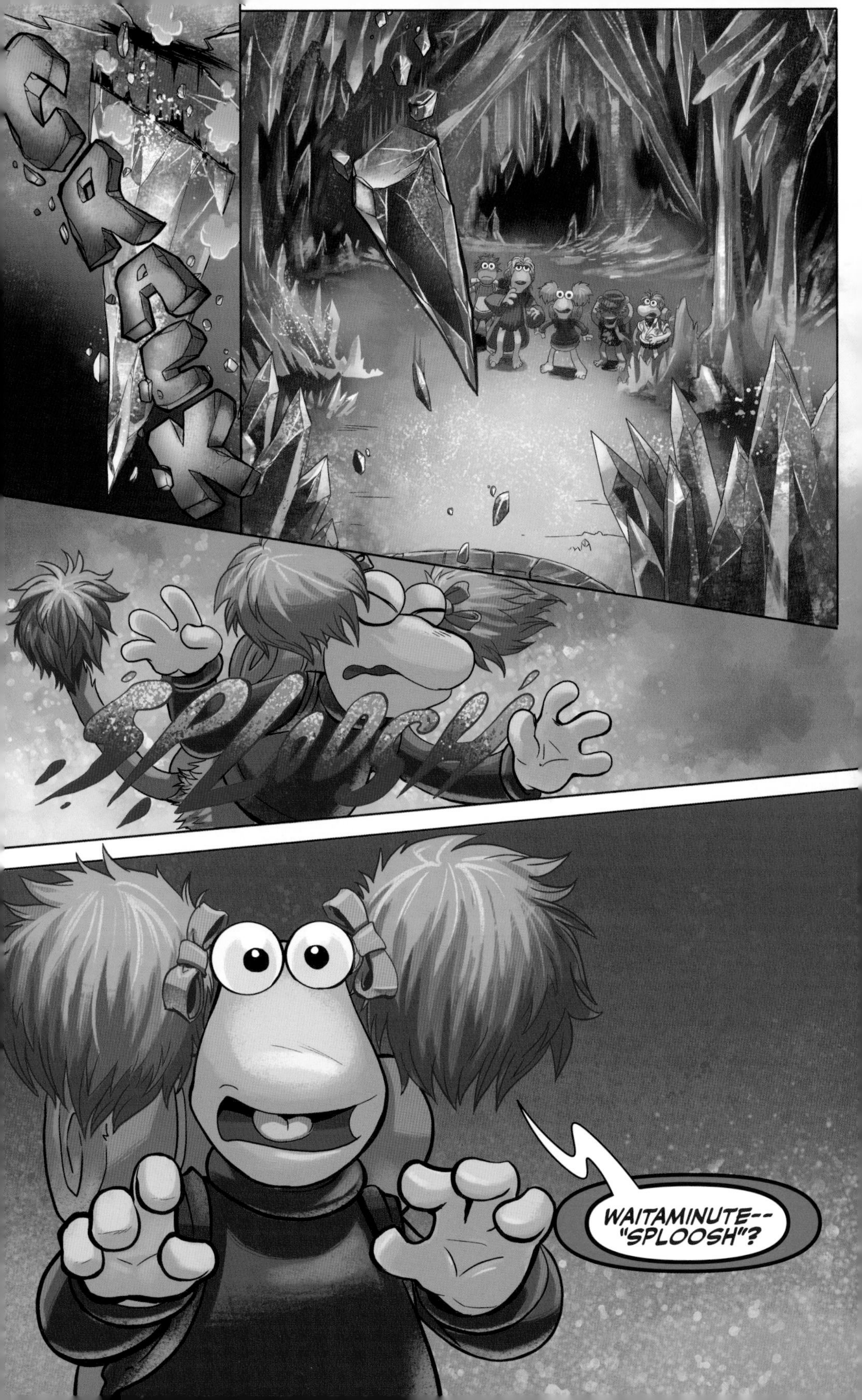
CRACK
SPLOOSH
WAITAMINUTE-- "SPLOOSH"?

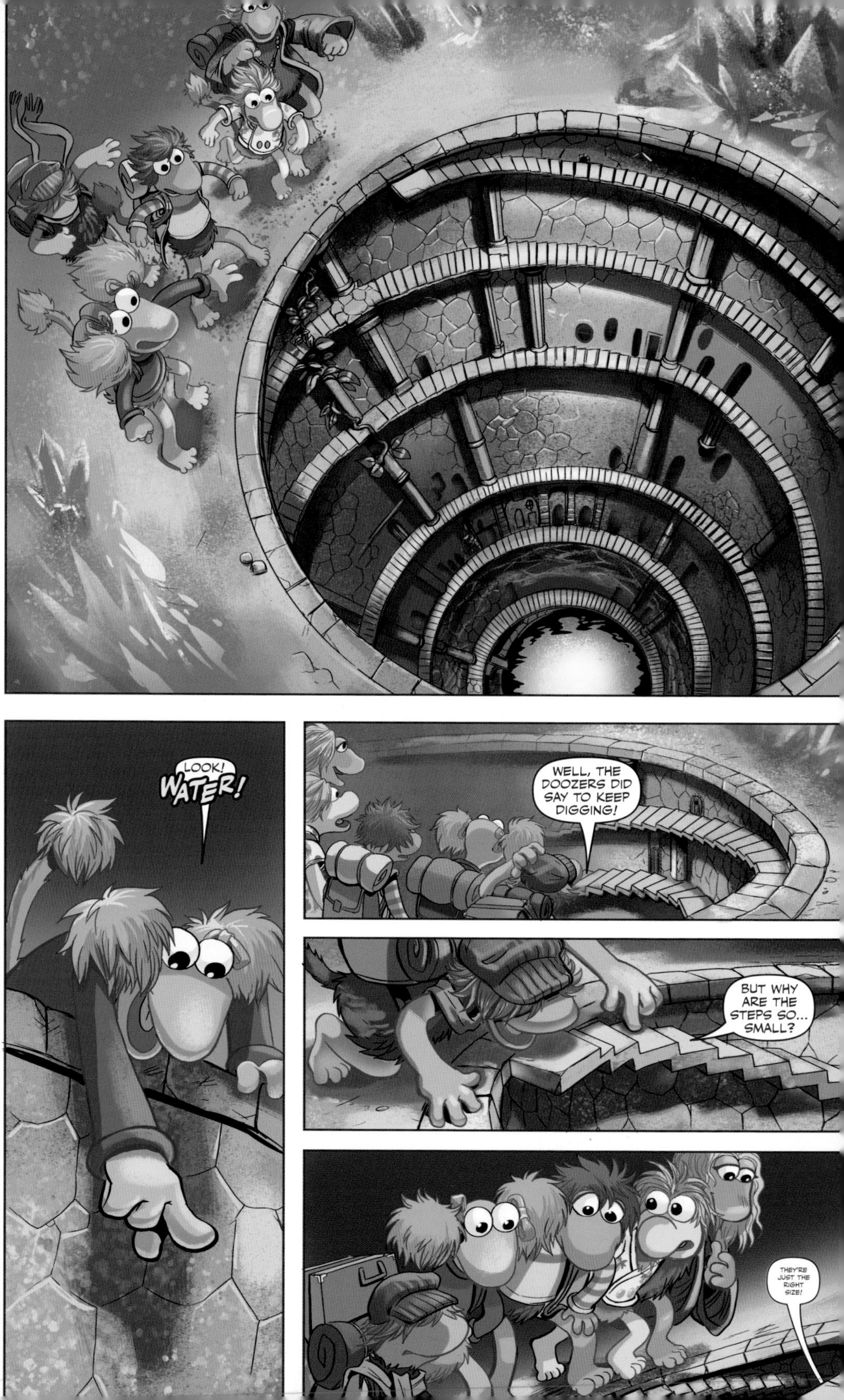
LOOK! WATER!
WELL, THE DOOZERS DID SAY TO KEEP DIGGING!
BUT WHY ARE THE STEPS SO... SMALL?
THEY'RE JUST THE RIGHT SIZE!

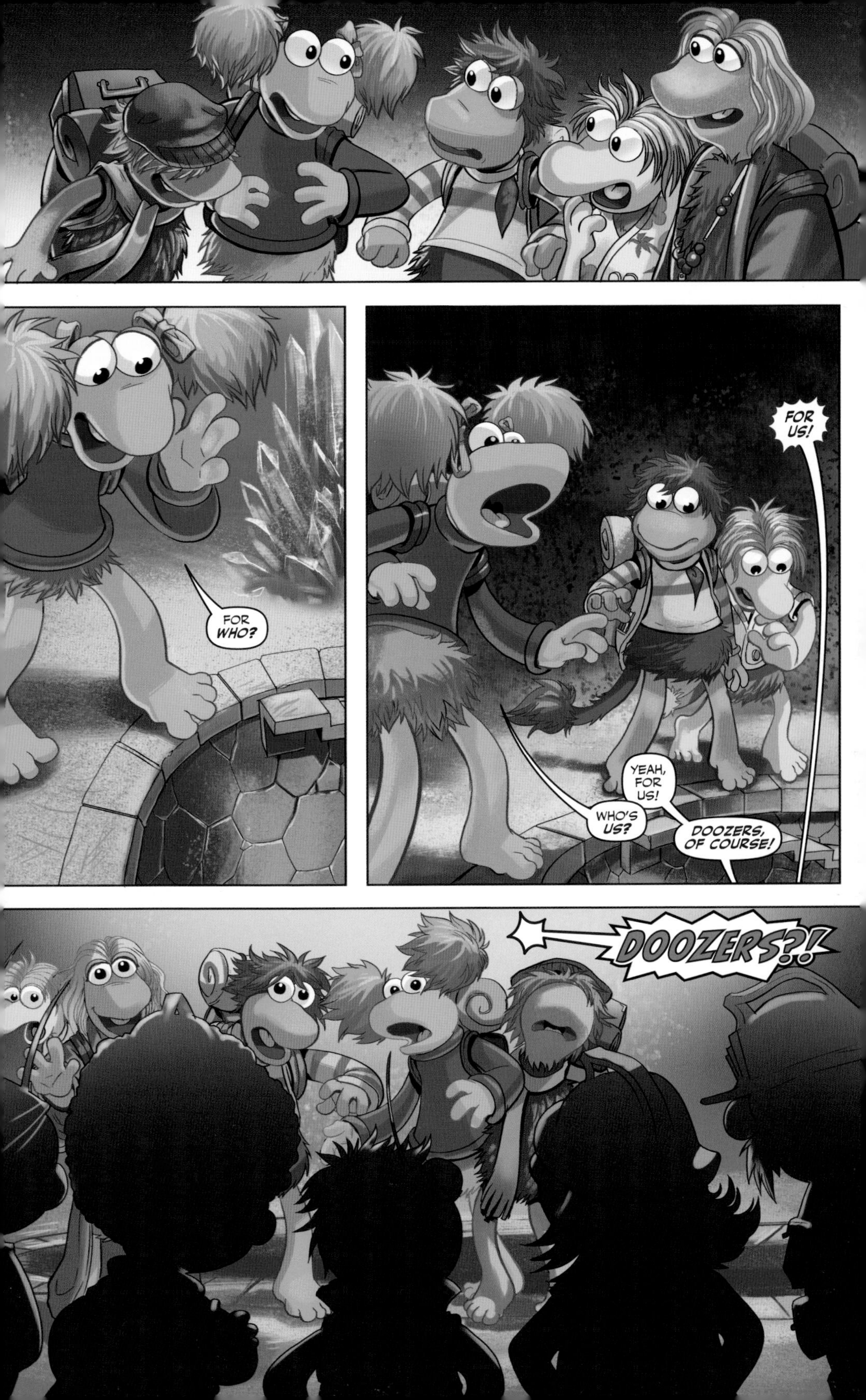
FOR WHO?
FOR US!
YEAH, FOR US!
WHO'S US?
DOOZERS, OF COURSE!
DOOZERS?!

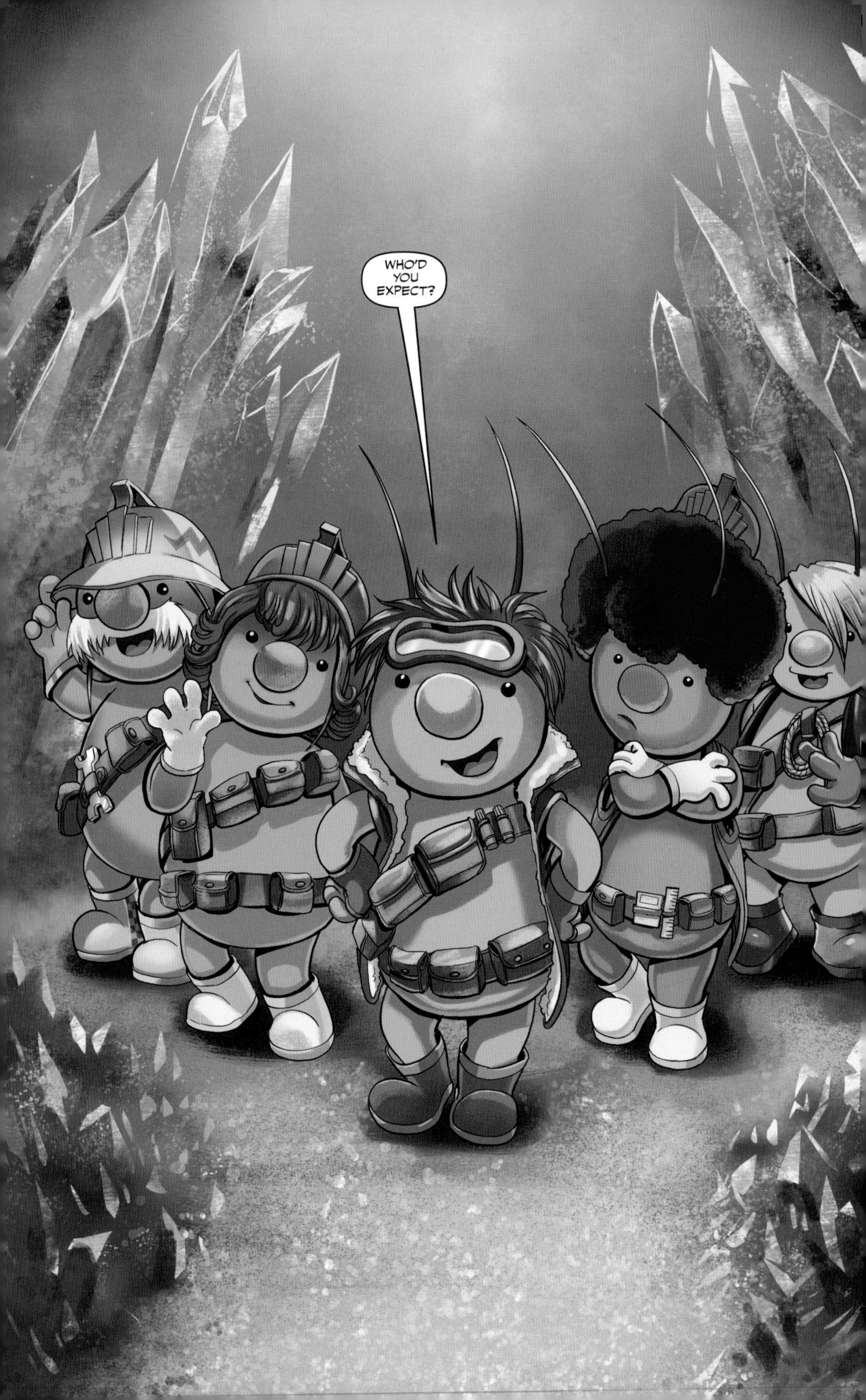
WHO'D YOU EXPECT?

LET THE MUSIC PLAY

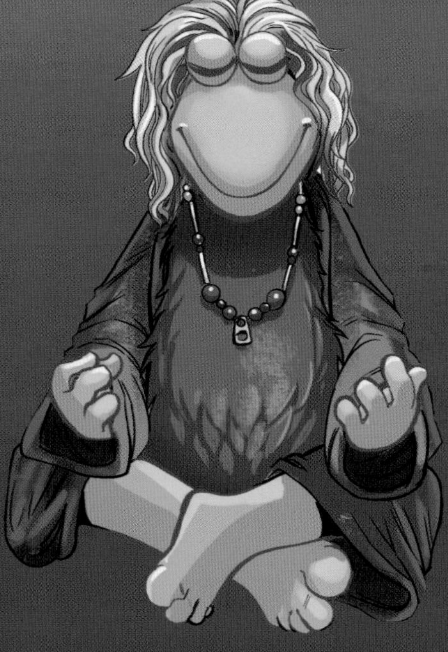

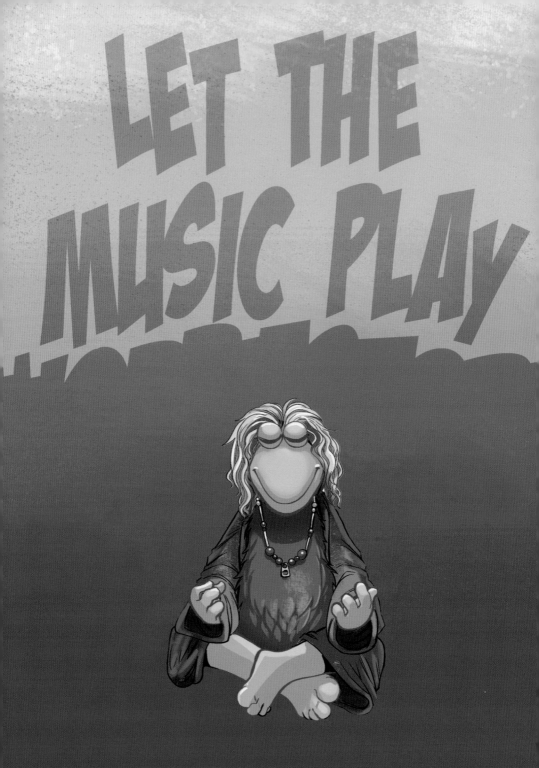

CHAPTER THREE

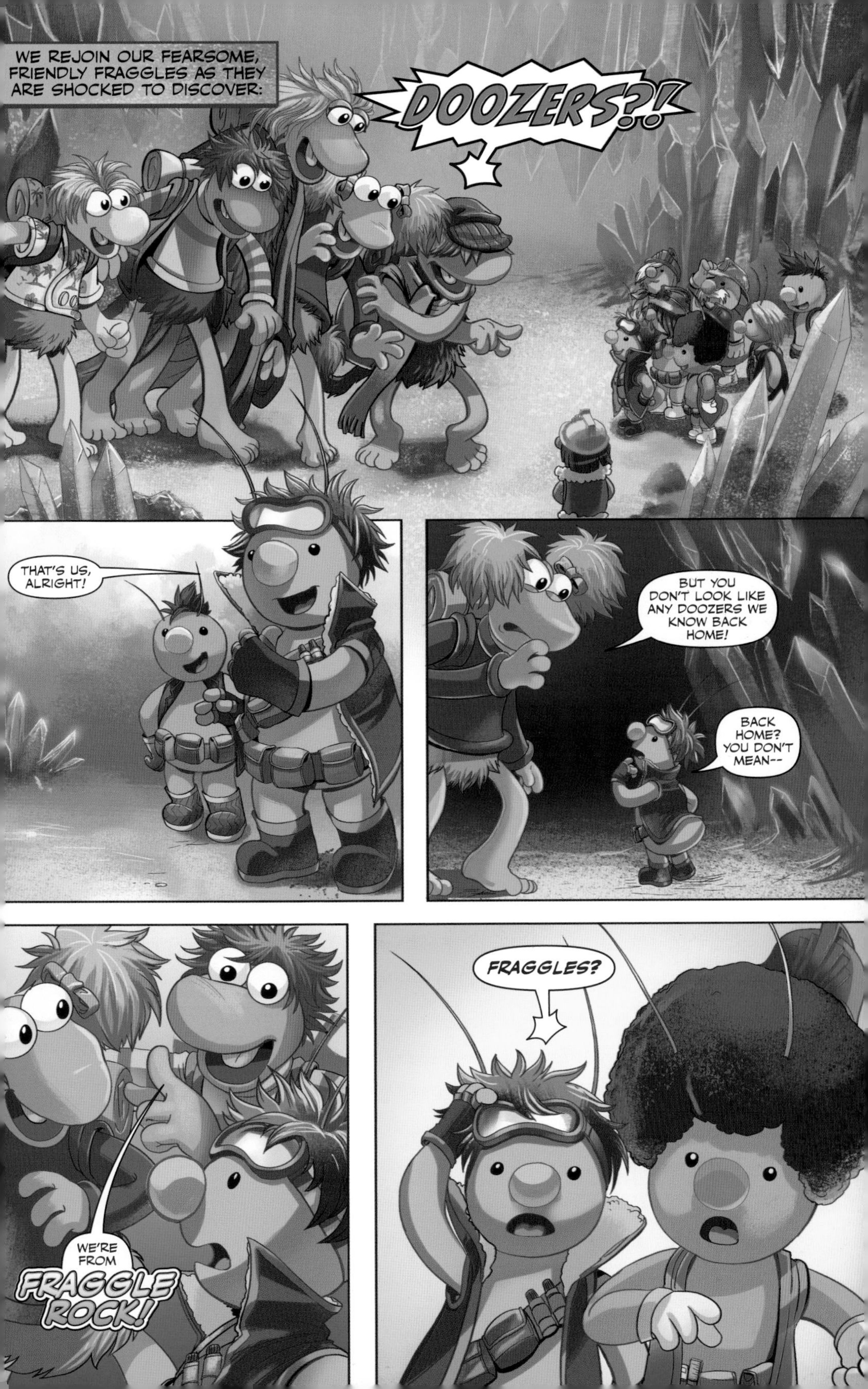
WE REJOIN OUR FEARSOME, FRIENDLY FRAGGLES AS THEY ARE SHOCKED TO DISCOVER:
DOOZERS?!
THAT'S US, ALRIGHT!
BUT YOU DON'T LOOK LIKE ANY DOOZERS WE KNOW BACK HOME!
BACK HOME? YOU DON'T MEAN--
WE'RE FROM
FRAGGLE ROCK!
FRAGGLES?

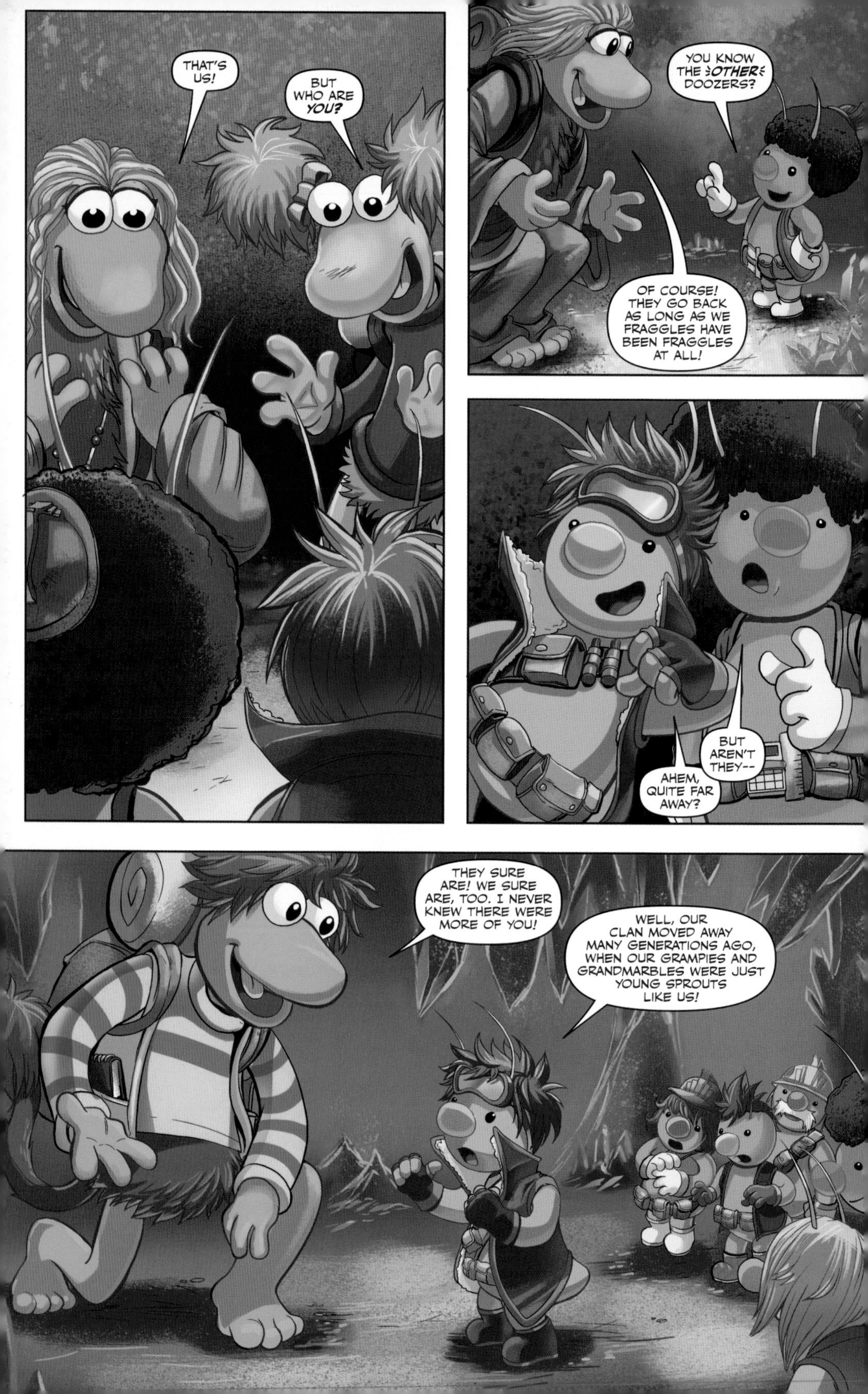
THAT'S US!
BUT WHO ARE *YOU?*
YOU KNOW THE *OTHER* DOOZERS?
OF COURSE! THEY GO BACK AS LONG AS WE FRAGGLES HAVE BEEN FRAGGLES AT ALL!
BUT AREN'T THEY--
AHEM, QUITE FAR AWAY?
THEY SURE ARE! WE SURE ARE, TOO. I NEVER KNEW THERE WERE MORE OF YOU!
WELL, OUR CLAN MOVED AWAY MANY GENERATIONS AGO, WHEN OUR GRAMPIES AND GRANDMARBLES WERE JUST YOUNG SPROUTS LIKE US!

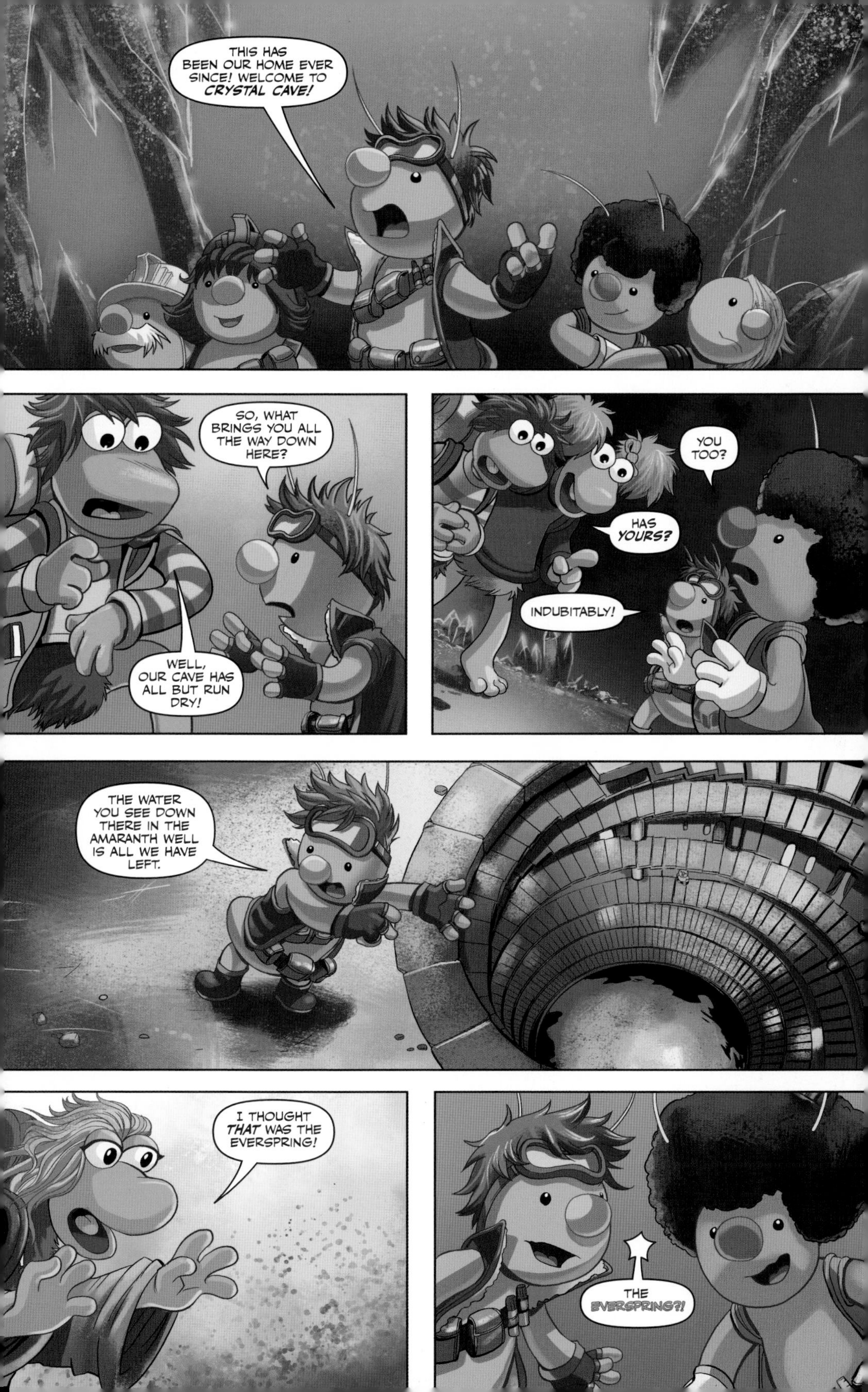
THIS HAS BEEN OUR HOME EVER SINCE! WELCOME TO *CRYSTAL CAVE!*
SO, WHAT BRINGS YOU ALL THE WAY DOWN HERE?
WELL, OUR CAVE HAS ALL BUT RUN DRY!
YOU TOO?
HAS *YOURS?*
INDUBITABLY!
THE WATER YOU SEE DOWN THERE IN THE AMARANTH WELL IS ALL WE HAVE LEFT.
I THOUGHT *THAT* WAS THE EVERSPRING!
THE EVERSPRING?!

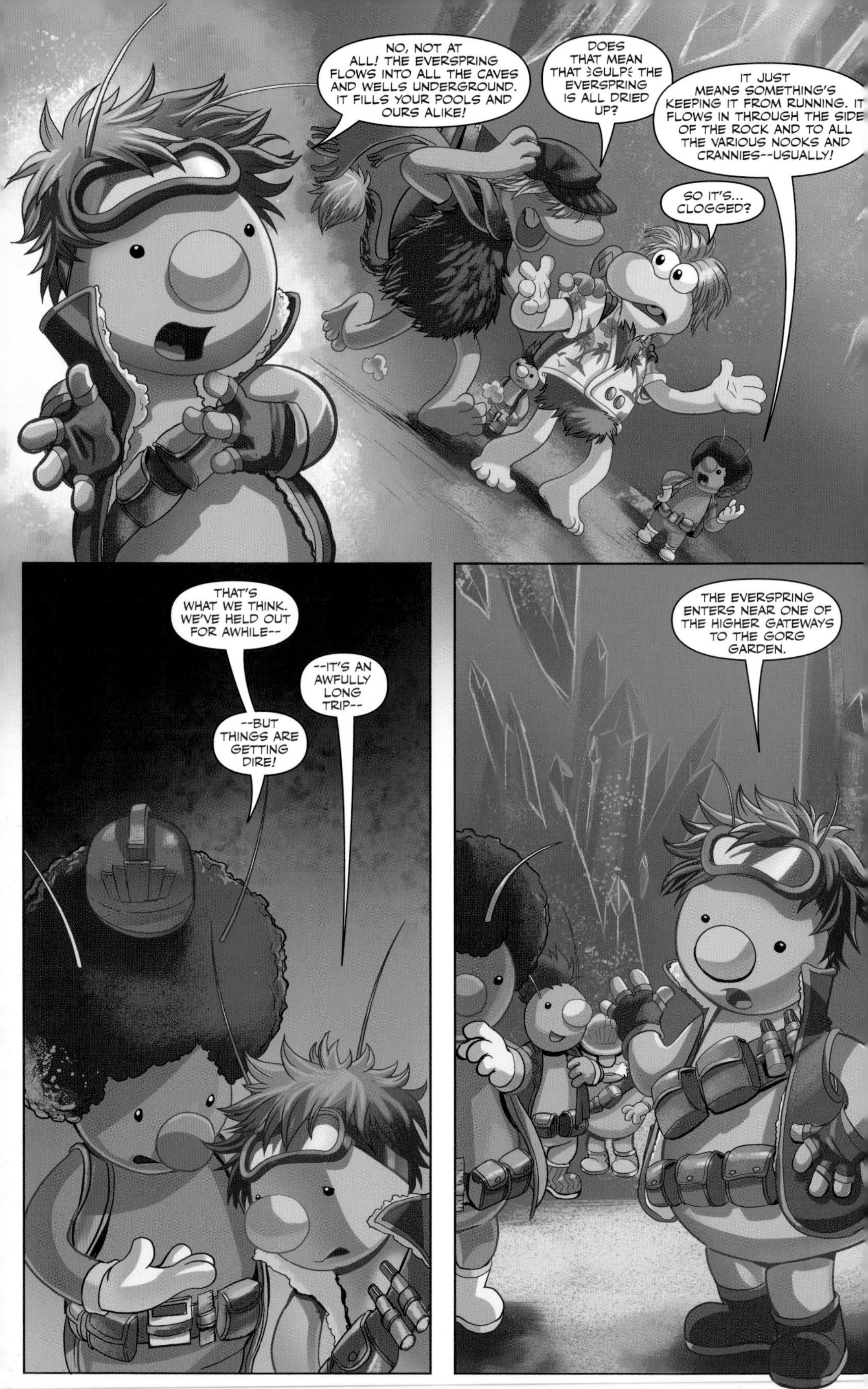
NO, NOT AT ALL! THE EVERSPRING FLOWS INTO ALL THE CAVES AND WELLS UNDERGROUND. IT FILLS YOUR POOLS AND OURS ALIKE!
DOES THAT MEAN THAT *GULP* THE EVERSPRING IS ALL DRIED UP?
IT JUST MEANS SOMETHING'S KEEPING IT FROM RUNNING. IT FLOWS IN THROUGH THE SIDE OF THE ROCK AND TO ALL THE VARIOUS NOOKS AND CRANNIES--USUALLY!
SO IT'S... CLOGGED?
THAT'S WHAT WE THINK. WE'VE HELD OUT FOR AWHILE--
--IT'S AN AWFULLY LONG TRIP--
--BUT THINGS ARE GETTING DIRE!
THE EVERSPRING ENTERS NEAR ONE OF THE HIGHER GATEWAYS TO THE GORG GARDEN.

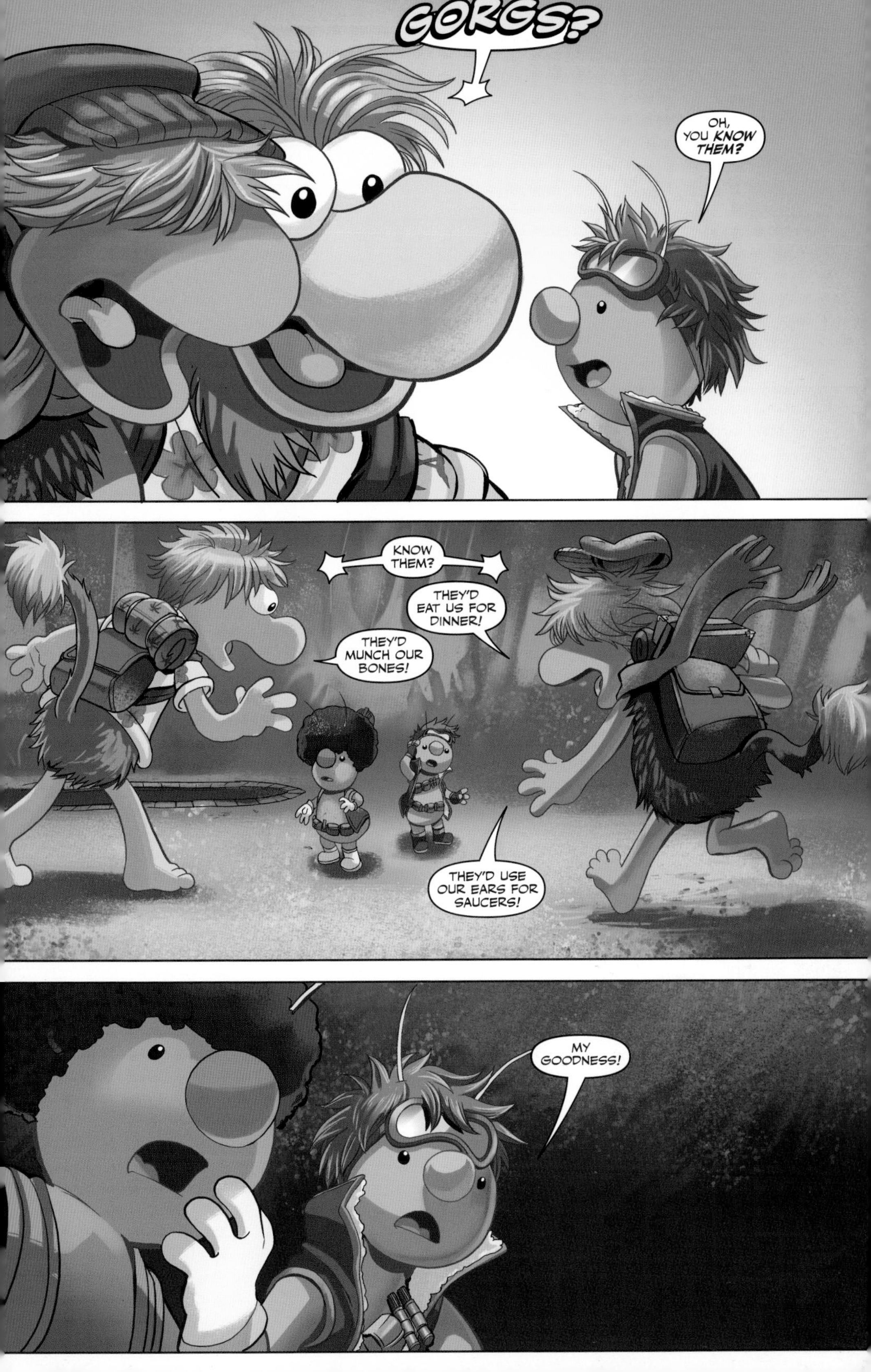
GORGS?
OH, YOU KNOW THEM?
KNOW THEM?
THEY'D EAT US FOR DINNER!
THEY'D MUNCH OUR BONES!
THEY'D USE OUR EARS FOR SAUCERS!
MY GOODNESS!

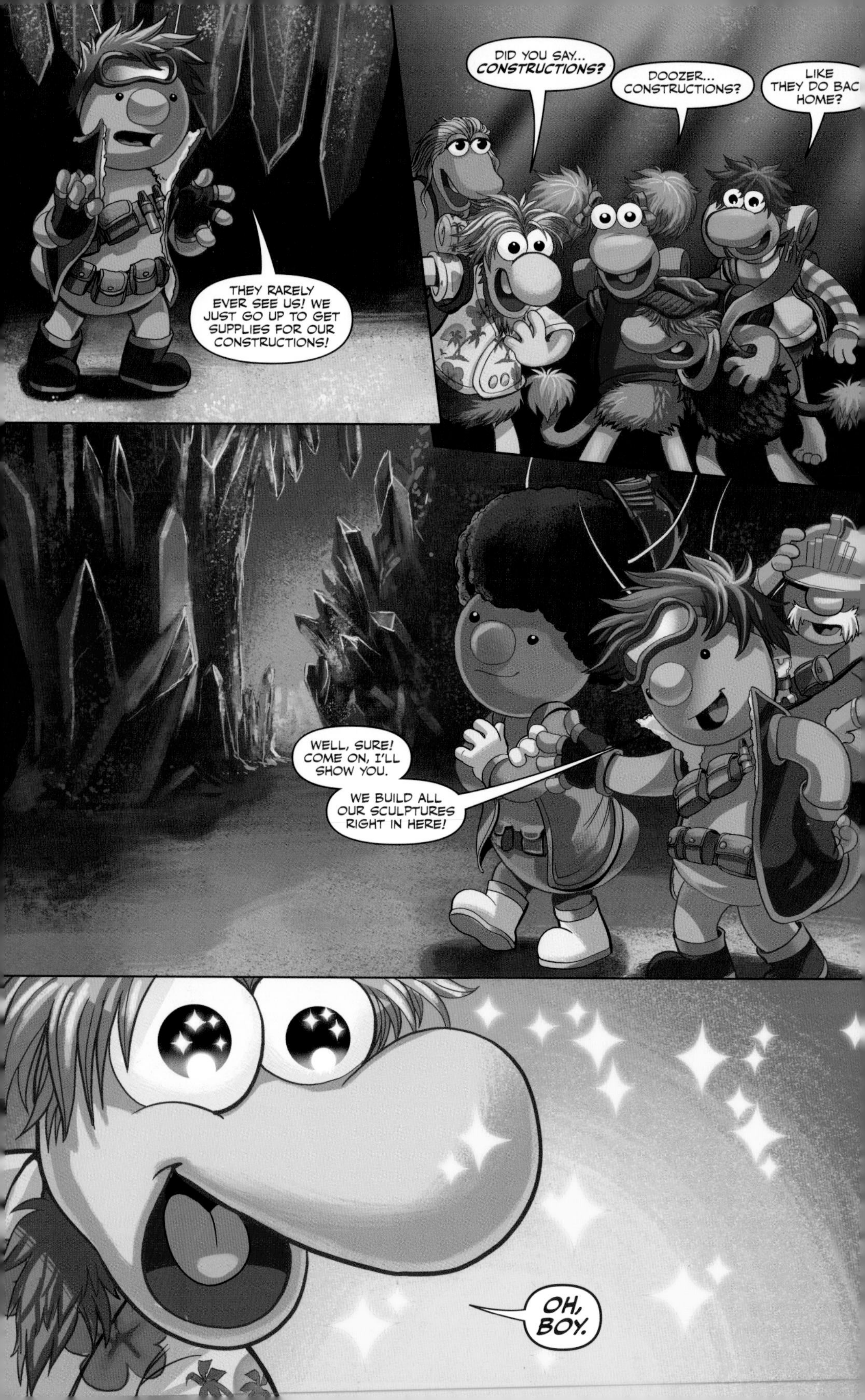
THEY RARELY EVER SEE US! WE JUST GO UP TO GET SUPPLIES FOR OUR CONSTRUCTIONS!
DID YOU SAY... CONSTRUCTIONS?
DOOZER... CONSTRUCTIONS?
LIKE THEY DO BAC HOME?
WELL, SURE! COME ON, I'LL SHOW YOU.
WE BUILD ALL OUR SCULPTURES RIGHT IN HERE!
OH, BOY.

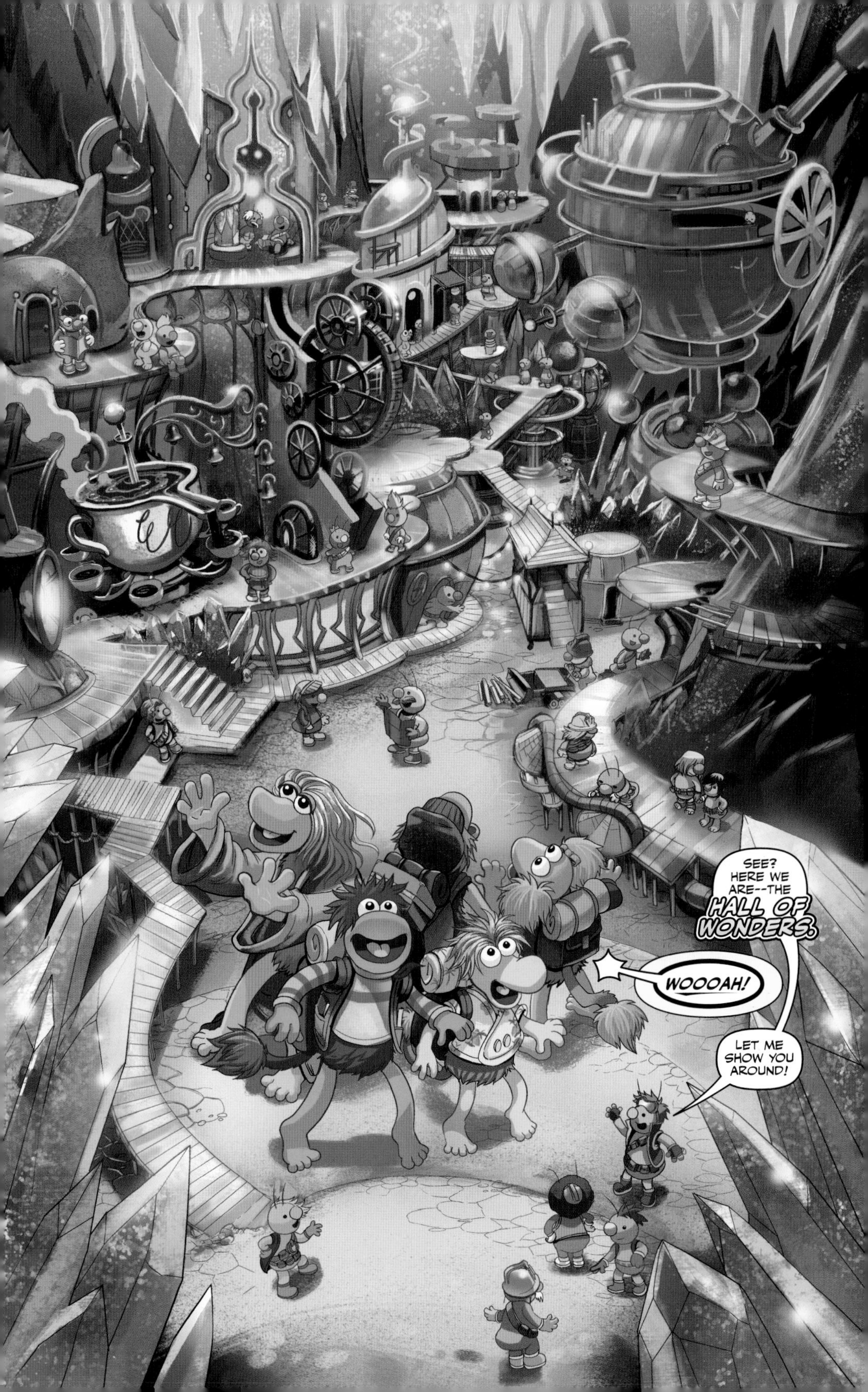
SEE? HERE WE ARE--THE HALL OF WONDERS.
WOOOAH!
LET ME SHOW YOU AROUND!

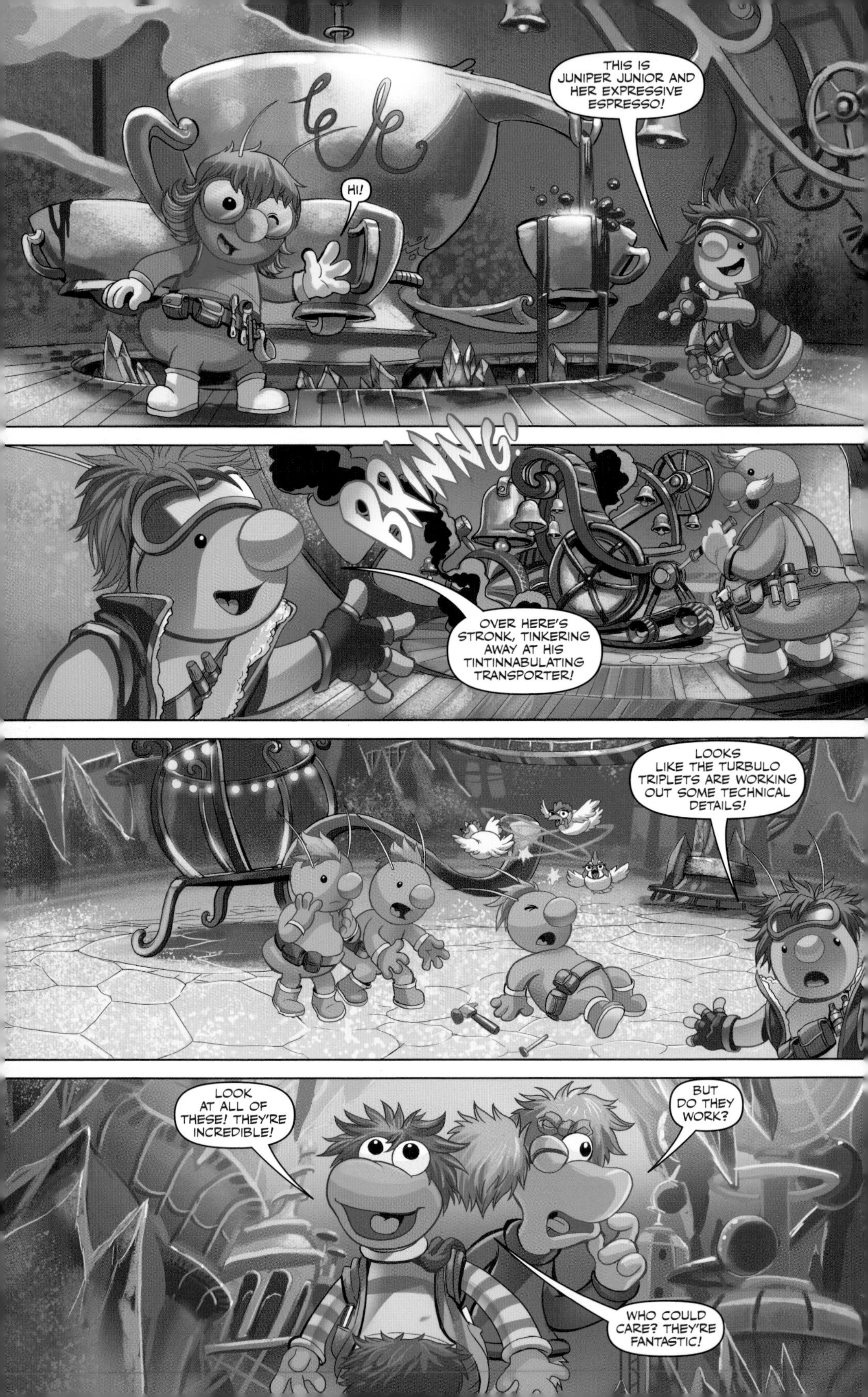
THIS IS JUNIPER JUNIOR AND HER EXPRESSIVE ESPRESSO!
HI!
BRIIING!
OVER HERE'S STRONK, TINKERING AWAY AT HIS TINTINNABULATING TRANSPORTER!
LOOKS LIKE THE TURBULO TRIPLETS ARE WORKING OUT SOME TECHNICAL DETAILS!
LOOK AT ALL OF THESE! THEY'RE INCREDIBLE!
BUT DO THEY WORK?
WHO COULD CARE? THEY'RE FANTASTIC!

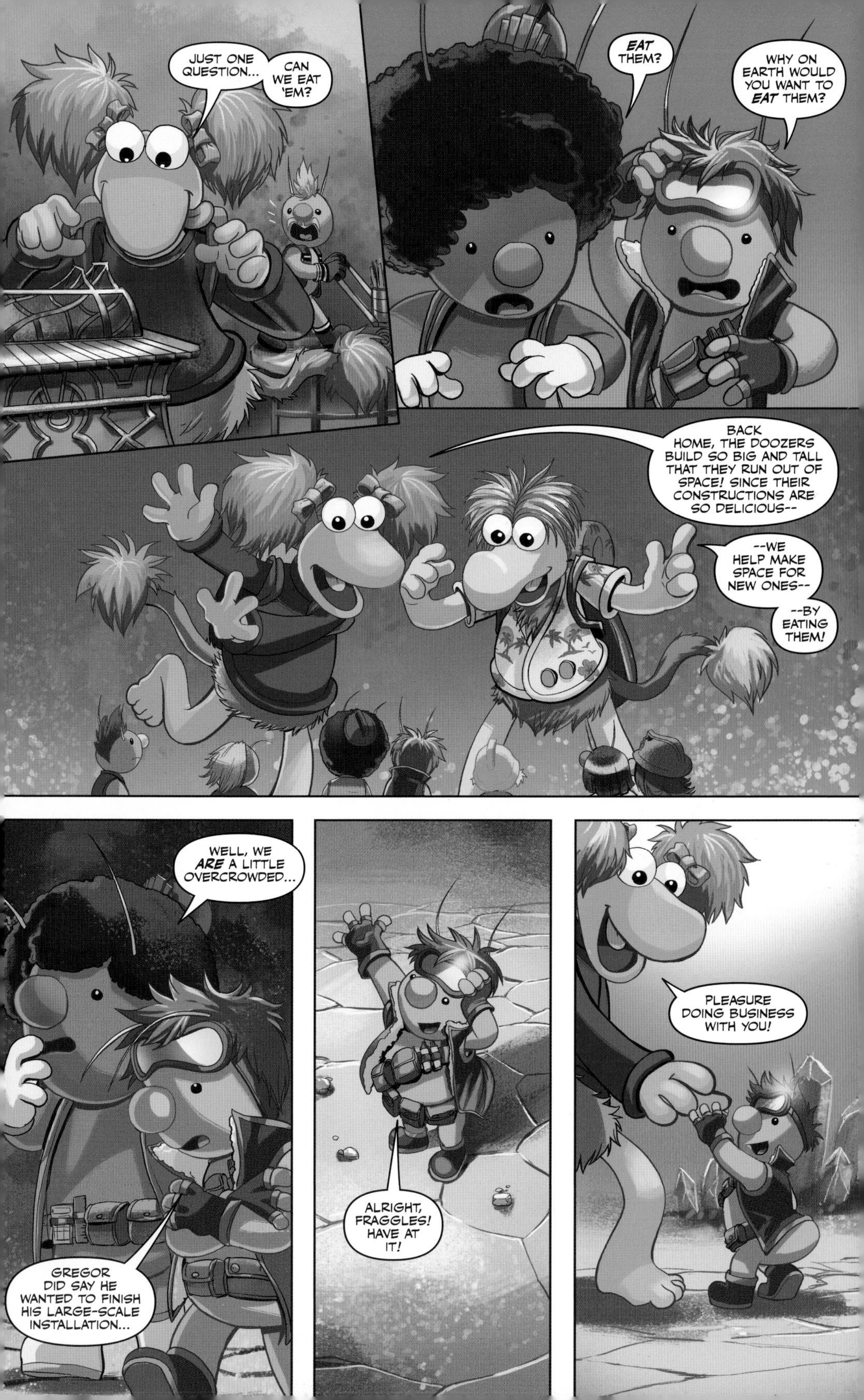
JUST ONE QUESTION...
CAN WE EAT 'EM?
EAT THEM?
WHY ON EARTH WOULD YOU WANT TO EAT THEM?
BACK HOME, THE DOOZERS BUILD SO BIG AND TALL THAT THEY RUN OUT OF SPACE! SINCE THEIR CONSTRUCTIONS ARE SO DELICIOUS--
--WE HELP MAKE SPACE FOR NEW ONES--
--BY EATING THEM!
WELL, WE ARE A LITTLE OVERCROWDED...
GREGOR DID SAY HE WANTED TO FINISH HIS LARGE-SCALE INSTALLATION...
ALRIGHT, FRAGGLES! HAVE AT IT!
PLEASURE DOING BUSINESS WITH YOU!

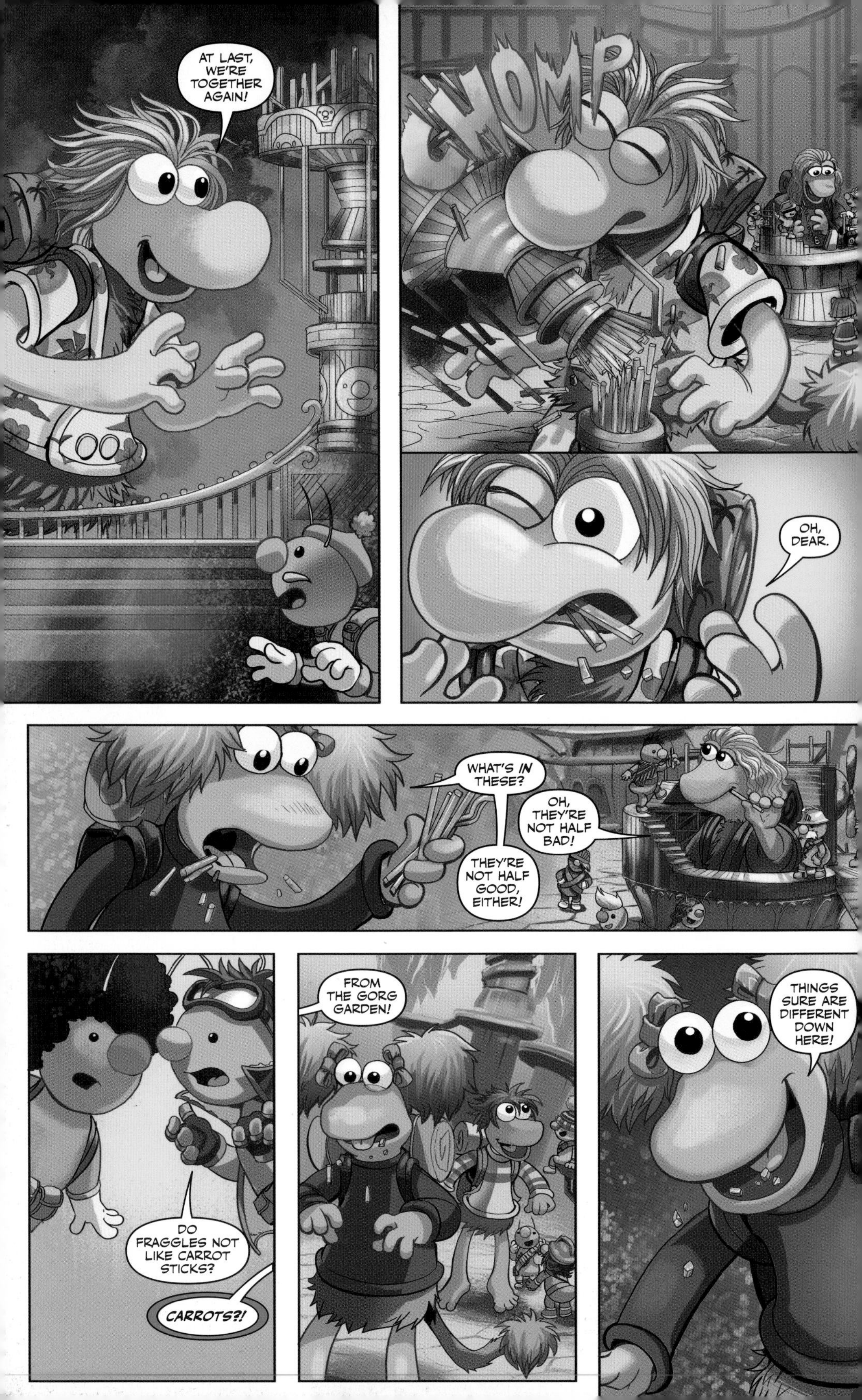
AT LAST, WE'RE TOGETHER AGAIN!
CHOMP
OH, DEAR.
WHAT'S IN THESE?
OH, THEY'RE NOT HALF BAD!
THEY'RE NOT HALF GOOD, EITHER!
DO FRAGGLES NOT LIKE CARROT STICKS?
CARROTS?!
FROM THE GORG GARDEN!
THINGS SURE ARE DIFFERENT DOWN HERE!

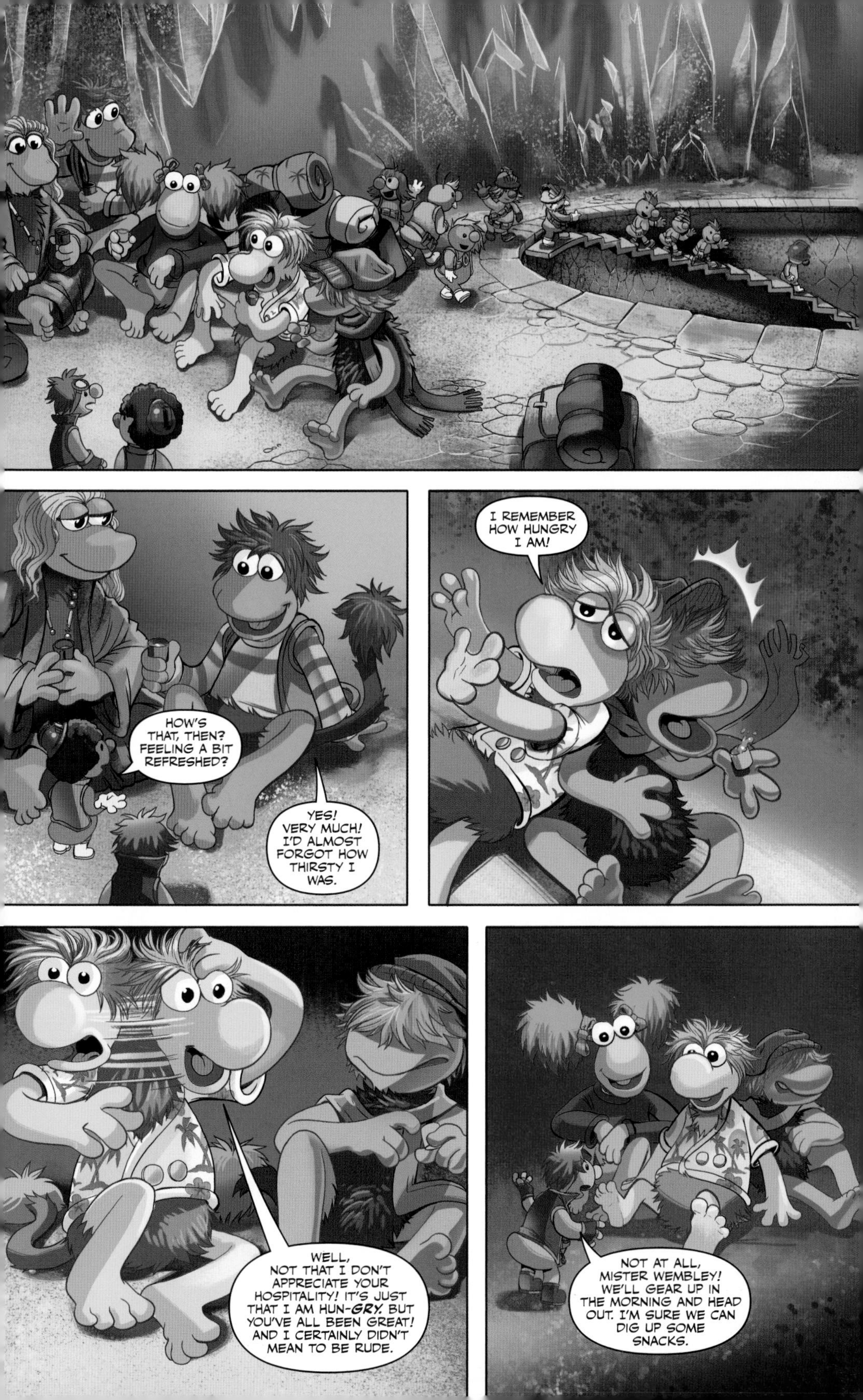
HOW'S THAT, THEN? FEELING A BIT REFRESHED?
YES! VERY MUCH! I'D ALMOST FORGOT HOW THIRSTY I WAS.
I REMEMBER HOW HUNGRY I AM!
WELL, NOT THAT I DON'T APPRECIATE YOUR HOSPITALITY! IT'S JUST THAT I AM HUN-GRY. BUT YOU'VE ALL BEEN GREAT! AND I CERTAINLY DIDN'T MEAN TO BE RUDE.
NOT AT ALL, MISTER WEMBLEY! WE'LL GEAR UP IN THE MORNING AND HEAD OUT. I'M SURE WE CAN DIG UP SOME SNACKS.

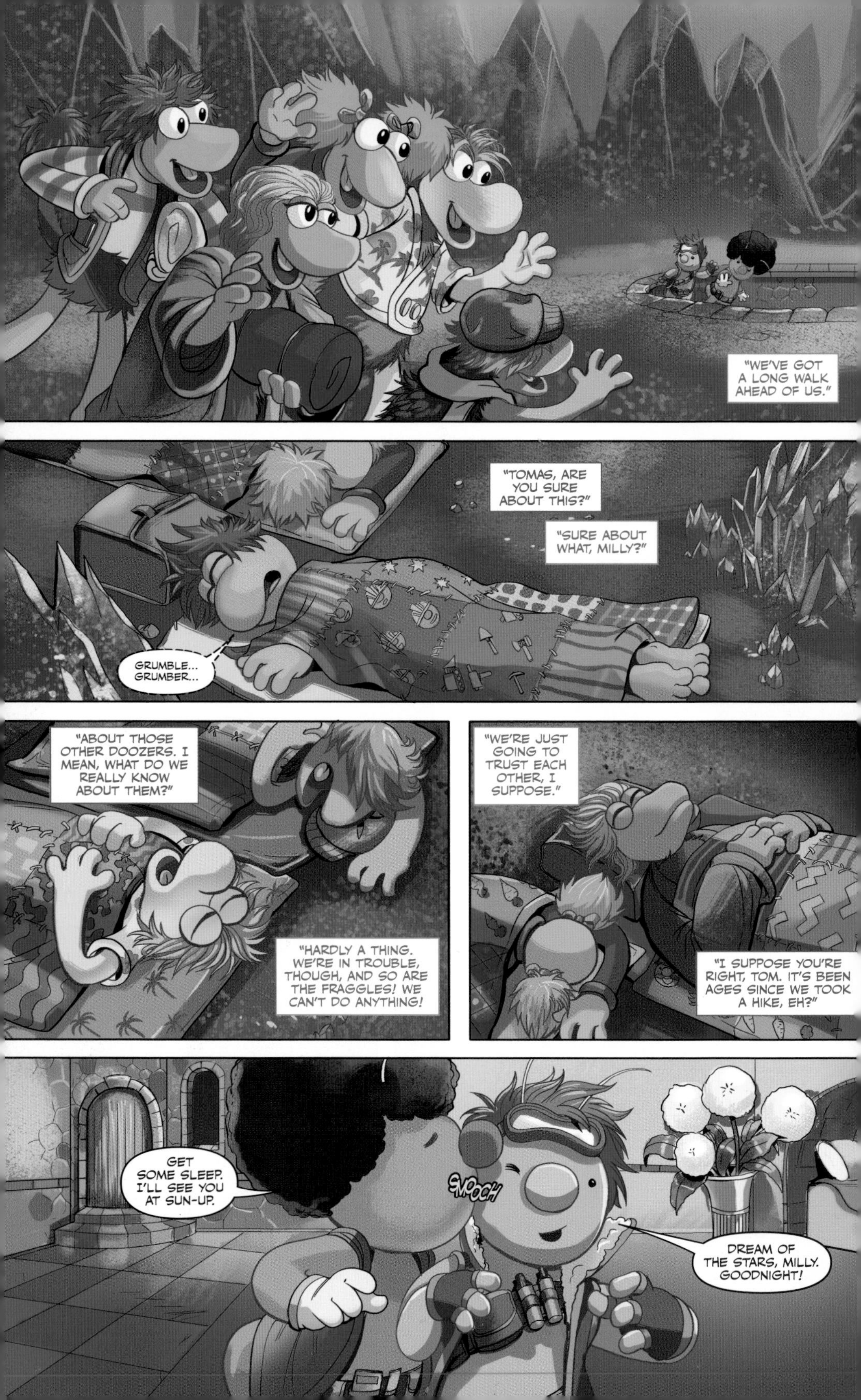
"WE'VE GOT A LONG WALK AHEAD OF US."
"TOMAS, ARE YOU SURE ABOUT THIS?"
"SURE ABOUT WHAT, MILLY?"
GRUMBLE... GRUMBER...
"ABOUT THOSE OTHER DOOZERS. I MEAN, WHAT DO WE REALLY KNOW ABOUT THEM?"
"HARDLY A THING. WE'RE IN TROUBLE, THOUGH, AND SO ARE THE FRAGGLES! WE CAN'T DO ANYTHING!
"WE'RE JUST GOING TO TRUST EACH OTHER, I SUPPOSE."
"I SUPPOSE YOU'RE RIGHT, TOM. IT'S BEEN AGES SINCE WE TOOK A HIKE, EH?"
GET SOME SLEEP. I'LL SEE YOU AT SUN-UP.
SMOOCH
DREAM OF THE STARS, MILLY. GOODNIGHT!

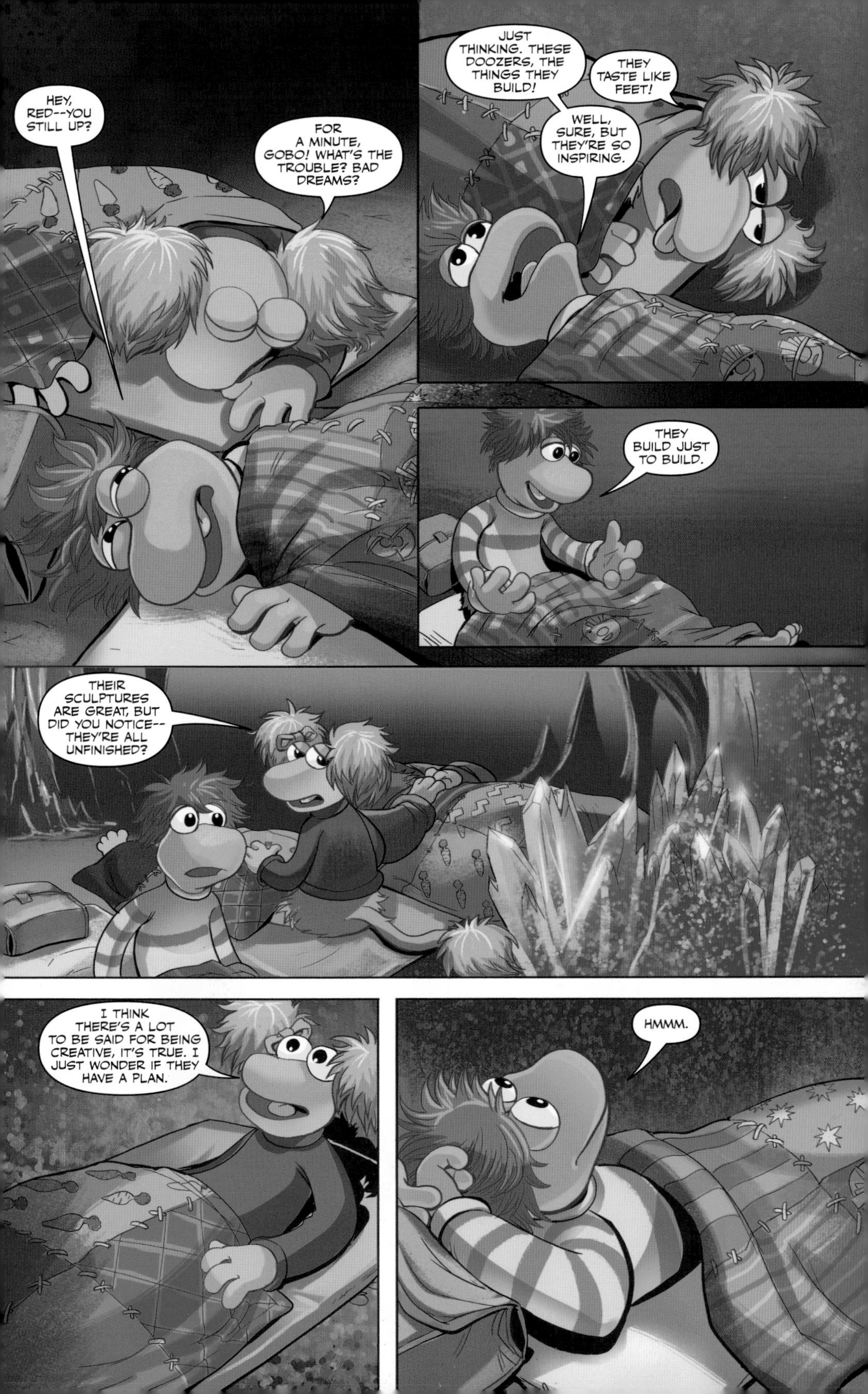
HEY, RED--YOU STILL UP?
FOR A MINUTE, GOBO! WHAT'S THE TROUBLE? BAD DREAMS?
JUST THINKING. THESE DOOZERS, THE THINGS THEY BUILD!
THEY TASTE LIKE FEET!
WELL, SURE, BUT THEY'RE SO INSPIRING.
THEY BUILD JUST TO BUILD.
THEIR SCULPTURES ARE GREAT, BUT DID YOU NOTICE-- THEY'RE ALL UNFINISHED?
I THINK THERE'S A LOT TO BE SAID FOR BEING CREATIVE, IT'S TRUE. I JUST WONDER IF THEY HAVE A PLAN.
HMMM.

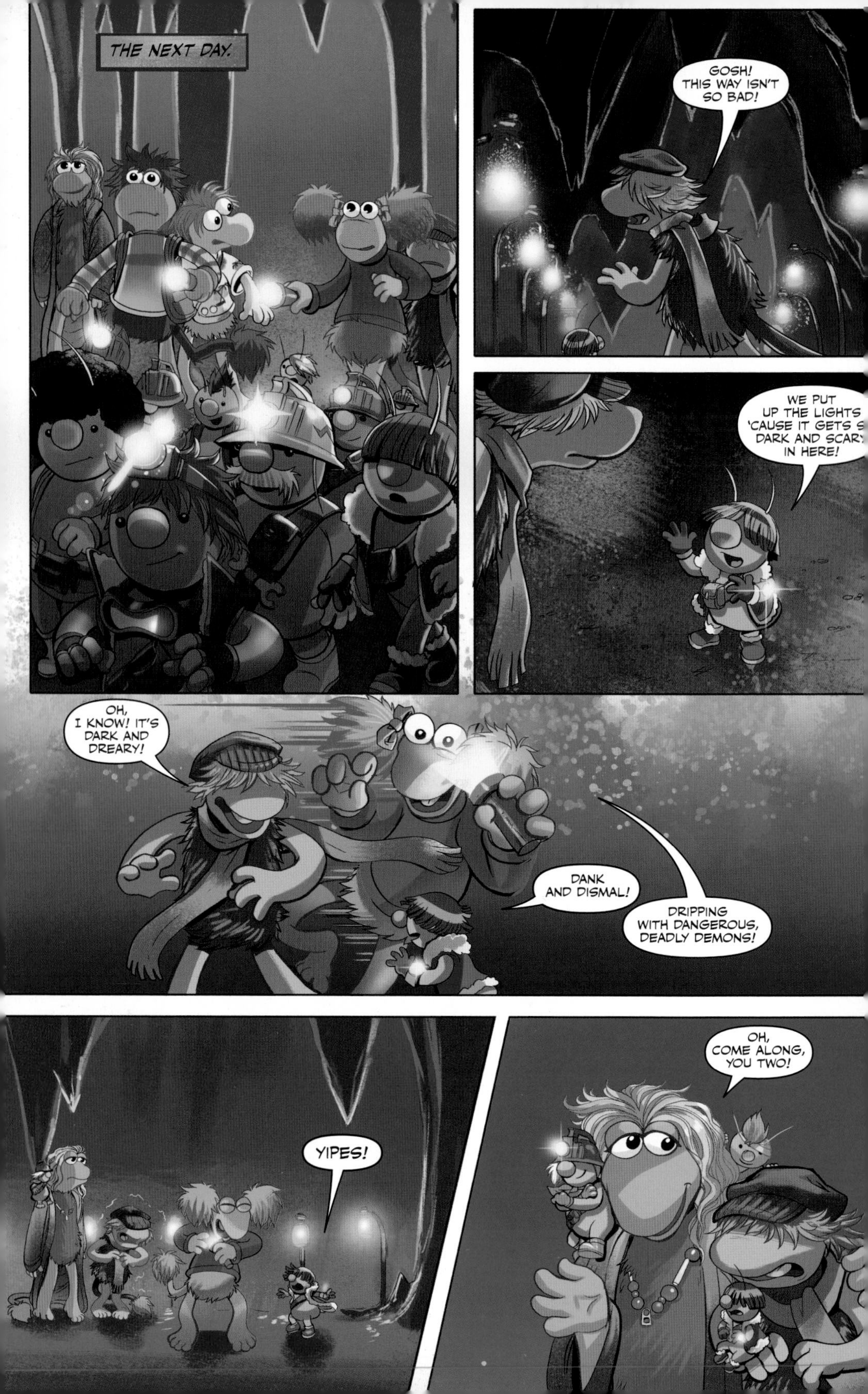
THE NEXT DAY.
GOSH! THIS WAY ISN'T SO BAD!
WE PUT UP THE LIGHTS 'CAUSE IT GETS S DARK AND SCAR IN HERE!
OH, I KNOW! IT'S DARK AND DREARY!
DANK AND DISMAL!
DRIPPING WITH DANGEROUS, DEADLY DEMONS!
YIPES!
OH, COME ALONG, YOU TWO!

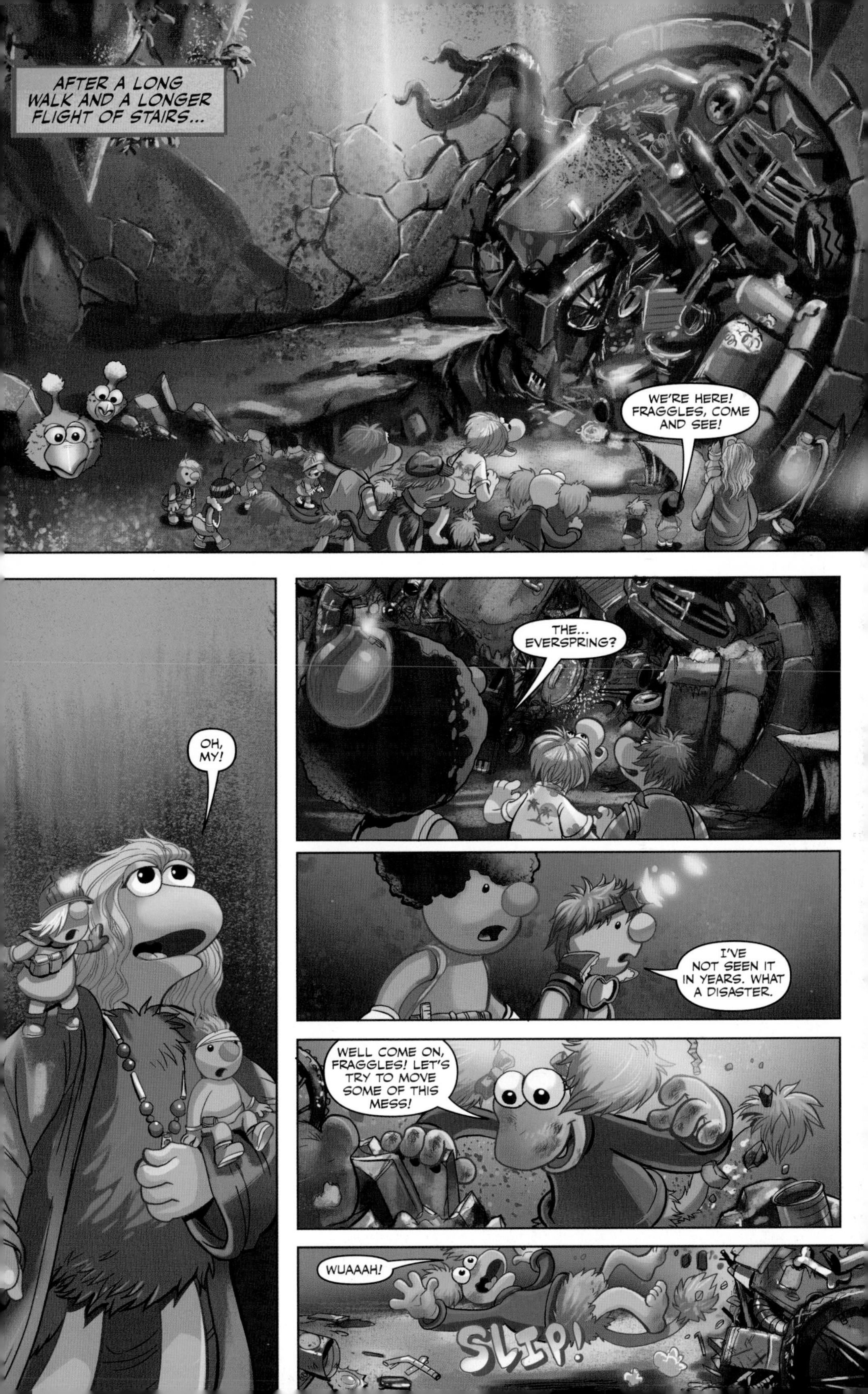
AFTER A LONG WALK AND A LONGER FLIGHT OF STAIRS...
WE'RE HERE! FRAGGLES, COME AND SEE!
OH, MY!
THE... EVERSPRING?
I'VE NOT SEEN IT IN YEARS. WHAT A DISASTER.
WELL COME ON, FRAGGLES! LET'S TRY TO MOVE SOME OF THIS MESS!
WUAAAH!
SLIP!

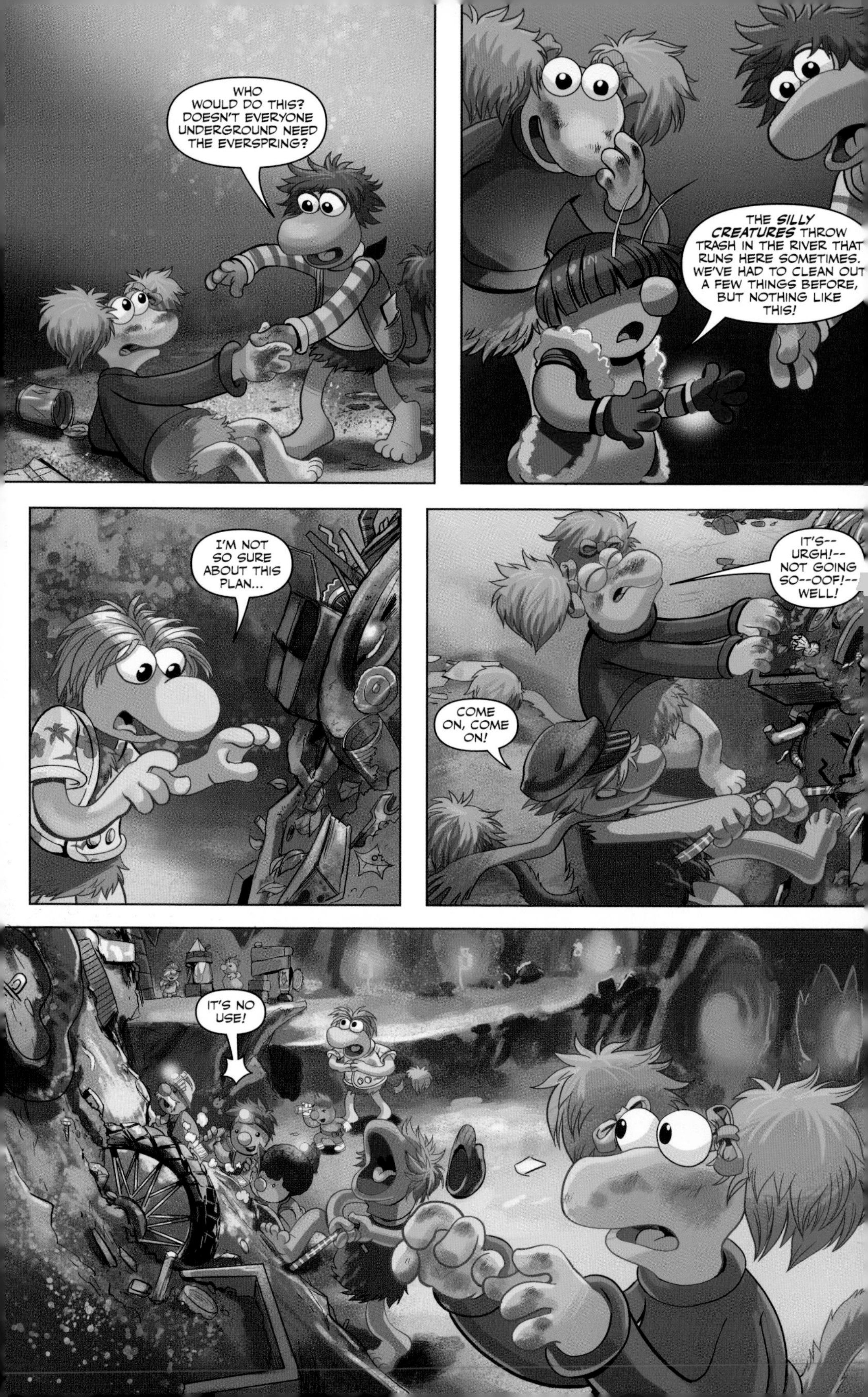
WHO WOULD DO THIS? DOESN'T EVERYONE UNDERGROUND NEED THE EVERSPRING?
THE *SILLY CREATURES* THROW TRASH IN THE RIVER THAT RUNS HERE SOMETIMES. WE'VE HAD TO CLEAN OUT A FEW THINGS BEFORE, BUT NOTHING LIKE THIS!
I'M NOT SO SURE ABOUT THIS PLAN...
IT'S-- URGH!-- NOT GOING SO--OOF!-- WELL!
COME ON, COME ON!
IT'S NO USE!

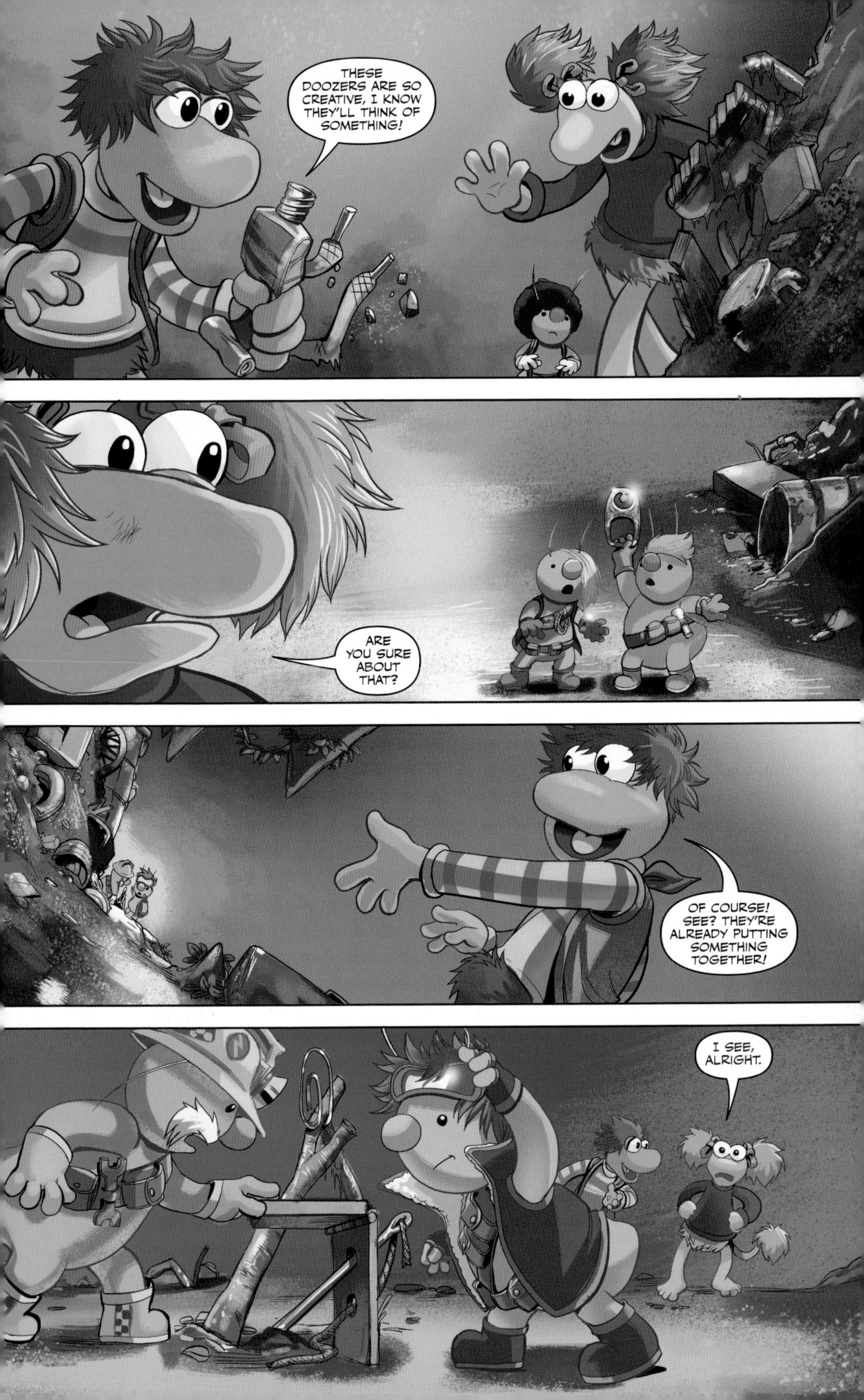
THESE DOOZERS ARE SO CREATIVE, I KNOW THEY'LL THINK OF SOMETHING!
ARE YOU SURE ABOUT THAT?
OF COURSE! SEE? THEY'RE ALREADY PUTTING SOMETHING TOGETHER!
I SEE, ALRIGHT.

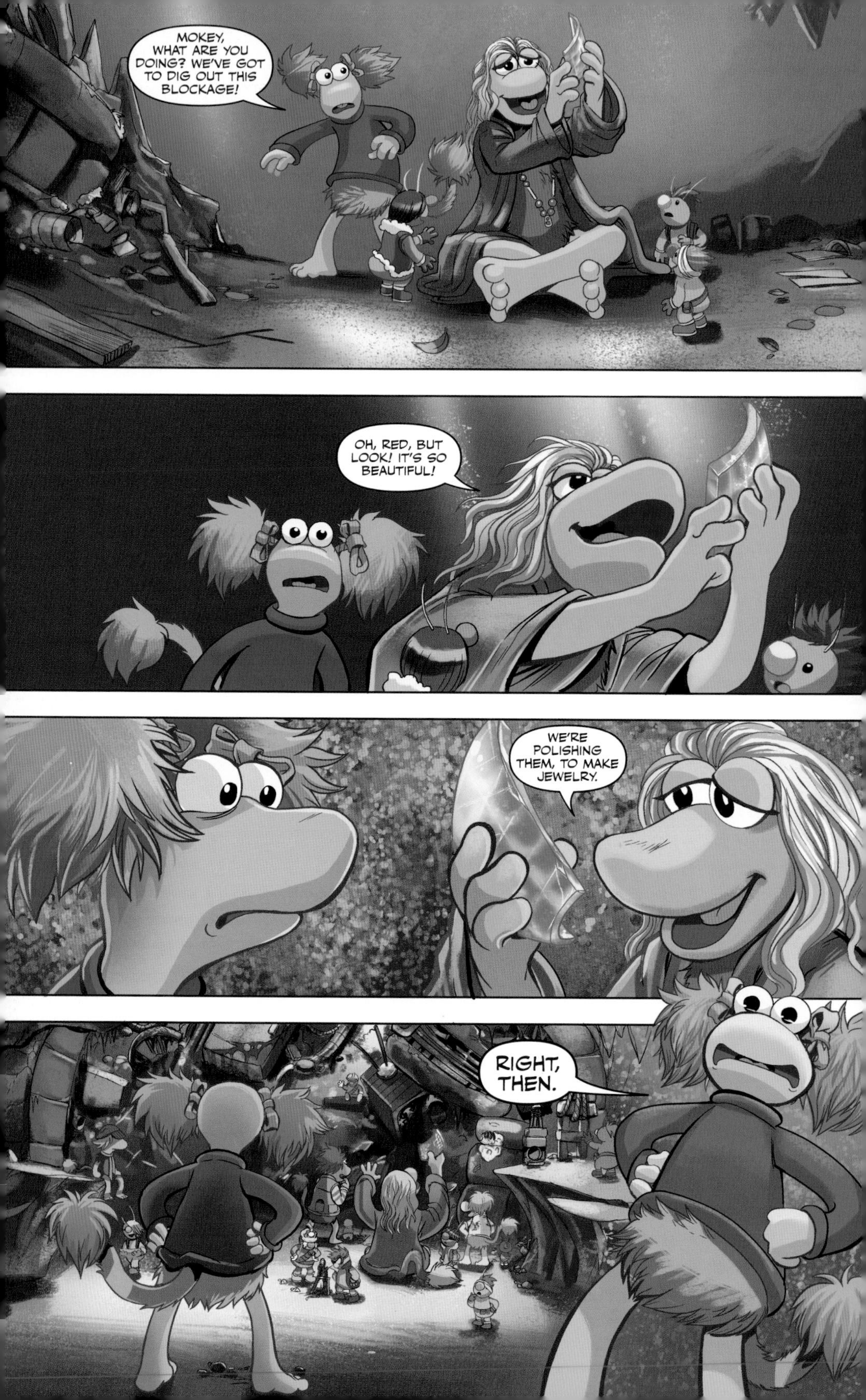
MOKEY, WHAT ARE YOU DOING? WE'VE GOT TO DIG OUT THIS BLOCKAGE!
OH, RED, BUT LOOK! IT'S SO BEAUTIFUL!
WE'RE POLISHING THEM, TO MAKE JEWELRY.
RIGHT, THEN.

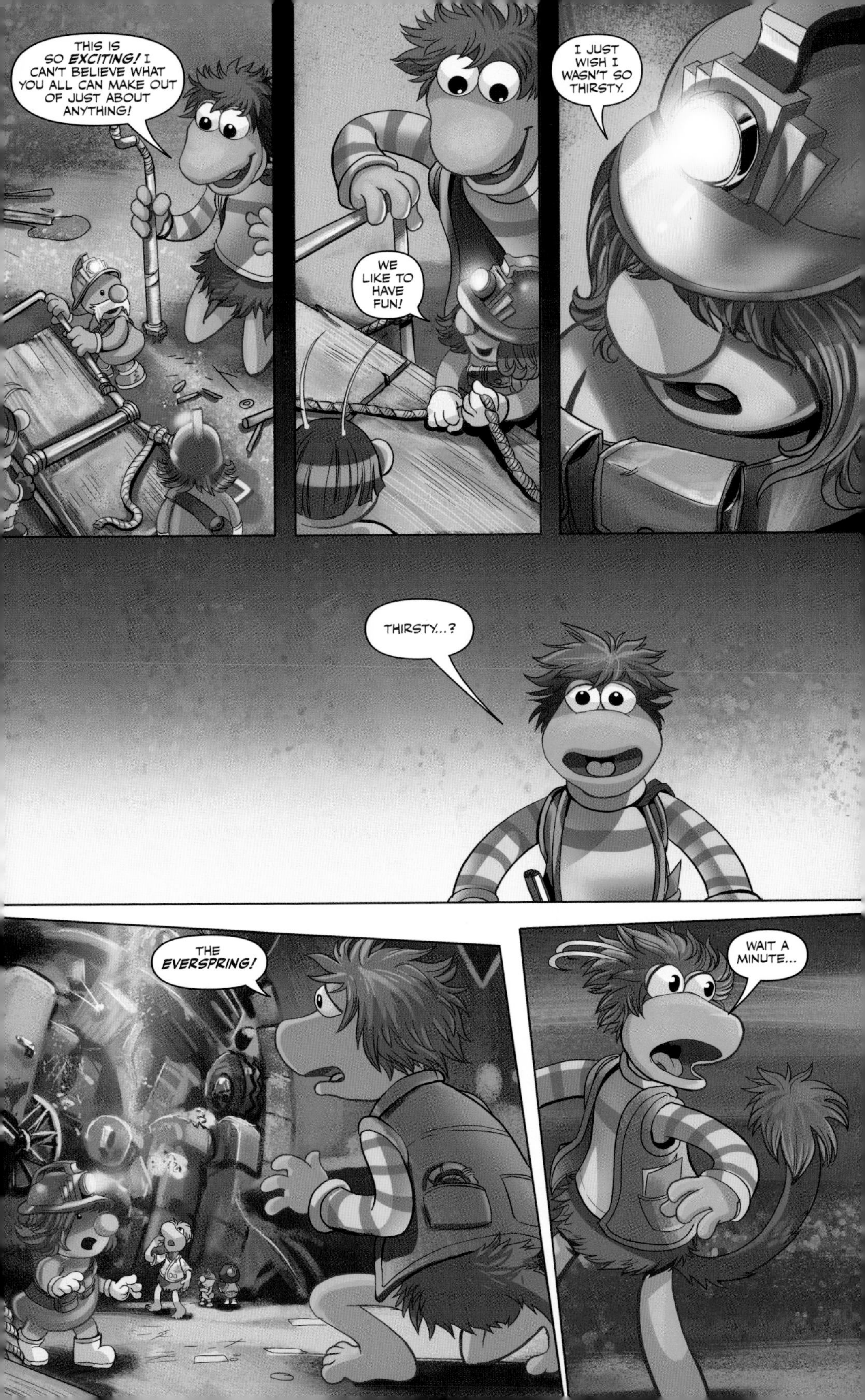
THIS IS SO ***EXCITING!*** I CAN'T BELIEVE WHAT YOU ALL CAN MAKE OUT OF JUST ABOUT ANYTHING!
WE LIKE TO HAVE FUN!
I JUST WISH I WASN'T SO THIRSTY.
THIRSTY...?
THE ***EVERSPRING!***
WAIT A MINUTE...

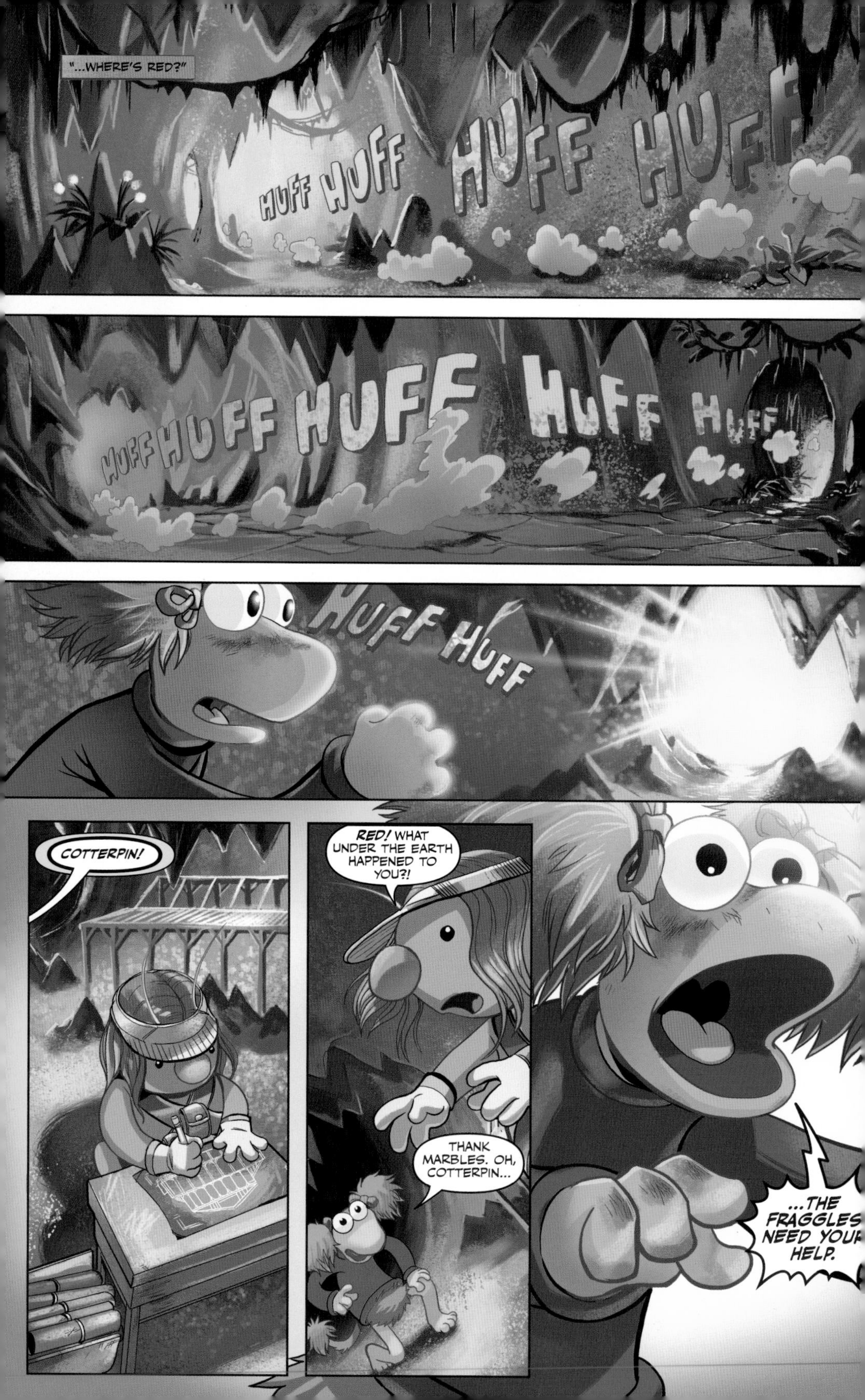
"...WHERE'S RED?"
HUFF HUFF HUFF HUFF
HUFF HUFF HUFF HUFF HUFF
HUFF HUFF
COTTERPIN!
RED! WHAT UNDER THE EARTH HAPPENED TO YOU?!
THANK MARBLES. OH, COTTERPIN...
...THE FRAGGLES NEED YOUR HELP.

DOWN AT FRAGGLE ROCK

CHAPTER FOUR

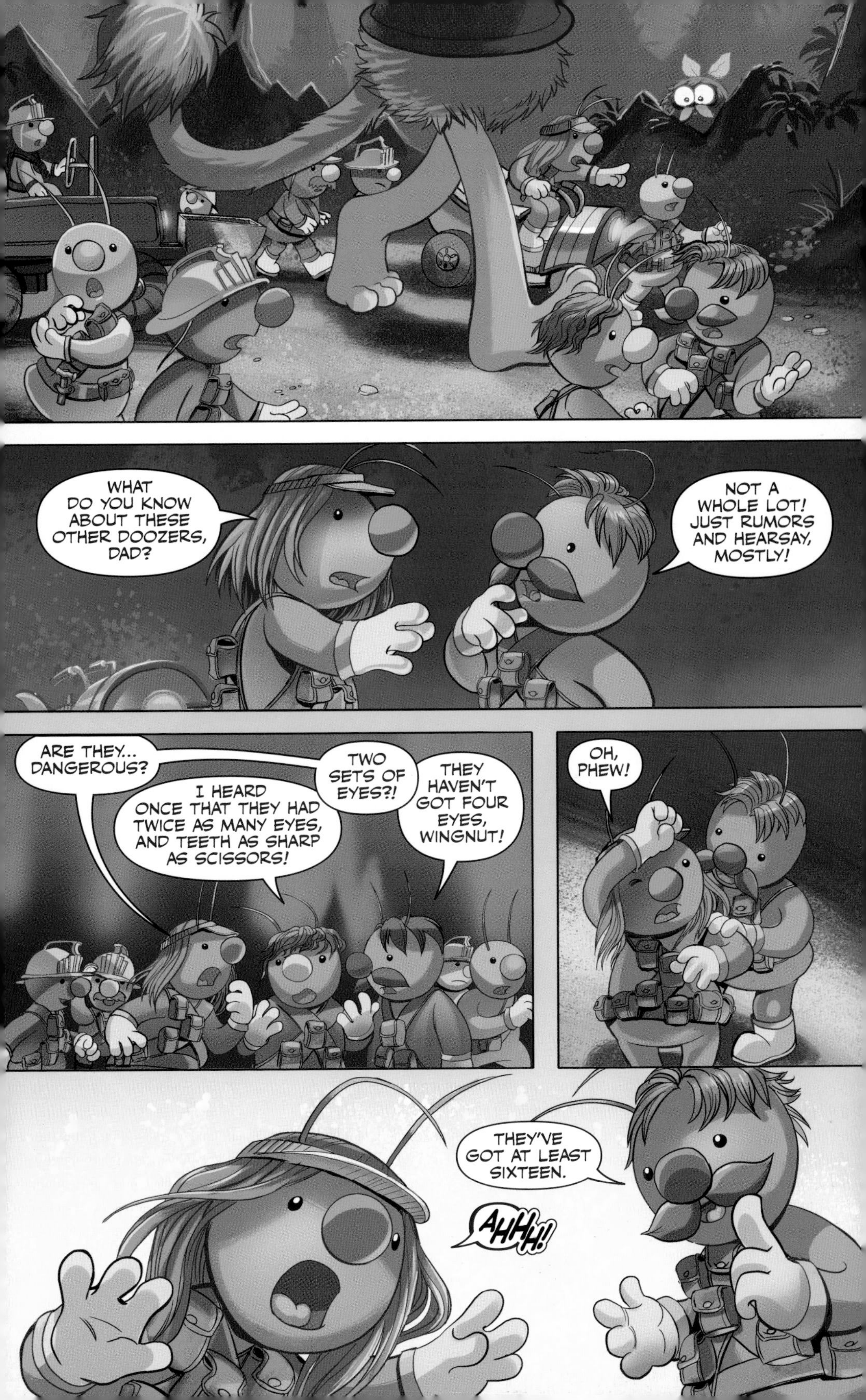
WHAT DO YOU KNOW ABOUT THESE OTHER DOOZERS, DAD?
NOT A WHOLE LOT! JUST RUMORS AND HEARSAY, MOSTLY!
ARE THEY... DANGEROUS?
I HEARD ONCE THAT THEY HAD TWICE AS MANY EYES, AND TEETH AS SHARP AS SCISSORS!
TWO SETS OF EYES?!
THEY HAVEN'T GOT FOUR EYES, WINGNUT!
OH, PHEW!
THEY'VE GOT AT LEAST SIXTEEN.
AHHH!

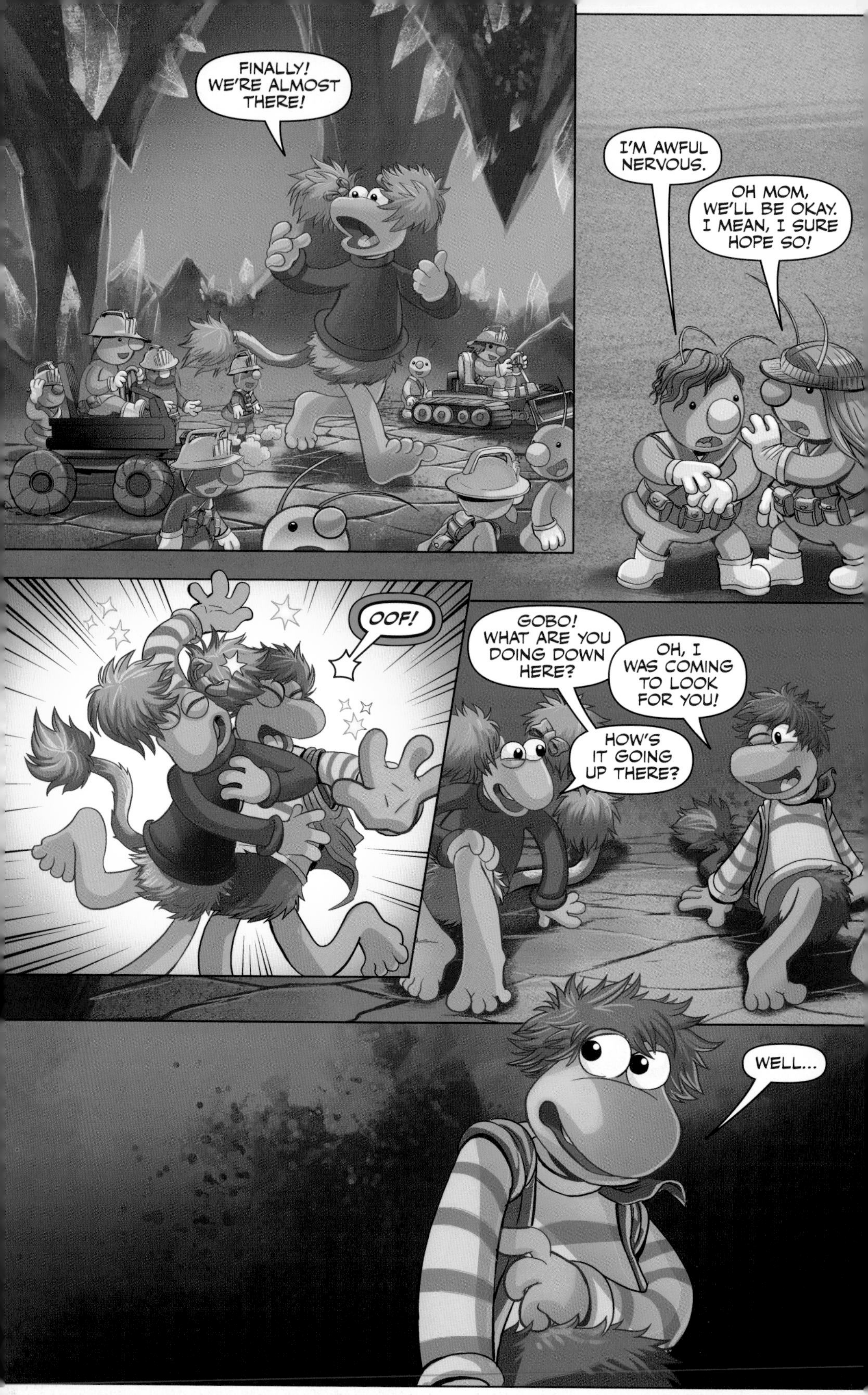
FINALLY! WE'RE ALMOST THERE!
I'M AWFUL NERVOUS.
OH MOM, WE'LL BE OKAY. I MEAN, I SURE HOPE SO!
OOF!
GOBO! WHAT ARE YOU DOING DOWN HERE?
OH, I WAS COMING TO LOOK FOR YOU!
HOW'S IT GOING UP THERE?
WELL...

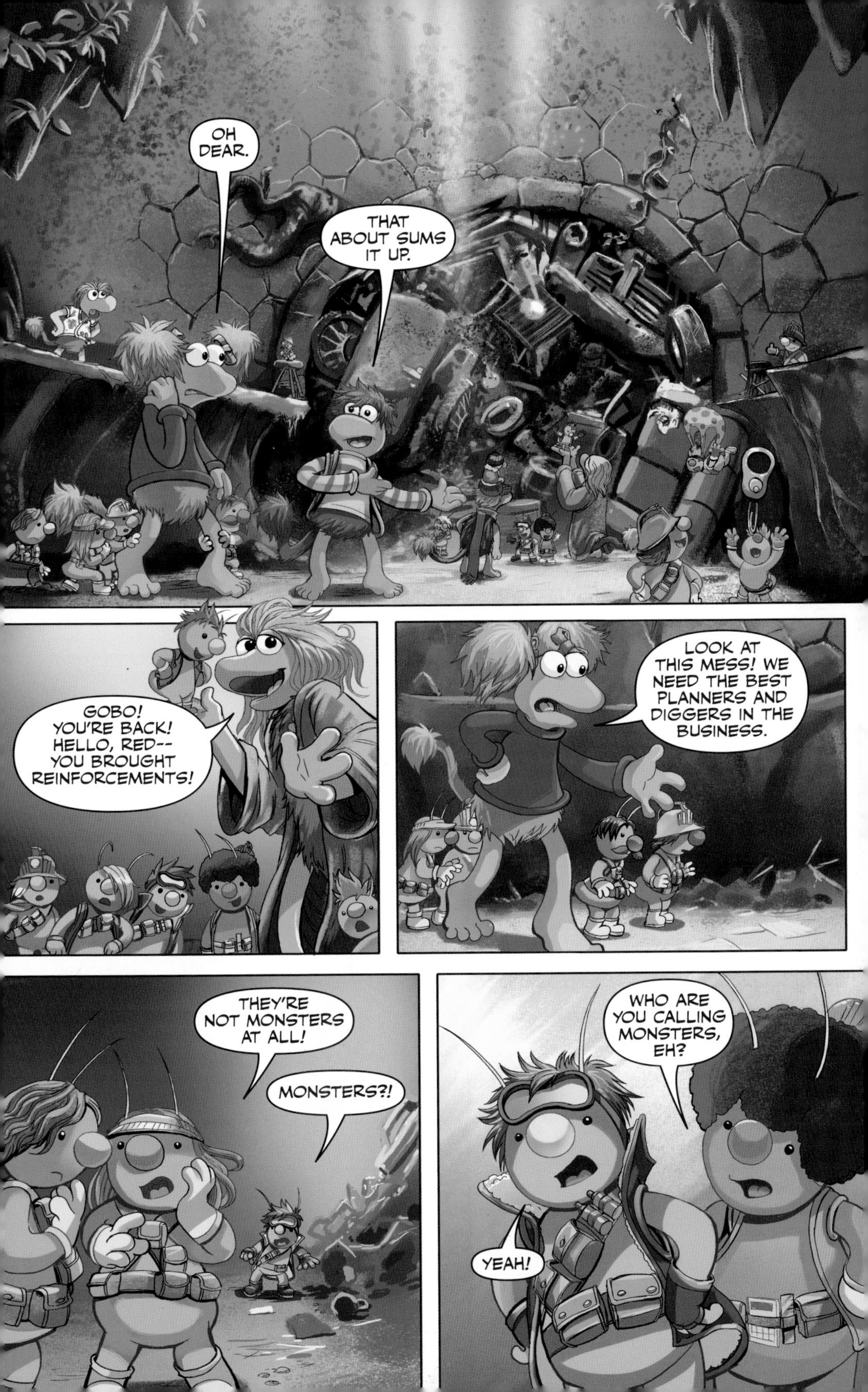
OH DEAR.
THAT ABOUT SUMS IT UP.
GOBO! YOU'RE BACK! HELLO, RED-- YOU BROUGHT REINFORCEMENTS!
LOOK AT THIS MESS! WE NEED THE BEST PLANNERS AND DIGGERS IN THE BUSINESS.
THEY'RE NOT MONSTERS AT ALL!
MONSTERS?!
WHO ARE YOU CALLING MONSTERS, EH?
YEAH!

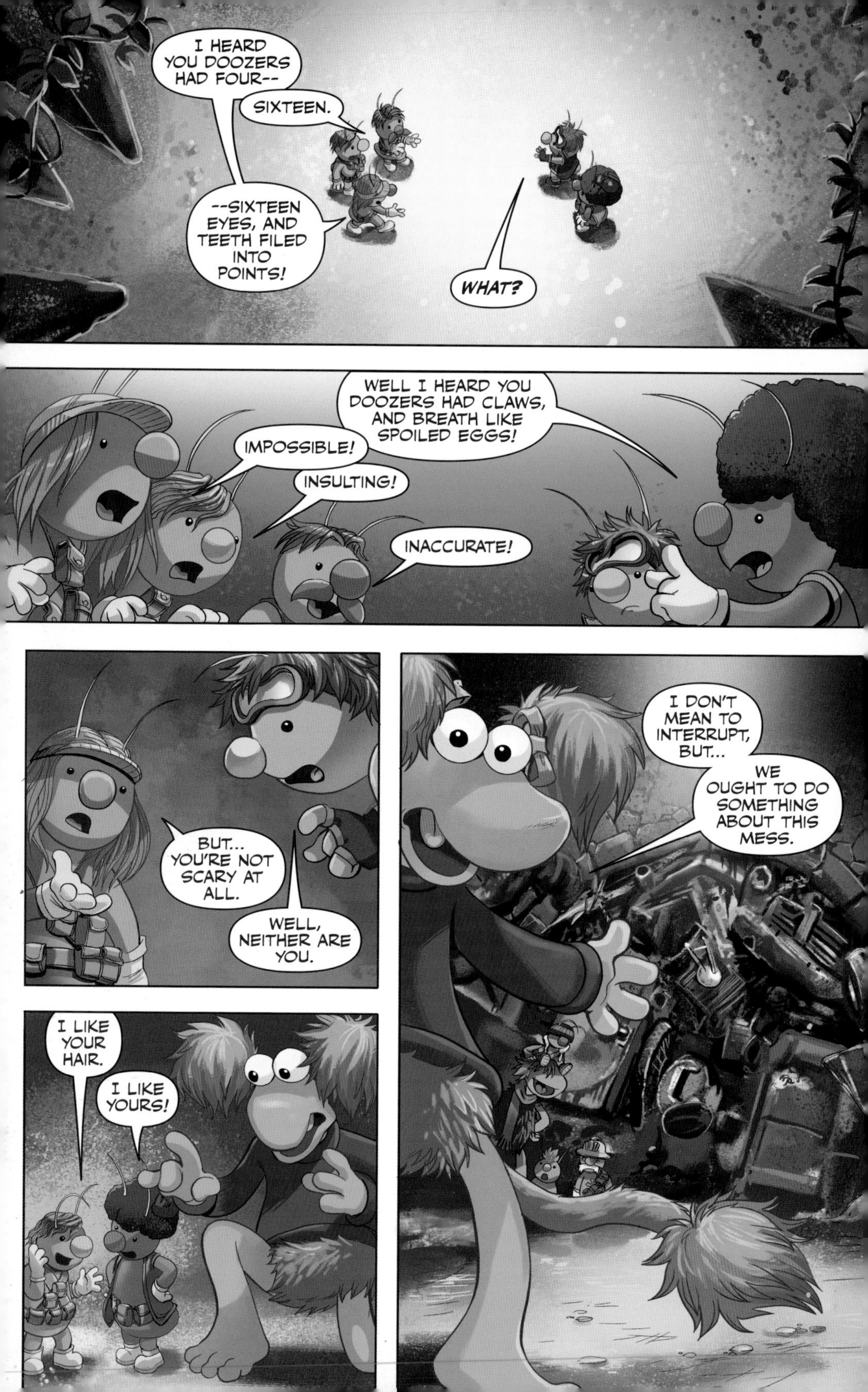
I HEARD YOU DOOZERS HAD FOUR--
SIXTEEN.
--SIXTEEN EYES, AND TEETH FILED INTO POINTS!
WHAT?
IMPOSSIBLE!
INSULTING!
INACCURATE!
WELL I HEARD YOU DOOZERS HAD CLAWS, AND BREATH LIKE SPOILED EGGS!
BUT... YOU'RE NOT SCARY AT ALL.
WELL, NEITHER ARE YOU.
I LIKE YOUR HAIR.
I LIKE YOURS!
I DON'T MEAN TO INTERRUPT, BUT...
WE OUGHT TO DO SOMETHING ABOUT THIS MESS.

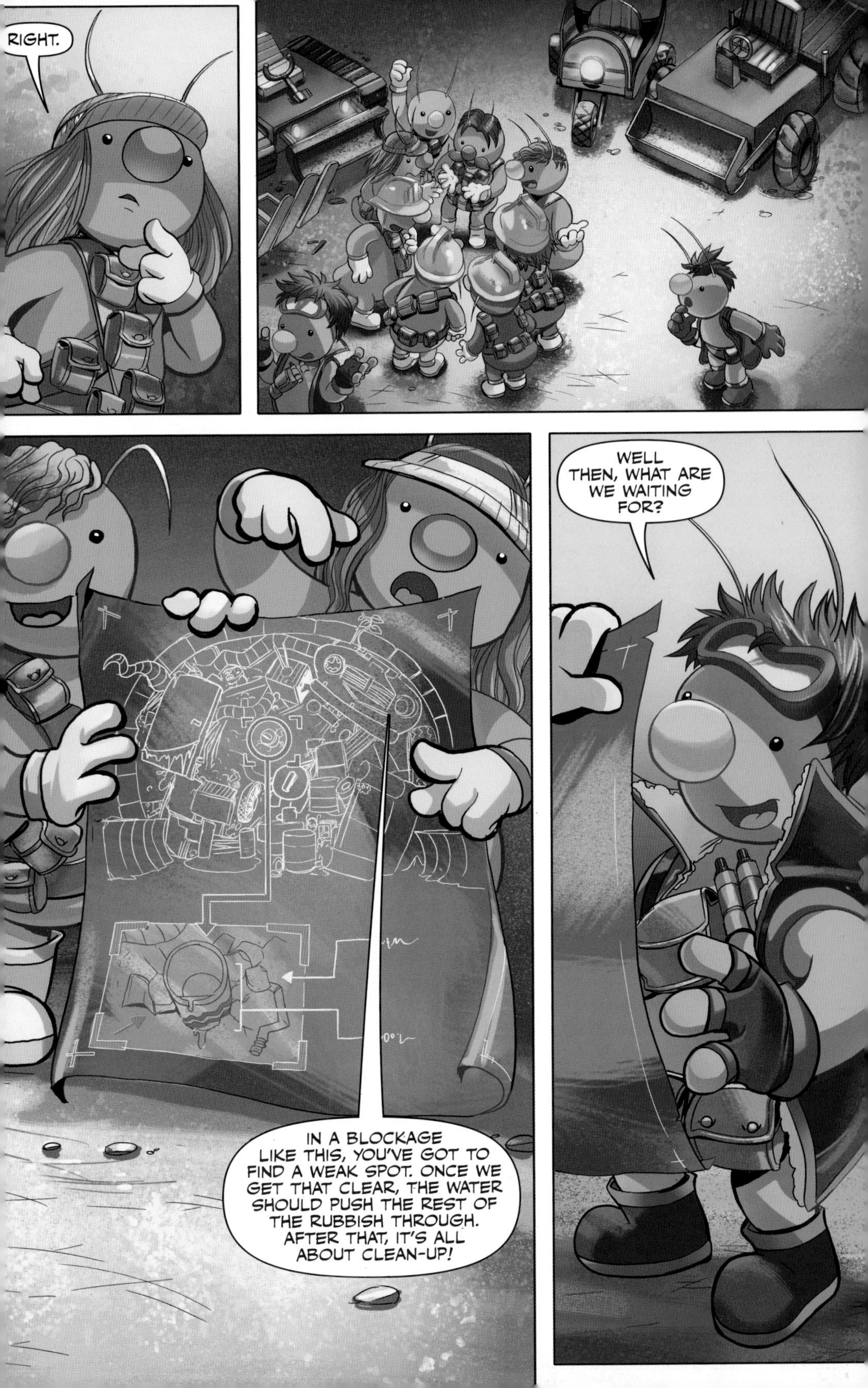
RIGHT.
IN A BLOCKAGE LIKE THIS, YOU'VE GOT TO FIND A WEAK SPOT. ONCE WE GET THAT CLEAR, THE WATER SHOULD PUSH THE REST OF THE RUBBISH THROUGH. AFTER THAT, IT'S ALL ABOUT CLEAN-UP!
WELL THEN, WHAT ARE WE WAITING FOR?

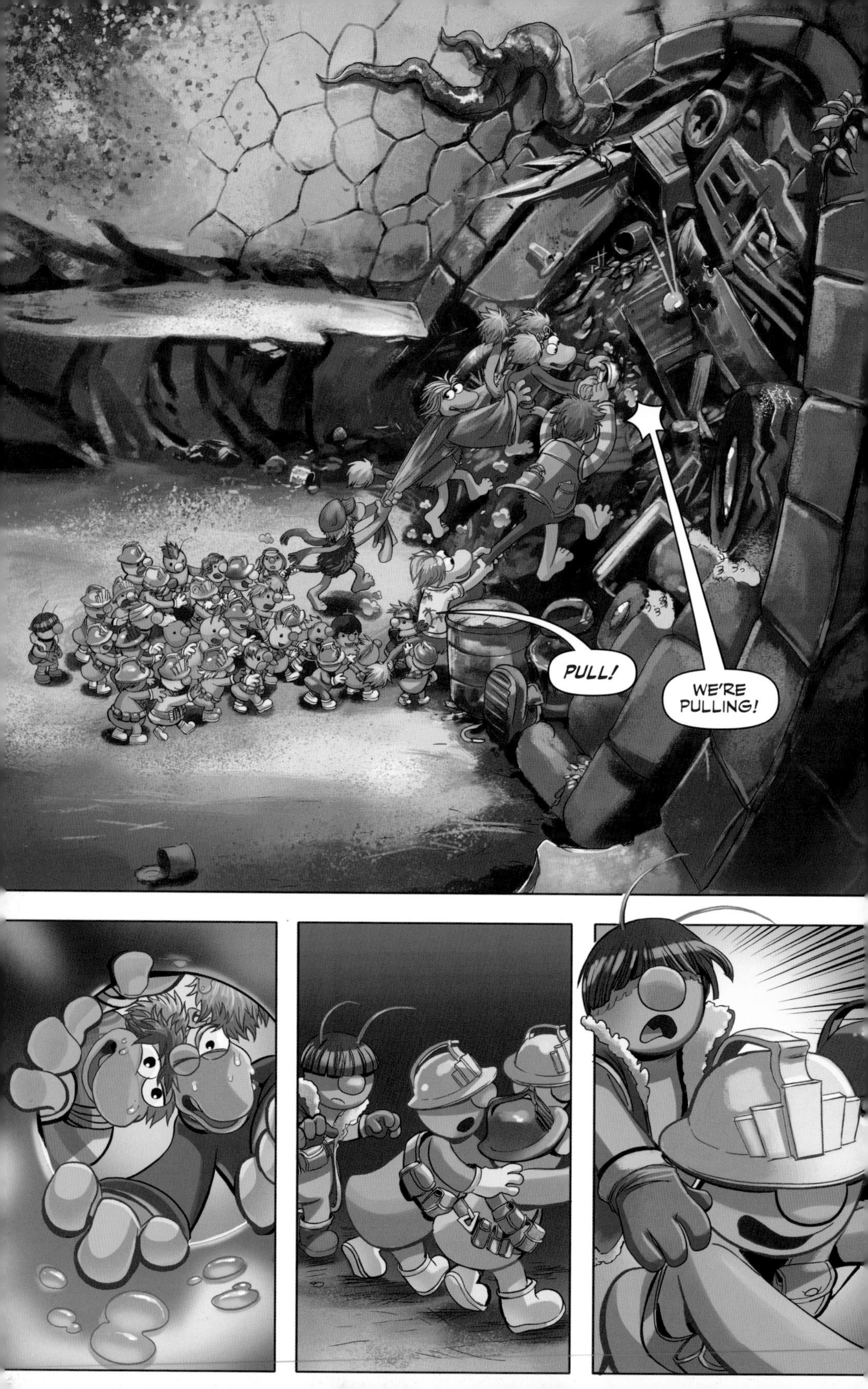
PULL!
WE'RE PULLING!

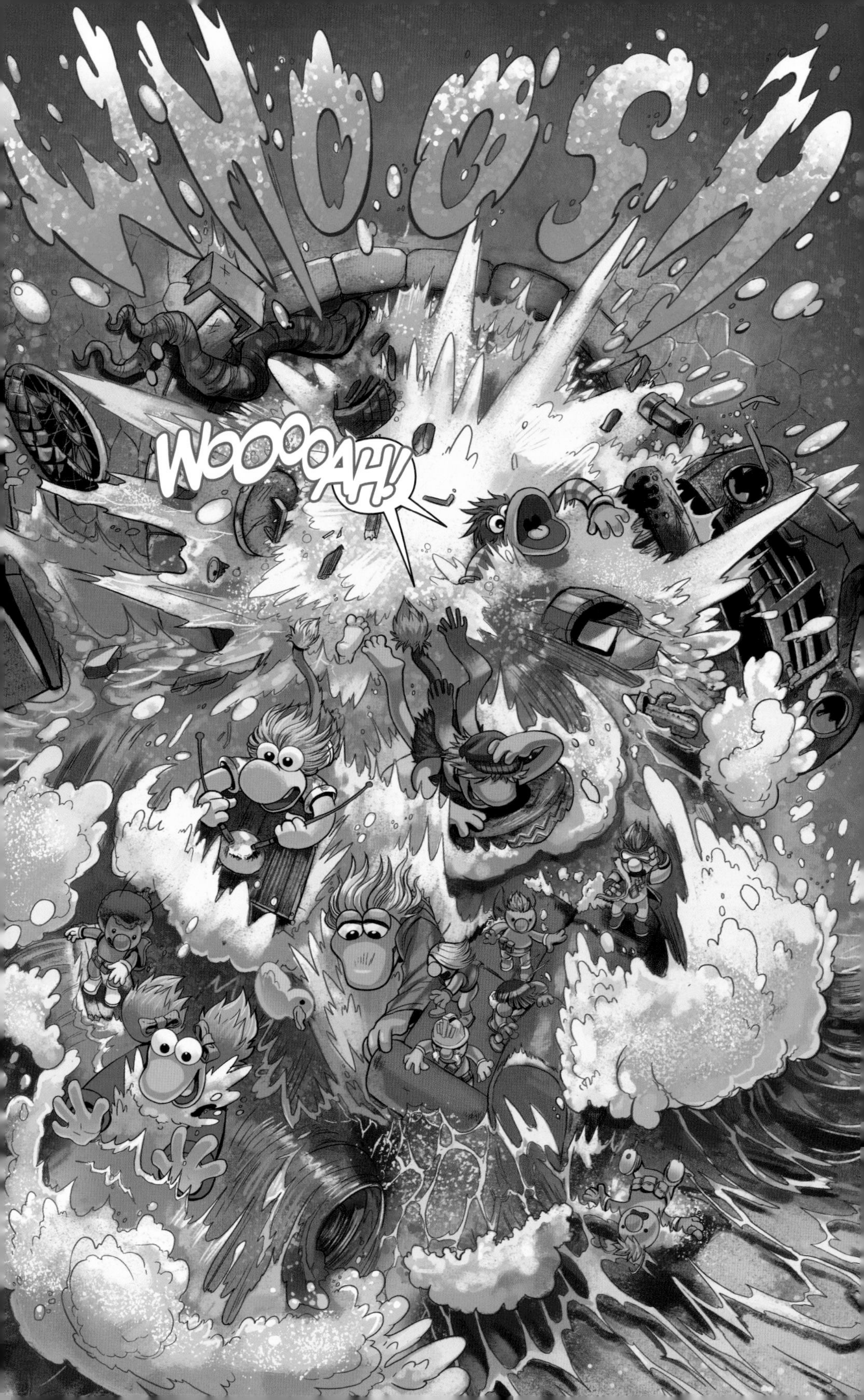
WHOOSH
WOOOOAH!

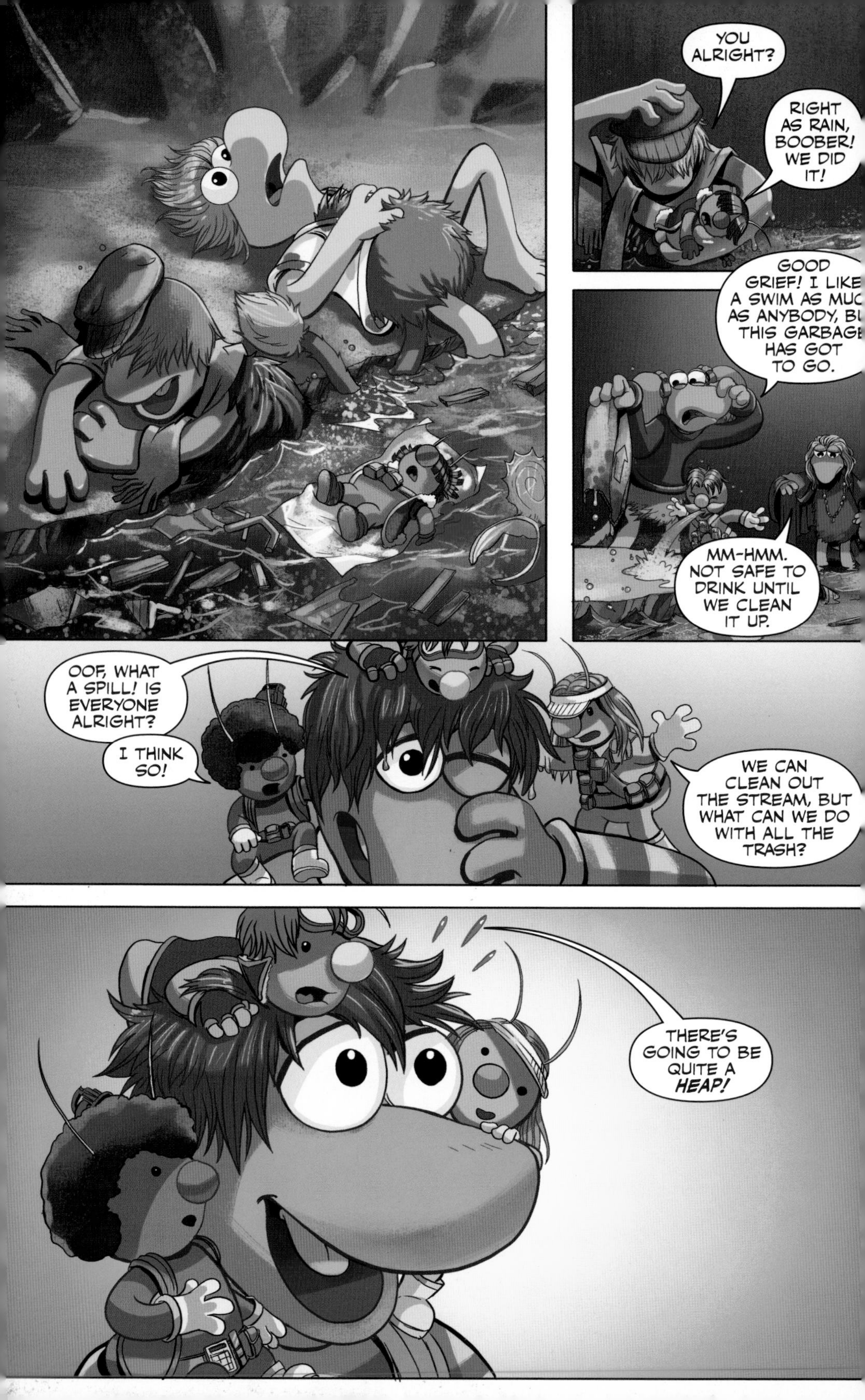
YOU ALRIGHT?
RIGHT AS RAIN, BOOBER! WE DID IT!
GOOD GRIEF! I LIKE A SWIM AS MUC AS ANYBODY, BU THIS GARBAGE HAS GOT TO GO.
MM-HMM. NOT SAFE TO DRINK UNTIL WE CLEAN IT UP.
OOF, WHAT A SPILL! IS EVERYONE ALRIGHT?
I THINK SO!
WE CAN CLEAN OUT THE STREAM, BUT WHAT CAN WE DO WITH ALL THE TRASH?
THERE'S GOING TO BE QUITE A *HEAP!*

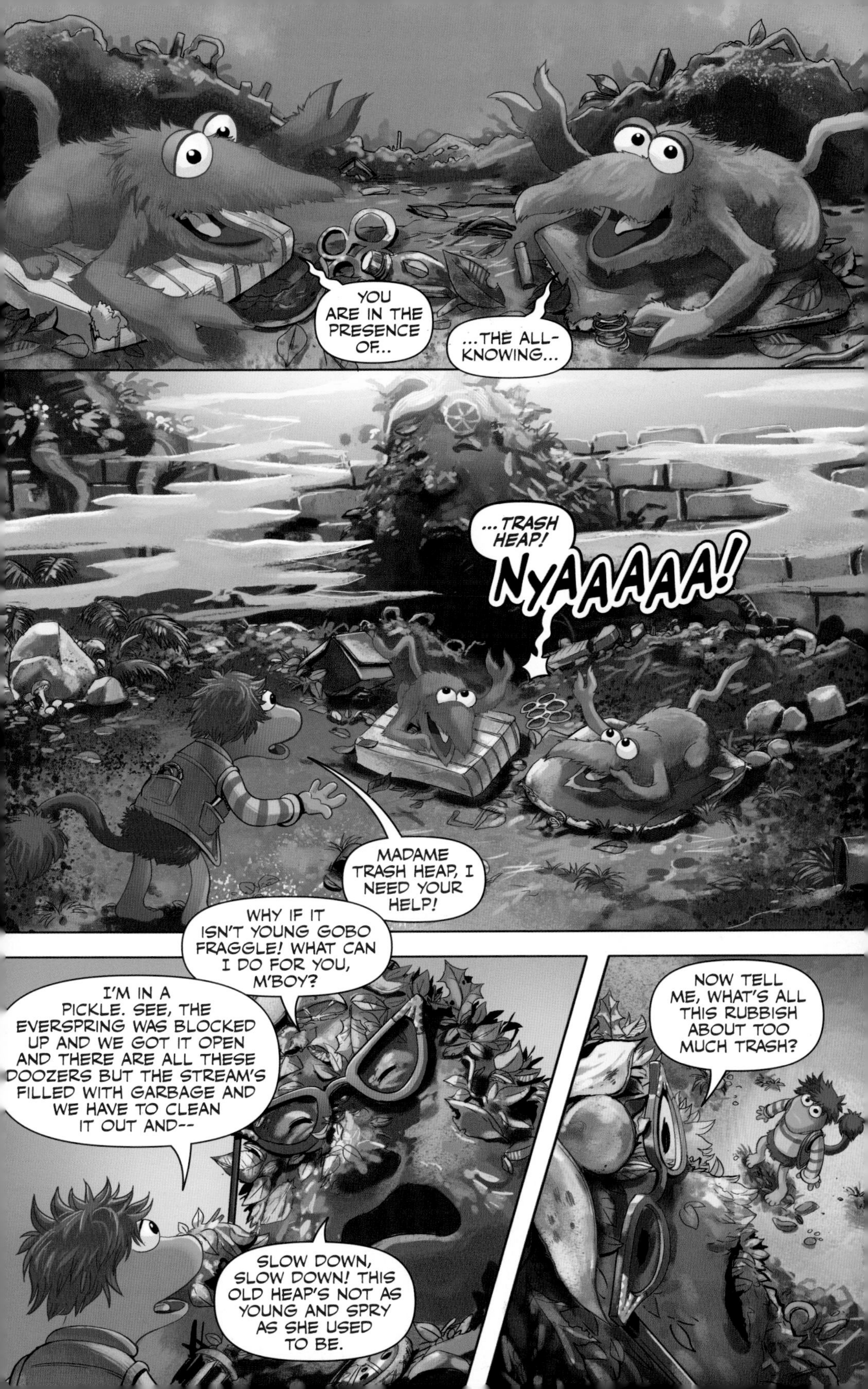
YOU ARE IN THE PRESENCE OF...
...THE ALL-KNOWING...
...TRASH HEAP!
NYAAAAA!
MADAME TRASH HEAP, I NEED YOUR HELP!
WHY IF IT ISN'T YOUNG GOBO FRAGGLE! WHAT CAN I DO FOR YOU, M'BOY?
I'M IN A PICKLE. SEE, THE EVERSPRING WAS BLOCKED UP AND WE GOT IT OPEN AND THERE ARE ALL THESE DOOZERS BUT THE STREAM'S FILLED WITH GARBAGE AND WE HAVE TO CLEAN IT OUT AND--
SLOW DOWN, SLOW DOWN! THIS OLD HEAP'S NOT AS YOUNG AND SPRY AS SHE USED TO BE.
NOW TELL ME, WHAT'S ALL THIS RUBBISH ABOUT TOO MUCH TRASH?

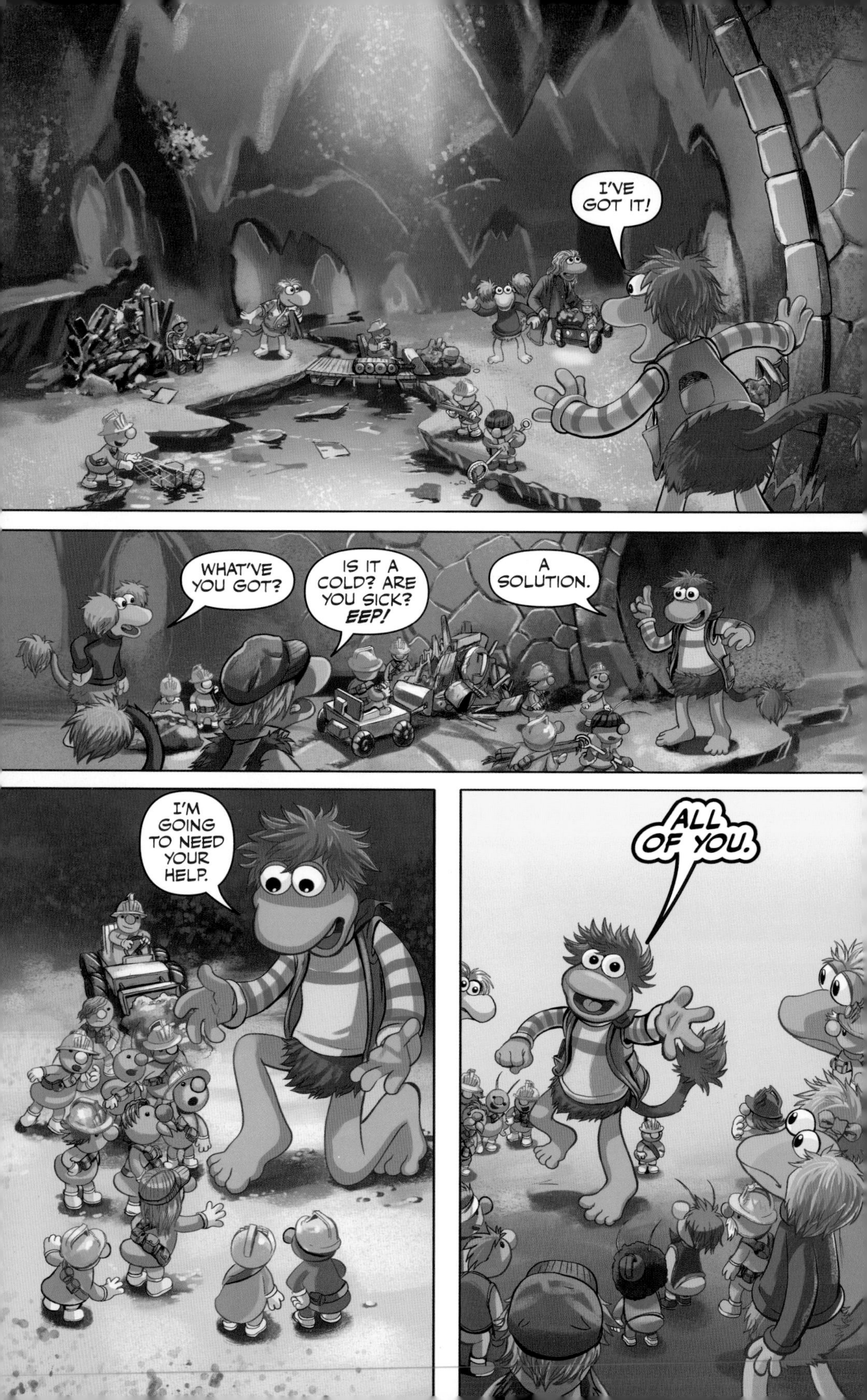
I'VE GOT IT!
WHAT'VE YOU GOT?
IS IT A COLD? ARE YOU SICK? *EEP!*
A SOLUTION.
I'M GOING TO NEED YOUR HELP.
ALL OF YOU.

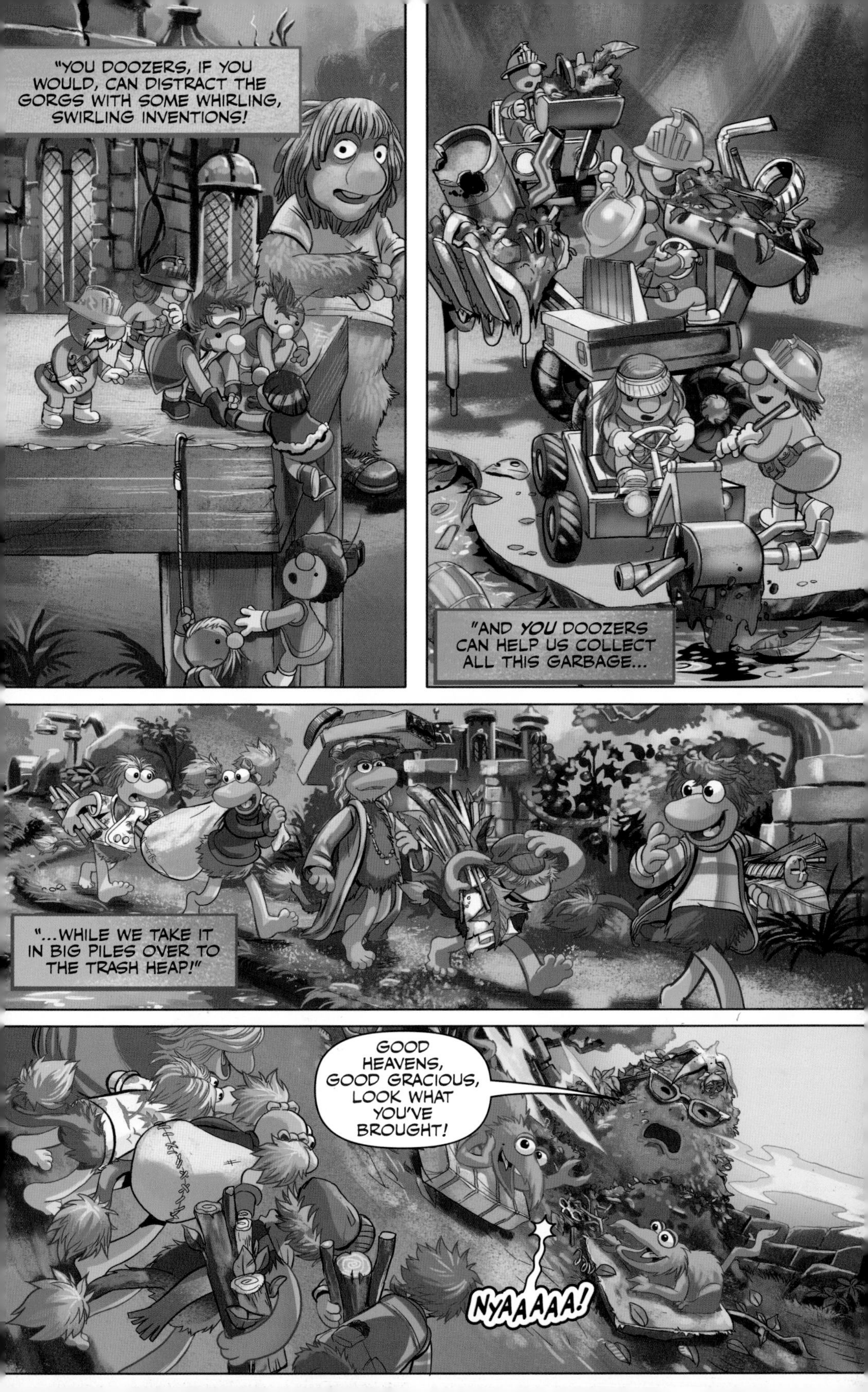
"YOU DOOZERS, IF YOU WOULD, CAN DISTRACT THE GORGS WITH SOME WHIRLING, SWIRLING INVENTIONS!
"AND *YOU* DOOZERS CAN HELP US COLLECT ALL THIS GARBAGE...
"...WHILE WE TAKE IT IN BIG PILES OVER TO THE TRASH HEAP!"
GOOD HEAVENS, GOOD GRACIOUS, LOOK WHAT YOU'VE BROUGHT!
NYAAAAA!

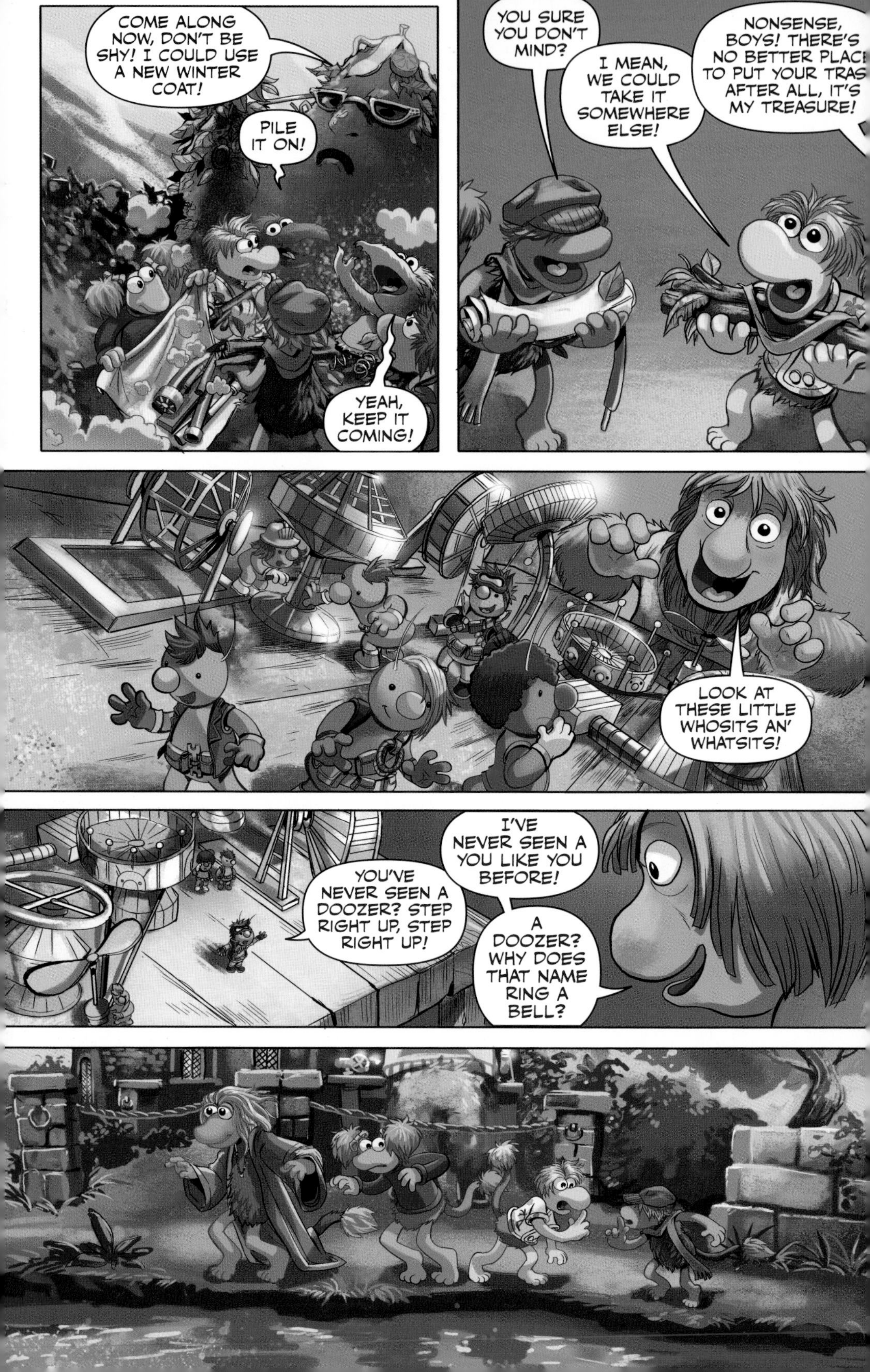
COME ALONG NOW, DON'T BE SHY! I COULD USE A NEW WINTER COAT!
PILE IT ON!
YEAH, KEEP IT COMING!
YOU SURE YOU DON'T MIND?
I MEAN, WE COULD TAKE IT SOMEWHERE ELSE!
NONSENSE, BOYS! THERE'S NO BETTER PLAC TO PUT YOUR TRAS AFTER ALL, IT'S MY TREASURE!
LOOK AT THESE LITTLE WHOSITS AN' WHATSITS!
I'VE NEVER SEEN A YOU LIKE YOU BEFORE!
YOU'VE NEVER SEEN A DOOZER? STEP RIGHT UP, STEP RIGHT UP!
A DOOZER? WHY DOES THAT NAME RING A BELL?

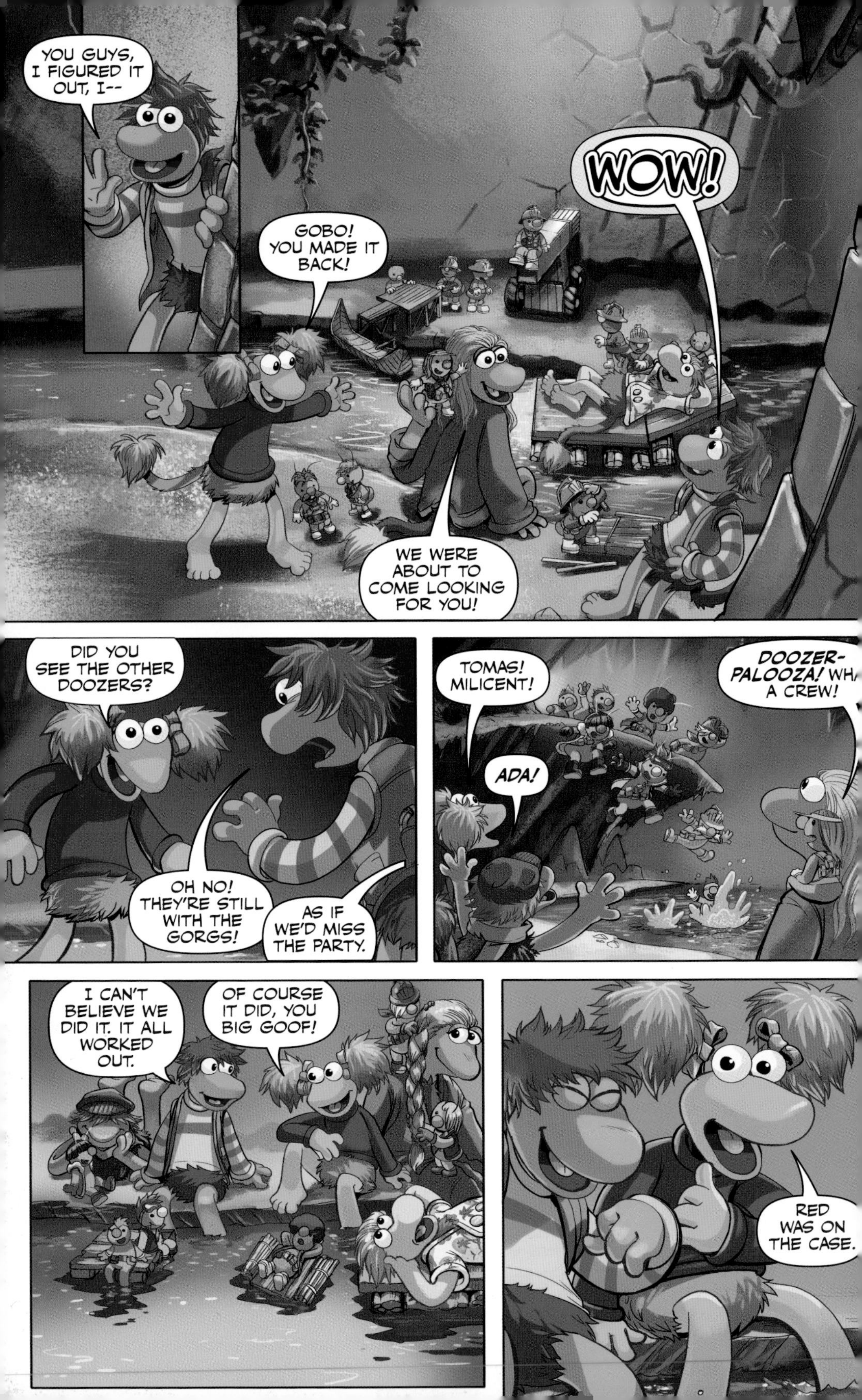
YOU GUYS, I FIGURED IT OUT, I--
GOBO! YOU MADE IT BACK!
WOW!
WE WERE ABOUT TO COME LOOKING FOR YOU!
DID YOU SEE THE OTHER DOOZERS?
OH NO! THEY'RE STILL WITH THE GORGS!
AS IF WE'D MISS THE PARTY.
TOMAS! MILICENT!
ADA!
DOOZER-PALOOZA! WHA
A CREW!
I CAN'T BELIEVE WE DID IT. IT ALL WORKED OUT.
OF COURSE IT DID, YOU BIG GOOF!
RED WAS ON THE CASE.

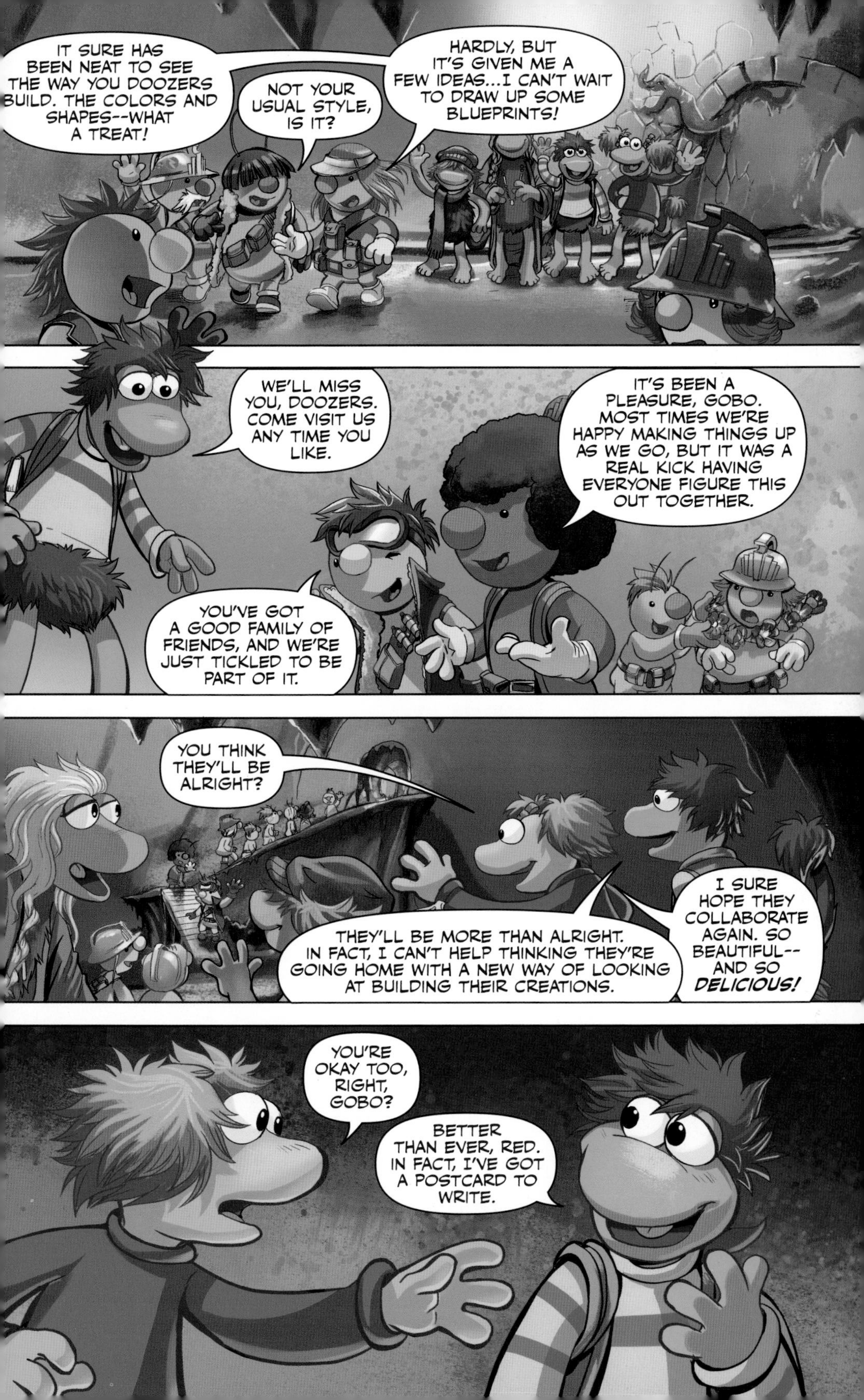

IT SURE HAS BEEN NEAT TO SEE THE WAY YOU DOOZERS BUILD. THE COLORS AND SHAPES--WHAT A TREAT!
NOT YOUR USUAL STYLE, IS IT?
HARDLY, BUT IT'S GIVEN ME A FEW IDEAS...I CAN'T WAIT TO DRAW UP SOME BLUEPRINTS!
WE'LL MISS YOU, DOOZERS. COME VISIT US ANY TIME YOU LIKE.
IT'S BEEN A PLEASURE, GOBO. MOST TIMES WE'RE HAPPY MAKING THINGS UP AS WE GO, BUT IT WAS A REAL KICK HAVING EVERYONE FIGURE THIS OUT TOGETHER.
YOU'VE GOT A GOOD FAMILY OF FRIENDS, AND WE'RE JUST TICKLED TO BE PART OF IT.
YOU THINK THEY'LL BE ALRIGHT?
THEY'LL BE MORE THAN ALRIGHT. IN FACT, I CAN'T HELP THINKING THEY'RE GOING HOME WITH A NEW WAY OF LOOKING AT BUILDING THEIR CREATIONS.
I SURE HOPE THEY COLLABORATE AGAIN. SO BEAUTIFUL--AND SO DELICIOUS!
YOU'RE OKAY TOO, RIGHT, GOBO?
BETTER THAN EVER, RED. IN FACT, I'VE GOT A POSTCARD TO WRITE.

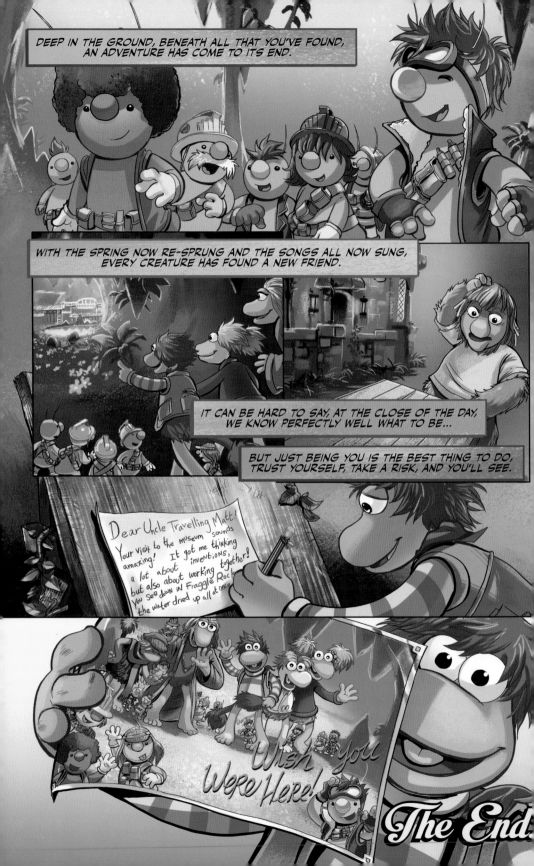

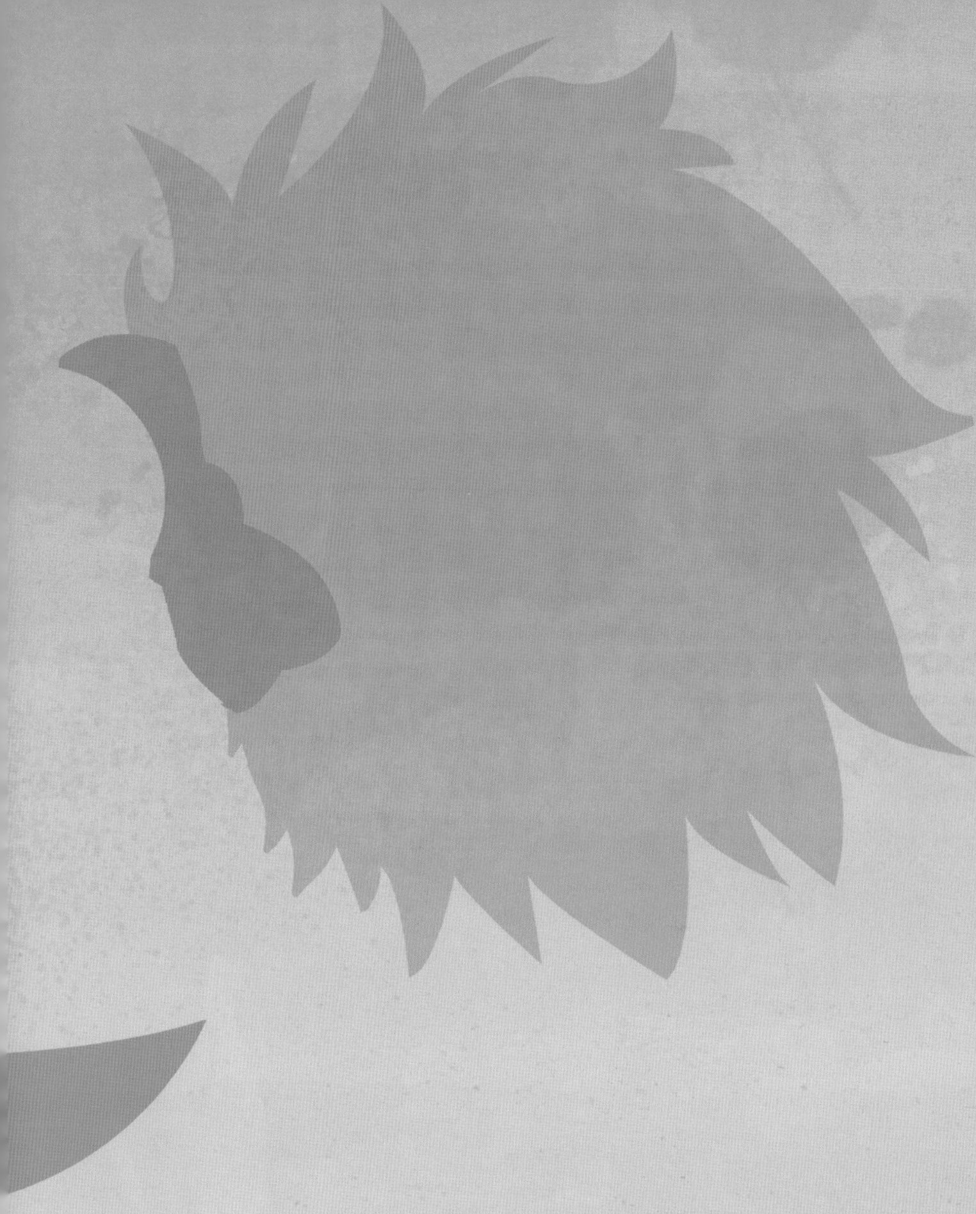

COVER GALLERY

VARIANT COVER BY JAKE MYLER WITH A PHOTO FROM THE JIM HENSON COMPANY ARCHIVES

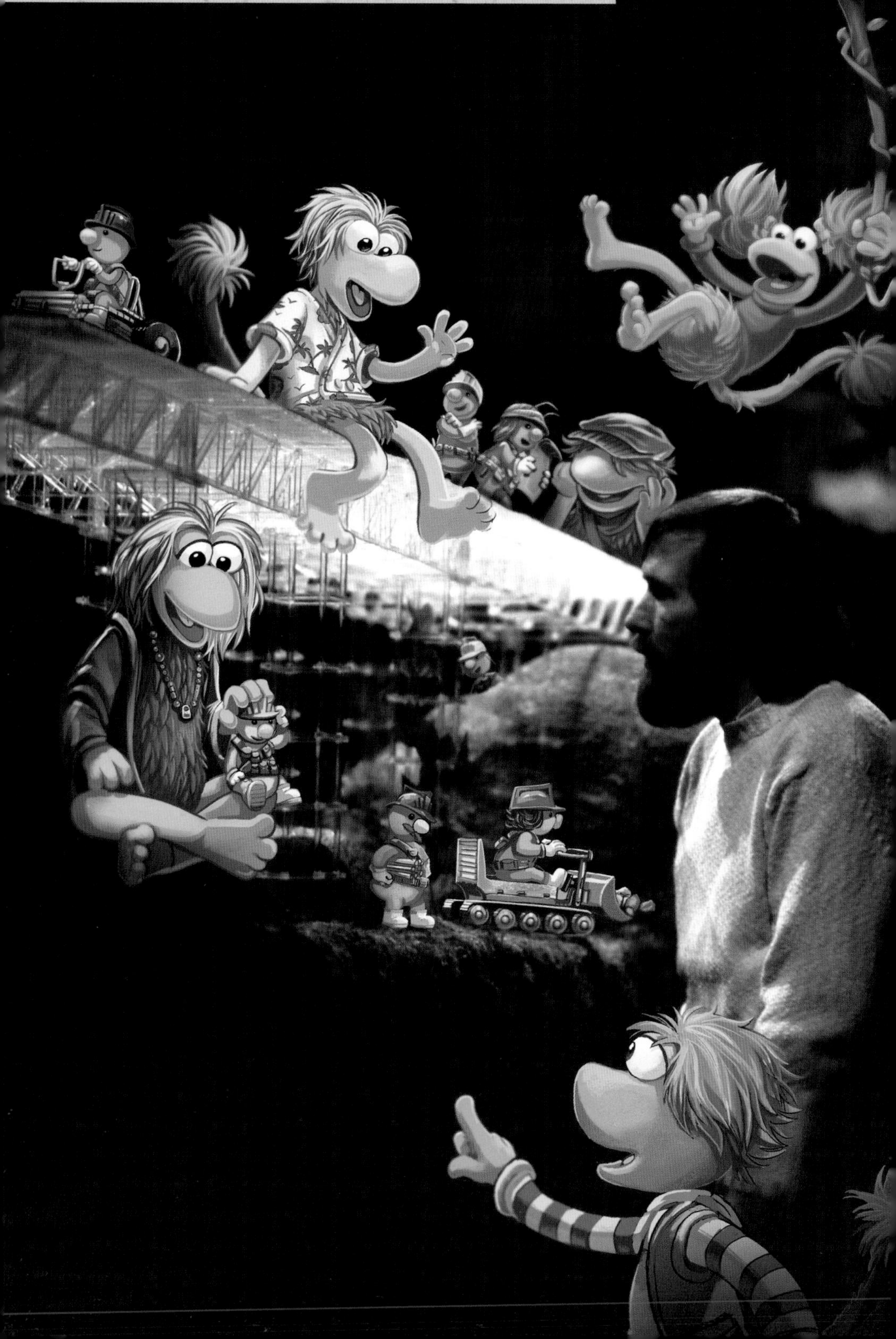

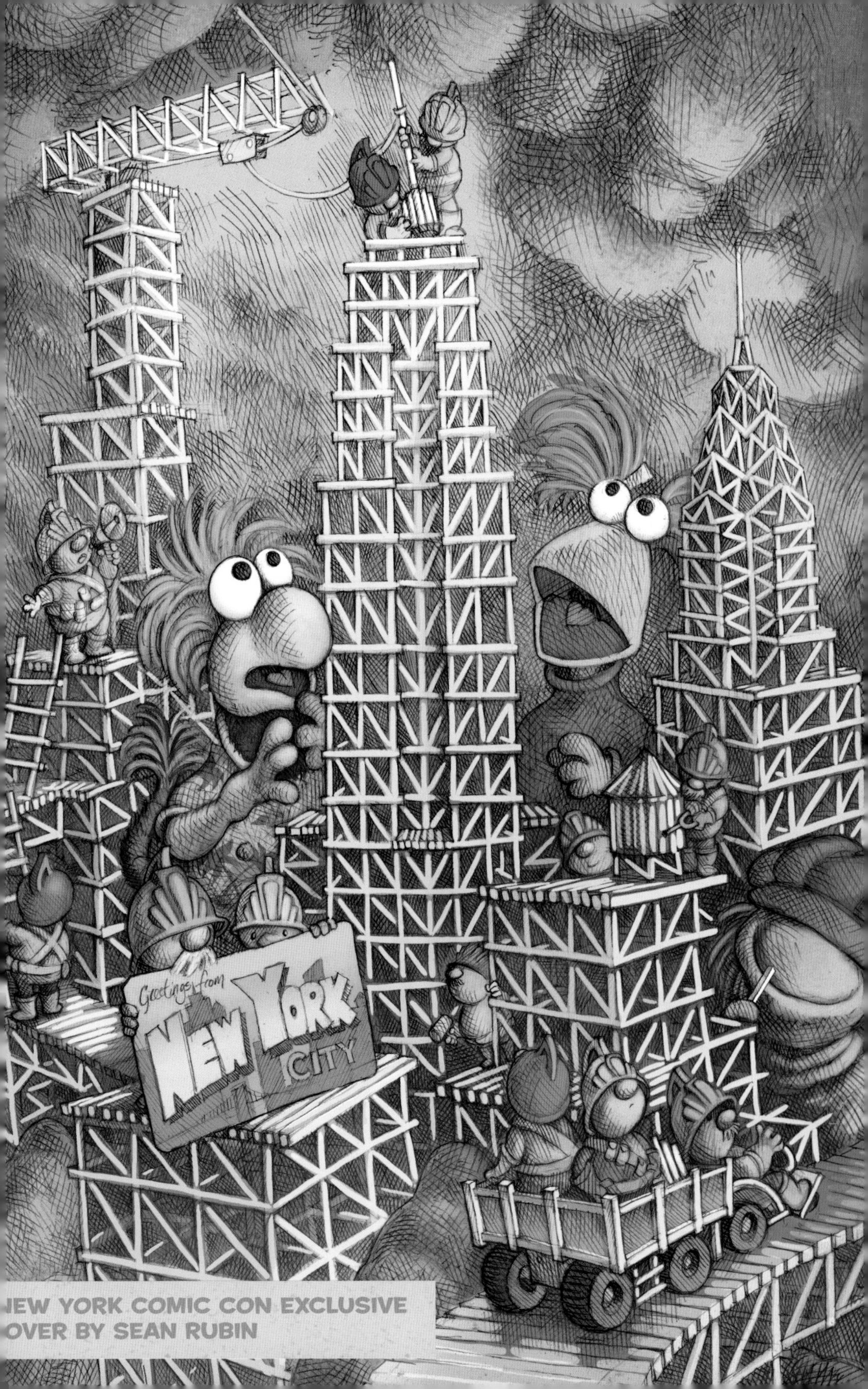
Greetings from
NEW YORK
CITY

NEW YORK COMIC CON EXCLUSIVE
COVER BY SEAN RUBIN

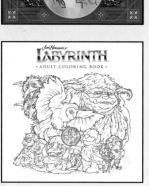

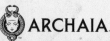